THE ENGLISH BILLIONAIRE

by

SERENITY WOODS

Copyright © 2021 Serenity Woods
All rights reserved.
ISBN: 9798479236648

DEDICATION

To Tony & Chris, my Kiwi boys.

CONTENTS

Chapter One 1
Chapter Two 16
Chapter Three 24
Chapter Four 32
Chapter Five 46
Chapter Six 53
Chapter Seven 59
Chapter Eight 69
Chapter Nine 76
Chapter Ten 84
Chapter Eleven 92
Chapter Twelve 99
Chapter Thirteen 106
Chapter Fourteen 113
Chapter Fifteen 120
Chapter Sixteen 126
Chapter Seventeen 133
Chapter Eighteen 141
Chapter Nineteen 148
Chapter Twenty 155
Chapter Twenty-One 163
Chapter Twenty-Two 169
Chapter Twenty-Three 178
Chapter Twenty-Four 187
Chapter Twenty-Five 194
Chapter Twenty-Six 200
Chapter Twenty-Seven 209
Epilogue 216
Newsletter 221
About the Author 222

Chapter One

Twelve years ago

Callum

It was a crazy New Year's Eve.

I don't know whether it was because I had jetlag, if it was the notion of being upside down on the bottom of the world, or if the searing heat had boiled my brain, but I felt as if I'd passed through a mirror into an alternative universe.

We were on our way to a party in the subtropical Northland of New Zealand, at a place called Matai Bay. It was at the end of a long peninsula, five hours' drive from Auckland, through countryside filled with flat-topped volcanoes, forested hills, and roads lined with huge palms and ferns.

I didn't really want to go. I'd rather have stayed in Auckland and seen the New Year in at my mate Rob's dad's place. I could have pleaded tiredness, snuck off to my room, and spent a pleasant couple of hours catching up on the emails I hadn't had time to touch since we landed in the country. But Rob told me I was being a boring old fart and I needed to loosen up, which I conceded was probably true, so in the end I gave in.

We stopped on the way at a tiny convenience store—which Rob informed me the Kiwis called a dairy even though there wasn't a cow in sight—to stock up on beer and snacks.

"This is possibly the most bizarre thing I've ever done," I told him as we carried the groceries back to the car. "I mean, look." I pointed

1

at the window of the dairy in which a picture of Santa dressed in a vest and shorts and carrying a beach umbrella gave us a thumbs-up. "It makes my head hurt."

"It does take some getting used to." Rob squeezed his crate of beers next to my pack of water bottles and shut the boot, and we got back in the car. He started the engine and pulled out onto the state highway. "When families go to the beach in December, they often stick Christmas trees in the sand, complete with tinsel and baubles. It's very alien to the Brits."

Rob was a well-spoken, upper-middle-class guy whose Kiwi father was a politician, and whose English mother was a barrister. When his parents divorced, his mum went back to the UK and Rob grew up there, but he visited New Zealand every year to see his dad, so he was used to the way everything was similar and yet so different.

In many ways the country felt familiar. Its partly European heritage meant Kiwis drove on the left, their food sported many English brand names, and they had similar systems of justice and government. But, like a distant dear cousin who'd left home and had to cope on his own for years, they'd developed a distinct personality as a result of being so far from Europe, plus of course the indigenous Maori gave the Kiwi culture a fascinating twist.

We arrived around six p.m. and parked in the car park. The place heaved with guys and girls of around our own age—early twenties—retrieving bags and boxes from their cars and carrying them down to the beach. It was only a few minutes before someone called out, "Rob!" and we turned to see a Maori guy running up to us, who promptly threw his arms around Rob and gave him a big bear hug.

"This is Mikaere," Rob said when the guy eventually released him. "Mik, this is Callum."

"From England!" Mik shook my hand. He wore a pair of swim shorts and nothing else, and his brown skin glittered with sand. "G'day, Callum. Great to have you here, eh!"

I smiled at the warm welcome. "It's good to be here."

"You guys got any beer?"

"There's a crate in the back," Rob said.

"We weren't sure if you had enough," I added, grinning at the sight of several crates being carried to the beach.

"Yeah, nah," Mik said, confusingly. "We always need more!" He guffawed and beckoned over another couple of guys to help us collect our bags and the two-person tent we'd bought for the event, and together we headed down the path.

I stopped at the top, where the scrubby grass turned into white sand, and stared at the scene. We stood at the bottom end of the bay, which curved up and to the right like a capital letter C. In the shallows, the sea was the color of the greenstone pendant that Rob called a *taonga* which Mik wore around his neck, although the water turned to a deep azure farther out, and then to burnished copper as the sun sank toward the horizon.

Tents clustered in groups, with battery-powered fairy lights strung between them. A beach cricket match provoked much laughter and shouting, while girls screamed in the sea as the guys inevitably splashed them. The smell of barbecued food filtered to my nostrils, along with the salty smell of the ocean.

Summer. On New Year's Eve. My head spun.

"Come on." Mik took the crate of beer from Rob's hands. "You're late getting started and you've got to catch up!"

We set up our tent near his and ate a 'sausage sizzle'—a barbecued sausage wrapped in a slice of bread with fried onions—as we chatted to some of Mik's friends. Then it was time for a swim, and we ran into the sea and dived in headfirst, emerging from the warm water to join in with throwing a beach ball around.

About fifty young men and women were gathered in groups, and it was impossible to speak to everyone, so I didn't see her until much later. By then, the sun had set, and someone had opened a box of citronella candles, which they placed in the sand to give light and keep some of the insects away. One of the guys drove his car close to the beach and played songs on his stereo, and the portable barbecues threw up delicious smells of sausages, burgers, prawns, and even a kingfish someone had caught for them that morning. Drinks flowed, and the distinct smell of weed filled the air as people passed joints around.

I was standing a little away from the main crowd, talking to Rob and a couple of Mik's friends, when I saw her coming out of the sea after a swim. She was small and slender with cropped blonde hair, wearing an aqua-blue bikini that shimmered so it looked like scales. Very young, probably no more than eighteen or nineteen. I had the odd notion that she was a mermaid who'd swum to shore, and I'd just missed seeing her magical form.

She accepted a beer someone held out to her and stood talking to them, but I could see she was looking at me.

"Who's that?" I murmured to Rob. He glanced over.

"Dunno," he said. "Mik? Who's that?"

Mik also looked over. "Her name's Kora. She's up from Wellington. She's here with her twin brother, Theo. He's the dude who brought the kingfish."

I'd met Theo earlier—a good-looking guy with an affable manner I'd liked very much.

Rob slung his arm around Juniper—a cousin of Mik's who he'd been glued to since we got there—and said to me, "Want anything else to eat? They're barbecuing some bananas with chocolate in the middle."

"I'm good, thanks."

He nodded, and he and Juniper wandered off to the barbecue.

I stayed where I was, swigging from my water bottle, watching the girl called Kora. She glanced over at me, saw I was on my own and looking at her, and left her group to wander across the sand toward me.

My pulse picked up a little, but I stayed relaxed as she approached.

"Hey," she said.

"Hey."

"I've been watching you for a while," she said, surprising me with her honesty. "I'm Kora."

"Callum MacDuff." I held out my hand, and she slid her smaller one into it.

"You're English," she stated as I released her hand, surprising me, as most people ask whether I'm Scottish because of my surname.

"The accent give me away?"

"That and the white skin."

"It's winter in the UK. I haven't had a chance to build up my summer tan." I didn't add that I was like a vampire and rarely ventured outdoors.

She smiled. "Fair enough. You here on vacation?"

"Yeah. Do you know Rob Brown?"

"The guy in the blue shorts—Mik's friend?"

"Yeah. His dad's a Kiwi. We've just graduated from Oxford and thought we'd celebrate by going traveling. We've been around the world and New Zealand is our last stop before we fly home in the New Year."

"Cool." She had pretty eyes the color of the sky behind her, high cheekbones, and a mouth that curved up more on one side than the other when she smiled, giving it a sultry twist. "What's your degree in?" she asked.

"Land and property management, development, and valuation. I can't make it sound any more interesting than that, sorry."

She gave a light laugh that sent the hairs rising on the back of my neck. "I'm sure it's fascinating. What are you going to do now you've qualified?"

"Buy and sell property. I seem to have a knack for it."

"Oh, is it a family business?"

"No." The last thing I wanted to think about on that beautiful summer night was my father.

She blinked at my abrupt answer, then dropped her gaze to the water bottle in my hand. "Do you want a beer?" she asked.

"No thanks. I don't drink."

"Not at all?"

I shook my head.

"Why not?"

I tipped my head to the side, not used to people speaking so frankly. "I'd be happy to get *you* one," I stated.

She lifted her bottle. "Still half full. I prefer champagne, but I wouldn't admit that here. You can't bring champagne to a beach party."

"No, I guess not." Even if I had touched alcohol, my family couldn't have afforded champagne. My grandmother sometimes bought cheap sparkling wine if it was a special occasion.

One of Kora's friends came over to us and held up a joint. Kora took a puff and passed it to me. I shook my head.

"You don't smoke either?" she asked, giving it back to her friend, who wandered on.

"Not my scene. I prefer to keep a clear head." As I said it, I realized how dull I sounded. I didn't do it for effect. Everyone at uni knew my background and didn't question my personal choices, but I could see how here I'd look like a right party pooper.

But Kora gave me a curious look. "You don't drink, you don't smoke. You listen, but you don't say much. You don't even smile. You're so serious. Are you shy?"

"No. I'm not used to… uh…"

"Parties?"

"Relaxing."

"Oh?" Now she looked really interested. "You're a workaholic?"

"You could say that." It was a good attempt at describing my work ethic, but it didn't come close to encompassing my seventy-hour weeks, or the fact that I would have worked eighty except that Rob forced me to take Saturdays off to play football.

"Did you get an honors degree?" she asked.

"Yeah."

"First class?"

"Yeah." I came top in my class in three out of the four subjects I took, but I wasn't going to tell her that.

"First class from Oxford is pretty good. You must be one smart guy."

"I do okay."

She smiled. "Modest too. I like that." Her eyes glowed with admiration, and something else. Desire. She found my admission hot.

I wasn't inexperienced with women, but I didn't have a girlfriend back in the UK, and, if I was honest, dating wasn't high on my list of priorities. But this wasn't about dating. Kora knew I was on holiday, and yet still she lingered. Her tanned skin glittered with sand in the firelight. She looked young and healthy and sexy. I felt dizzy, and I wasn't sure whether it was the jetlag, the smell of the weed, or the fact that my heart was racing.

"Are you at university?" I asked.

"I'm about to start at Vic in February. Victoria University in Wellington," she added at my puzzled look. "I'll be studying Art History." So I was right; she must be around eighteen.

"What do you want to do? You want to be a curator?"

"Well, actually, I'm interested in antiques and collectibles. I'd like a job at an auction house."

"That sounds interesting."

"I think so." The way she said it suggested others she'd spoken to hadn't felt the same way. She took a breath, hesitating for a moment, then said, "I collect antique toys. Teddy bears, dolls, that kind of thing."

"Oh? What a great hobby."

"It is." She lit up like one of the candles in the sand. "I've even got a 1978 Luke Skywalker action figure in its original box—it's one of only twenty in the world."

"Now that is cool."

It was difficult to tell who had money in New Zealand as there was no class system like there was in the UK. Not that being English upper class meant a person had money—quite the opposite at times—but it was often a pointer. In this country though, people who owned a boat or a swimming pool spoke and dressed the same as everyone else. Wearing designer labels seemed less important amongst the young people I'd met, and nearly everyone drove pickups or 'utes' rather than sports cars.

But part of my valuation course had been about antiques, and I knew enough to guess that Kora's Skywalker doll would have cost her serious money. "How much is that worth?" I asked. "My guess is… twenty thousand dollars?"

Her expression turned guarded. "Around that," she said.

She looked at her feet, and I followed her gaze and watched her curl her toes in the sand. Her toenails were painted a golden brown several shades darker than the sand, and they were super sexy. I liked this girl. She interested me. The last thing I wanted to do was insult her.

"I'm going to be a billionaire by the time I'm thirty," I revealed.

She lifted an amused gaze to mine. "That's quite a statement."

"I felt I owed an explanation after being so rude. I have a fascination with money. Rob calls me Scrooge."

That made her laugh. "Now I'm going to call you Callum McDuck."

I grinned. "I'll take it. I am sorry though. I'm always interested in how people make their fortunes, and I forget other people can be sensitive about it."

She gave me an appraising look, maybe surprised at my honesty. "I come from a rich family," she said eventually. "We're from the UK originally. My great-great-great-grandfather owned a toyshop. He sold a doll to Queen Victoria at the Great Exhibition in 1851, and she gave him a royal warrant, which meant he could advertise that he supplied to the Royal Family. After that, every upper-class family in London went to his shop for presents for their children at Christmas."

That fascinated me. "So that's why you're interested in toys?"

She nodded. "He knew how to invest the money he made, too. He became a very wealthy man. His sons and grandsons opened more shops in the UK and continued to invest their money, and the business boomed."

"What about the Wall Street Crash? Didn't that affect them?"

"My great-grandfather, Henry, was very astute, and he saw trouble coming. He got out of the market in early 1929 and kept the fortune intact. He's the one who moved to New Zealand and began a Kiwi chain of shops, investing in New Zealand real estate during a time when few people had money, and the fortune just kept growing. He was called King Midas by his family and friends because he sometimes invested in risky ventures but they hardly ever failed—everything he touched turned to gold. That luck, if you like—although I don't like the word because it doesn't take into account the hard work they've done, so let's call it business acumen—has continued down through the generations. The family knows how to take care of what they have, and none of us are big spenders, so the family fortune continues to grow. My father and brothers are similarly smart."

"And so are you," I said softly, impressed by her understanding. A stellar intellect turned me on so much more than a pretty face or a curvy figure. Not that Kora wasn't beautiful, because she was.

She met my eyes, and in the semi-darkness I saw a touch of color appear on her cheekbones. "That's possibly the nicest thing anyone has ever said to me," she admitted, not shyly exactly, but more with a sense of wonder that anyone could think that of her.

I held her gaze, desire growing within me. I'd never been as fascinated by a woman as I was at that moment by Kora.

She turned her head to look at the car as the music changed to Wham's *Last Christmas*, then moistened her lips with the tip of her tongue as her gaze came back to me. "They always drag the old ones out at this time of year," she said.

"The old ones are the best. Gotta love George Michael."

She chuckled. "Yeah."

"Wanna dance?" I asked on the spur of the moment.

Her face lit up. "Really? I wouldn't have thought you were the dancing type."

"I am if there's a smart woman to dance with."

Her lips curved up at how I described her. I could have called her gorgeous or beautiful, but I could see she preferred the compliment to her intelligence.

I moved toward her and put my hand on her hip, and she lifted one arm around my neck, still holding her bottle with the other. Then we began to move to the music.

We danced for hours, while the stars popped out on the black velvet sky and the moon rose above the sea, as if Nature herself was decorating the sky with her own silver Christmas bauble.

As we danced, we talked a little about this and that, but mostly we just turned together slowly in the sand while the cool sea breeze blew across us, listening to the music and the conversation and laughter from the people around us. Gradually, we moved closer together until her soft body pressed against mine and her cheek rested on my shoulder. I touched my lips to her hair, remembering my first impression that she was like a mermaid who'd turned into her human form as she came onto land. My hand rested in the middle of her back, and I itched to stroke her skin, to explore her curves, but I refrained, contenting myself by brushing my thumb across her spine and enjoying her answering shiver.

Then someone announced it was nearly midnight. A couple of the guys had organized some fireworks, and everyone got to their feet and opened a new beer bottle and joined in counting down. A huge cheer went up as we reached zero, and the rockets exploded above our heads in showers of gold and silver sparks.

Kora turned her face up to me. The exploding fireworks lit up one side, while the other was in shadow. "Happy New Year," she whispered. Her gaze dropped to my mouth.

"Happy New Year." I glanced around us. Everywhere, people were taking the opportunity to kiss those nearest to them in celebration. I looked back at Kora, and she moistened her lips with the tip of her tongue.

I moved closer, then lowered my lips to hers and held them there for a moment before lifting my head to look at her. My heart pounded, and my blood raced around my body.

To my surprise, she moved back. Disappointed, I watched as she walked over to a nearby fold-up table and placed her bottle there. Then she came back and, to my delight, threw her arms around my neck, lifted on tiptoes, and crushed her lips to mine.

Exultant, I slid my arms around her waist and gave in to the passion that had been building between us all evening. When I brushed her bottom lip with my tongue, she parted hers with a sigh, and we exchanged a long, luscious embrace that left me hard and aching.

Kora drew back, lowered her arms, and took my hand in hers. Without a word, she led me across the sand to a small red tent, saying a few brief words to another girl on the way, who just grinned and returned to kissing the guy she was with.

She unzipped the front of the tent, dropped to her knees, and crawled inside. Heart racing, I followed, maneuvering my big frame through the tiny gap with difficulty, then falling onto my back on one of the two sleeping bags with a laugh.

Kora picked up a tiny box that lay near the tent opening and flicked a switch. A trail of white fairy lights sprung on, turning the inside of the tent into a magical Christmas grotto.

"Gina's idea," she said, presumably naming the girl she was supposed to be sharing the tent with. "Don't worry, she won't interrupt."

"Pre-agreed rules?" I asked, amused.

She leaned on an elbow and looked down at me. "I didn't come here to get laid, if that's what you're asking. Theo and I have been working hard, and we came here with friends to see the New Year in."

"He's not about to come barging in with a shotgun?"

She chuckled. "He'll be too occupied with that blonde he's been talking to all evening. Not that it's any of his business anyway. I just want you to know… I don't usually do this…"

"Me neither."

"Really?"

I shook my head.

Her gaze dropped to my mouth. "Can I kiss you?"

"Yes, Kora, you can kiss me. As long as I can kiss you back."

"I should bloody hope so," she replied in a British accent. I laughed, and she grinned before lifting up to lie on top of me and covering my mouth with hers.

We kissed for ages, listening to the laughter outside and the crackling of the fire not far from the tent, our bodies molding together as she sank her hands into my hair and I stroked down her back, following the dip of her waist and the flare of her hips.

Eventually, I put a hand on the tie of her bikini top behind her neck and waited. When she lifted her head and gave a little nod, I tugged the tie undone. She pushed up, sitting astride me, her head brushing the top of the tent, and I peeled the triangles of cloth slowly down to reveal her small, firm, and high breasts, their attractive pink nipples begging to be kissed.

I was happy to oblige and covered one with my mouth while I teased the other with my thumb. Kora groaned and rocked her hips, arousing herself on me, and I dropped my hands to her hips to slow her movement, hoping to draw out our pleasure. I hadn't expected the evening to end like this, and I didn't want it all to be over in a minute or two.

Kora seemed to have other ideas, though, and she undid her bikini top at the back and tossed it aside, then lifted off to ease the bottom half down her legs. I gave in, grabbed a handful of my tee at the back of my neck, and tugged it off, then pushed my swim shorts down and kicked them off too.

"Shit," she said, "have you got a condom? I don't have one in my bag. Gina probably has one I could steal…"

"I've got one in my wallet," I replied, fished it out, and tore off the wrapping. I wouldn't have cared if she'd come to the beach with the intention of hooking up with one of the guys, but I had to admit to a small swell of pleasure that it didn't look as if that was the case, which meant she must really have liked me.

"Let me," she whispered. Resting on my elbows, I gave her the condom, and watched as she placed it on the tip of my erection and rolled it on slowly.

Flopping onto my back, I covered my face with my hands, struggling for control. I hadn't had sex for a while, and the whole situation was strangely erotic. I'd been captured by a mermaid in a fairy cave at the bottom of the world on New Year's Eve, with sand beneath the thin base of the tent and the sound of the sea just a hundred yards away.

I felt her climb on top of me, shift to get in the right position, and then slowly sink down, encasing me in her velvet warmth.

I let out a long groan, lifting my arms above my head and opening sleepy eyes to see her outlined by the light behind her as she began to rock her hips.

"Ooh," she murmured, "you're big. Mmm… that feels good…" She tipped her head back and cupped her breasts, brushing her thumbs across her nipples.

I watched her ride me, speechless with wonder, and more turned on than I would have thought possible at her unashamed display of passion. Man, she was sexy, and I hung on for as long as I could, wanting the night to go on forever.

But when her hips began to move faster, and she caught her bottom lip between her teeth and made little moaning noises, I lost the plot.

I growled, caught her around the waist, and flipped her beneath me. She squealed, laughed, then moaned again as I lifted up onto my hands and pushed my hips forward, burying myself in her moist warmth as deep as I could.

"Callum…" she whispered, closing her eyes. "Ohhh…"

I crushed my lips to hers and plunged my tongue into her mouth as I began to move with purpose, making sure I ground against her with every thrust.

"Mmm…" she moaned beneath my lips, and when I raised my head, she groaned loudly.

"Shh," I demanded, but she was too far gone, and as she came, her moans filled the little tent and no doubt echoed right along the beach.

I covered her mouth with my hand, trying not to laugh, and my jaw knotted as she bit into the soft flesh of my palm. But then my own body took over, and after a couple of hard thrusts my climax washed over me, hot, beautiful, and sweet, locking us together in a brief moment of bliss.

When it subsided, I opened my eyes, suddenly aware I was pressing down on her mouth and hoping I hadn't hurt or alarmed her. But her eyes sparkled in the dull light from the lamp, and when I lifted my hand, she was laughing.

"Sorry," she whispered, but the giggles rose inside her like bubbles in the champagne she loved, and wouldn't be suppressed.

I groaned as she clenched around me and I withdrew from her, then collapsed beside her and joined in with her laughter. She draped herself across me, resting her cheek on my chest, and I felt her lips touch my damp skin.

"Mmm," she murmured. "That was magnificent."

"My first time with a mermaid."

She giggled again, then sighed.

Within less than a minute, we were both asleep.

*

She was still there when I woke up later, needing to pee. I dressed awkwardly, then crept out of the tent as silently as I could. The beach was mostly deserted, everyone having retired to their tents, a couple of people sound asleep on the sand where they'd probably passed out. By the light of the moon and the dull glow from the fire, I walked away from the tents to the small toilet block near the car park, then came back along the beach, the sand cool between my toes. The sea was calm and silver, the view like a scene from a black-and-white movie. It was New Year's Day—the year newborn, filled with hope and promise. I had so much to do, so much I wanted to achieve, but at that moment all I could think about was the magical night and the girl who'd so willingly given herself to me. I hadn't thought I believed in love at first sight, but at that moment, I was completely convinced of its existence.

I crawled back into the tent, curled up around her, and fell back to sleep.

*

The next time I awoke, she was gone. I stretched, yawned, then sat up and unzipped the tent door a bit. Golden sunlight streamed in, along with the sound of conversation and laughter and the smell of coffee. Kora's bikini had vanished, so she'd obviously dressed before she exited the tent. I checked my phone—it was seven-thirty.

I crawled out, got to my feet, and stretched again. About two-thirds of the tent doors were open, and people were beginning to pick up the rubbish and put the empty beer bottles into recycling bags. A coffee van in the car park was already open and doing a roaring trade with both the partygoers and the holidaymakers from the nearby camping ground.

"Hey." It was Rob, who came over with a grin. "Good party, eh?"

"Fantastic. How's Juniper?"

"Gorgeous," he said, and laughed. "How's Kora?"

"Beautiful," I replied. "Is she around?"

"Somewhere. Look, we'll have to head off soon. We're supposed to be meeting Dad at one in Auckland and it's going to take us five hours to drive back."

"Sure. I'll start packing up."

"I'll help you with the tent."

We took down the tent that I don't think either of had used and packed up our things, but all the while I was looking for Kora. It was only as we took our stuff back to the car that I saw Mik, strapping down his tent in the back of his ute.

"Morning," I said, walking up to him.

"Morning, Callum. Had a good time?"

"Great, thanks. Have you seen Kora?"

"Yeah, she had to shoot. She said to say goodbye. She and Theo had to catch the seven a.m. flight."

I was shocked at the disappointment that knifed through me. She hadn't even bothered to say goodbye.

"Sorry, man," Mik said at the look on my face. "If it's any consolation, I saw her turn to go back to the beach, but Theo caught her hand and pulled her toward the car. She'd have missed the plane if she'd stayed."

I nodded. "Thanks for inviting me, anyway."

"No worries. Drive carefully, eh?"

We clasped hands and bumped shoulders, and then I returned to our car and got in the driver's side.

In the mirror, I watched Rob saying goodbye to Juniper, nuzzling her ear and making her laugh before giving her one last kiss. He came and got in and gave me a big grin. "All right?"

"Yeah, let's get going." I put the car in Drive and pulled away.

"Kora gone?" Rob asked.

"Yeah, had to catch an early flight."

"Sorry about that. She was cool."

"Yeah, she was." I adjusted the rear-view mirror. "So, what's going on today?"

While Rob chatted on about where his Dad was going to take us, I watched Matai Bay grow smaller in the mirror. My mermaid had vanished in the daylight. I knew then that I'd never see her again.

It was a crying shame, but what had I expected? She'd known nothing could come of it, so I guess she'd thought to save us a sad parting, and had left me instead with the memory of the night, warm and magical.

The road curved away from the sea, and in the mirror, the bay disappeared.

I turned my gaze to the road ahead, and settled back for the drive.

Chapter Two

Present Day

Kora

London is everything I expected it would be, and more. Busy. Fast. Cosmopolitan. I've seen it so often on the TV that I knew it would feel familiar and yet different, too. As I travel from Heathrow into the city, I see red buses, black cabs, and red telephone boxes. The Tower of London and Big Ben. The London Eye and the statue of Eros in Piccadilly Circus. Voices with the fantastic Cockney accent, and faces from every part of the world.

It's also extremely cold, even for me, coming from windy Wellington, and I'm glad I brought my big winter coat, bulky as it was to carry on the plane. It's February, and in New Zealand it's the height of summer, humid and hot. Here, it's below freezing, threatening snow. Snow! I've seen it on the mountains in the South Island, and once when I went to Queenstown in winter, but it so rarely snows in Wellington that it's going to be a novelty for me.

I'm not sure if it's the jetlag interfering with my system or if I picked a stomach bug up on the plane, but it takes me a few days of not wanting to be more than three feet from a bathroom before I finally feel well enough to go out and explore the city. As soon as I'm out, though, it doesn't take me long to adapt to London life.

At first, the Tube is scarily busy—everyone seems to know where they're going, and traveling anywhere near rush hour is a nightmare, but I find it exciting, so different from anything I'm used to at home. Trains rumble around and above me, and the wind blows along the tunnels. Soon I'm changing lines and reading maps as if I've lived there all my life.

Above ground, new, elaborate architecture and ancient buildings stand cheek by jowl, and I'm determined to see as many places as I can while I'm here. I go to Westminster Abbey, St Paul's Cathedral, The Tower of London, Madame Tussauds, the British Museum, the National Gallery, and numerous other places.

And then there's the shopping. At home, I occasionally fly up to Auckland and over to Sydney, but it's a real treat to go around Selfridges in Oxford Street and Harrods in Knightsbridge, and all the designer shops in Sloan Street. I treat myself to a bottle of Gardenia Les Exclusifs de Chanel, a pair of Jimmy Choo strappy sandals in platinum ice dusty glitter that catch my eye, and a Louis Vuitton Alma bag I've wanted for ages and decide to splash out on while I'm on my shopping binge. Despite my family's extensive wealth, it's rare that I spend so much money on myself in one go, and I return to Claridge's laden with boxes and the guilty gleefulness that only comes when you've spoiled yourself.

Dad was both thrilled and concerned when I announced I was thinking about going to London. Thrilled because I've been low since I broke up with Julian, and Dad's always believed in travel to take a person's mind off their problems. And concerned, because it's only been just over a month since Theo went missing off the coast of Fiji, and now Dad's terrified to let any of us out of his sight. He told me he'd agree to me going—not that he could have stopped me, but we both pretend he's still in charge even though I'm thirty—only if I let him book the trip. I agreed because I love him and I understood how much Theo's disappearance frightened him, but I have to admit I was unprepared for the level of ostentatiousness he'd organize. I had a First Class suite on the plane, which was like an enclosed hotel room, and a private chauffeur picked me up from Heathrow in a Mercedes-Benz E-Class that Theo would have killed for.

I'm staying in the Princess Eugenie suite at Claridge's, which is so lavish I feel as if I'm a member of the English Royal Family. It's only when I discovered that the Empress Eugenie of France entertained Queen Victoria in her winter quarters in Claridge's that I understood why Dad booked the suite. Ever since he told me as a girl that Arthur Prince sold a doll to Queen Victoria, I've been fascinated by her. He knew I'd be thrilled at the possibility that she might have visited this very room.

It's with some reluctance that, ten days after landing, I acknowledge it's time to do some work. I'm due to go to Prince's Toy Shop in Regent Street at three p.m. to meet my third cousin, Stephanie Prince, so I spend the morning lazing in bed, slowly making my way through a full English breakfast that the butler brings me on a tray—a real luxury.

After that, I shower and dress, then sit behind the Louis XV-style desk in the study to check my emails on my laptop and message my family on Facebook to give them an update on how I'm doing.

As three o'clock approaches, I go down to the lobby and out to where the chauffeur is waiting for me, and he drives me to Regent Street.

I get out of the car and stand on the pavement, looking up at the huge Prince's Toy Store sign. This is where it all began. Ben has a black-and-white photo of Arthur Prince's toy shop in his office, and it consisted of the workshop and storeroom out the back and the small shop at the front, with a bow window in which he displayed his dolls and rocking horses and toy soldiers.

Now, the store is set over seven floors covering fifty-four thousand square feet and selling more than fifty thousand lines of toys. Not bad considering Arthur made all his toys himself.

I'm not normally an overly emotional person, but I have to admit that tears prick my eyes as I look up at the sign, and I have to swallow hard and blink to stop them falling. I'm immensely proud of our family, from all the men who grew the business over the last two centuries, to Stephanie Prince, who now runs the London store.

"Ms. Prince?"

A man in a smart gray suit approaches me. He's around my age, with dark-brown skin and close-cropped black hair, and wearing glasses with fashionable rectangular frames.

"Yes," I reply, "I'm Kora Prince."

He holds out a hand. "I'm Will Cross, I'm Stephanie Prince's assistant. Welcome to London!"

"Thank you. Ooh, it's cold!"

He grins. "You happen to be visiting in the coldest winter for the last ten years. Come on, let's get you inside and I'll take you up to Stephanie's office."

I follow him through the huge revolving door that turns slowly, into the ground floor of the store. Just like in our store at home, the ground floor is devoted to stuffed toys, from teddy bears to plush fantasy and zoo animals, and there's even a life-sized lion attracting attention in the center.

Will leads me through the store to the escalators, passing a glass cabinet in which sits a lone teddy bear, looking somewhat forlorn. I stop and read the label, seeing that it's a Steiff bear—one of the most collectible soft toys in the world.

"He looks lonely," I say to Will as he joins me.

"It's all an act. He loves the attention." I chuckle, and he smiles.

"Is he for sale?" I ask.

"No, he's from the V&A," he says, shorthand for the Victoria and Albert Museum. "They loan us various toys throughout the year."

"What a great idea." I follow him to the elevators, which I must remember to call lifts while I'm here.

We go up to the seventh floor, and when the door opens, I can see this part of the building is all offices that keep the business running. Will leads me through along the corridor to the end. Here the door bears a sign declaring it belongs to Stephanie Prince, and Will knocks on it, then opens it and gestures for me to precede him. No modern chrome and glass partitions here—this is an old brick building, and Stephanie's large office has a gas fire set in one wall, the flames leaping over the fake coals. Its large windows overlook the bustling Regent Street.

I smile at the woman who gets up from her desk and comes forward to greet me. "Kora!" She takes my hand, then brings me close to kiss me on the cheek. "How lovely to meet you at last."

I've spoken to Stephanie a couple of times on Zoom, so I knew she was blonde like me and attractive, but she's much more stunning in the flesh. She's tall, whereas I'm only five-four, and she's model-slim, with a toned figure, immaculate makeup, and a bob so sharp you could cut yourself on it. Her complexion is very English rose, her skin a pale cream with a touch of pink. It wouldn't surprise me if she never goes out in the sun. I think I read somewhere that she's in her late thirties, but she doesn't look it—she's extremely chic and elegant. I feel like a country bumpkin in comparison, even though I've taken care with my appearance today, and I'm wearing my best suit.

"It's so good to be here," I tell her as she moves back.

She gestures toward a black leather sofa and chairs. I take off my coat, and Will hangs it on a coat stand by the door. I lower myself onto the sofa while she takes the chair opposite.

"Tea, coffee, hot chocolate?" she asks.

"Ooh, a hot chocolate would be lovely."

"A soy latte for me please." She nods at Will, who leaves the room. Then she smiles at me. "Ben told us all about his siblings when he came over, so it's lovely to meet you in the flesh."

My oldest brother came to England on his honeymoon, and he visited the UK Princes before going on his tour of Europe.

"I'm sorry to hear about the death of his wife," she adds.

"Yes, it was quite a shock," I say politely. I don't want to go into what a bitch Rebecca Prince was, and I'd never admit to anyone how, when she died, my main emotion was relief.

"And how wonderful that Theo was rescued after his adventures," she says. "We were watching with bated breath to see if they found him. I can't imagine what he went through, and you too, of course."

"It was a tough time," I say, which is the understatement of the year. I could never put into words the trauma of that Christmas, with the death of my grandfather being followed within hours by the news of Theo's disappearance.

"But now you're here," she announces, "and hopefully having a good time."

"I'm having a terrific time. Seeing the sights, shopping, going to shows…"

"You're alone, though?"

I nod. "I broke up with my boyfriend last year. It's not quite the same, traveling by yourself. Part of the enjoyment of sightseeing is sharing with another person. But it has been nice not to have to put anyone else's needs before my own." Those last six months with Julian were incredibly stressful, so I've enjoyed the peace of my own company.

"I understand how it's a double-edged sword," Stephanie replies. "I feel the same way."

"Oh, really?"

"Yes, my divorce came through a couple of months ago, although we've been separated for over a year now." She brushes at an imaginary piece of fluff on her immaculate skirt. I can't imagine her losing control over anything, but instinct tells me she's fighting emotion. She didn't want the separation. I feel a surge of pity for her. I can't imagine how hard it must be if one of you really doesn't want to break up.

"I'm sorry," I murmur. "It's tough. My breakup was acrimonious, but I still miss Julian at times."

"I didn't have to worry about hot tempers or arguments or anything like that," she says. "He froze me out. Our relationship was at absolute zero by the time we parted. The Ice King certainly earns his nickname."

She stops talking as Will comes back into the room with a tray bearing a steaming mug of hot chocolate and a coffee for Stephanie. I flick a curious glance at her as she leans forward to collect her cup. Why would a man leave such a beautiful woman? You never know what goes in a relationship, but she's gorgeous, elegant, intelligent, and extremely rich. How bad can their marriage have been for her husband to give up on her?

Two marshmallows nestle in the whipped cream on top of the hot chocolate. Stephanie's soy latte is no doubt much healthier, but mine must be more delicious. I have a large mouthful and sigh as it warms me through.

"So," Stephanie says, pinning a smile on her face, "to business. How are things going Down Under?"

We talk for a while about the company. Lucas, my older brother who is the company's Director of Finance, briefed me well before I left, and I'm able to compare sales and trends with relative ease providing I can refer to the sheets in the folder I brought. Clearly, though, I don't know as much about it as Stephanie. Facts and figures roll off her tongue without her having to look them up, and she has impressive insight into all the different departments of her company. I like her, but I'm a little in awe of her, to be honest. I can't ever imagine being so into the business. It's not where my passion lies.

But I'm able to hold my own enough to have a decent conversation, and I give her the report that Dad, Ben, and Lucas prepared and answer a few of her questions the best I can. It's close to four-thirty and I'm halfway through another hot chocolate by the time we finish. Outside, the light is beginning to fade, and the sky is the color of iron.

"We'll have snow before the weekend," she says as I close my folder and sit back. "When are you flying out?"

"In five days."

"Hopefully it'll be gone by then. It doesn't normally last long, if it does snow. Okay, so shall we say ten o'clock tomorrow? No point in rushing when you're supposed to be on holiday."

I smile. "Sounds great." I'm going to spend some time with each of her heads of department, and Stephanie herself is also going to give me a proper tour of the toy store.

"What do you have planned for the rest of your time here?" she asks.

"Oh, more sightseeing. I'd love to do a tour of the rest of England, but I'll have to come back for another visit for that."

"Yes, it is a beautiful country and there's so much to see. Do you—" She stops as Will knocks on the door and comes into the room.

"Excuse me," he says, "but Callum is here."

"Thank you, Will. I'll be out in a moment."

Will goes out, and Stephanie gives me an apologetic smile. "I'm so sorry, but it's my husband. I need to sign some papers for him." I note that she doesn't call him her ex.

"Oh. Of course." I pick up my bag and get to my feet. I'm curious to meet the guy who froze Stephanie out of their marriage. "Do I need to put on a crash helmet?"

She gives me a wry look. "Hardly. We're quite civil. Callum's far too much of a gentleman to be anything but. Sometimes, I wish he were more vocal. Maybe if we'd argued more, got it all out in the open, we wouldn't have broken up."

"I don't know," I mumble, "I'd have given anything for a bit of civility in my breakup." Julian had gone crazy when I told him it was over—he'd yelled at me, thrown things, even broken the TV. He'd scared me. I'll never forgive him for that.

"I'm setting up a branch of the toy store in South London," she states as I finish off the last mouthful of hot chocolate, tipping up the mug to collect the marshmallow at the bottom before I pick up my coat. "Callum found a suitable site for it and organized the sale, and he's brought the papers for me to sign."

"He's into real estate?"

"You could say that. The man has a knack for sniffing out bargains. He's made an absolute fortune over the years buying and selling property."

I wonder if he made a billion dollars, I think with amusement as I recall the Callum I met twelve years ago at the beach. As always when

I think of that night, I feel a touch of sadness. I've compared every guy I've been with to the man I met at Matai Bay, and all of them have failed to match up to him. But then he's suspended in my memory like a mosquito in amber, captured in perfection, and he's never had a chance to disappoint me and let me down like the others have.

We walk across to the waiting area in front of Will's desk where a man is sitting checking his phone. "Callum," Stephanie says, and he looks up and gets to his feet, sliding his phone into the pocket of his long black woolen coat. "Hello, darling," she coos, going over to him and reaching up to touch her lips to his cheek. "Oh, are those the papers?" She takes them out of his hand. "Here, let me sign them for you now. Oh, this is my cousin, Kora, by the way. Kora, Callum MacDuff." She turns away to place the file on the table, and begins to flick through it.

Beneath his coat, Callum is wearing an extremely well-fitting navy suit with a crisp white shirt and a light-blue tie. He has a modern haircut—short around the sides and up the back, longer on top, combed neatly, very sleek. He looks every inch a wealthy London businessman.

But the name confirms it, as do the widening of his eyes as his gaze falls on me.

He's taller. Broader. Obviously wealthier. There are small lines at the corner of his eyes.

But it's definitely the guy I had a one-night stand with twelve years ago on the other side of the world.

My heart skips a beat. Stephanie was married to Callum MacDuff? She uses her maiden name, so I could never have guessed.

The silence stretches out between us as he continues to stare at me, realization settling into his light-brown eyes the way a pebble would sink slowly into a vat of honey. He obviously can't believe it either.

I'm relieved he recognizes me. Maybe I haven't changed as much as I thought I had.

So, this is the civil gentleman who froze Stephanie out of their relationship? The Ice King? I can't match that person to the hot, sexy, passionate man who's haunted my dreams from time to time since that night on the beach.

Well. This is going to be interesting.

Chapter Three

Callum

Kora Prince couldn't be more different from her English cousin. They're both blonde, but there the similarity ends. Stephanie colors her hair ash blonde, and it's cut in a perfect bob, incredibly neat. She never goes out in the sun, so her skin is a creamy white. Her makeup, as always, is immaculate—finely applied eyeliner and gray eyeshadow, and neatly painted dark-pink lips to give her that permanent smoky allure. She's always been thin, but she's lost even more weight since we broke up, and there are hollows beneath her high cheekbones that give her a haunted look. Her suit is probably Ralph Lauren, a dusky pink, the skirt a couple of inches above her knees.

Kora's hair is a honey blonde, no longer cropped, but now hanging past her shoulders in soft waves. She's shorter than Stephanie and curvier, and her skin is a beautiful warm brown, speaking of summers spent swimming and playing sport outdoors. She's wearing a stylish beige woolen trouser suit with extremely sexy black high-heeled boots and a white silk shirt.

Stephanie is the moon and Kora is the sun, which seems appropriate considering what the weather was like that summer we first met.

Thinking of that, I glance at Stephanie, but she's still bent over the papers. I look back at Kora. I don't want Stephanie to know we know each other. I can't face the barrage of questions and the jealousy that will inevitably follow.

"Hello," Kora says. She shifts the coat she's holding to her left arm and holds out a hand. "I'm Kora Prince." I can see by her expression that she recognizes me, but clearly she's realized I want to keep our previous relationship—such as it was—to ourselves.

"Hello." I shake her hand, which is warm and feels small in my big paw. The last time we shook hands like this, she was wearing a very sexy aqua-blue bikini. "You have a cream mustache," I point out as I release her hand. "I'm guessing that's not permanent."

Her lips curve up, and then she sticks out her tongue and runs the tip above her top lip as far as she can, trying to lick off the cream. It's such an irreverent action, so unlike what Stephanie would have done, that it makes me laugh.

Stephanie looks over her shoulder, surprise on her face. I don't laugh often, and never with strangers.

"Better?" Kora asks, and I nod. "It's Will's fault," she states. "He tempted me with another hot chocolate, and he didn't warn me about the mustache factor."

Will chuckles from behind his desk, clearly won over by her.

"Where are you from?" I ask Kora. "Australia, by the sound of your accent."

She gives me a wry look at the teasing comment. "New Zealand," she scolds. "My father is the CEO of the Antipodean branch of Prince's."

Oh... Twelve years ago, Kora told me about her family's business, but I never made the connection with Stephanie's family. I don't know why. I didn't meet Stephanie until I was twenty-eight—six years after meeting Kora—and although Stephanie and I often talked about the business, she wasn't interested in the history of it the way Kora was. She never mentioned the details Kora told me that I can still remember—of her ancestor setting up the toy shop and getting a Royal Warrant after selling a doll to Queen Victoria.

"Are you here on holiday?" I ask, because I can't think what else to say. She's fried my brain, exactly the same way she did back on the beach.

"Ostensibly on business, but yes, I'm sightseeing too. Lots to see and do."

I nod, and then there's no time for more conversation because Stephanie has finished signing the papers. She turns, but doesn't hand them back yet. "Do you have anything planned for dinner tonight?" she asks. She sounds nonchalant, bored even, like she couldn't care less, but I know her better than that.

"A meeting with some Japanese investors," I reply.

Her eyes meet mine, flaring with annoyance that I've turned her down. She's about to accuse me of lying.

I narrow my eyes, and she bites her bottom lip and lowers her gaze. She knows there's nothing I'd dislike more than arguing in front of other people.

I agreed to find her a site for her new shop before we separated, and even though things have been extremely difficult between us, I decided to see it through because I'm a businessman first and foremost. However, I hadn't realized she'd be contacting me every five minutes to sort out insignificant details.

I was the one who applied for a divorce. Stephanie contested it, insisting to the court that our marriage hadn't broken down irretrievably, and she managed to drag out the proceedings for months before her lawyer finally convinced her that the court was never going to find in her favor. But although the divorce is final and I no longer wear a ring, she still hangs onto the idea that we could be a couple again, even though there's not a snowball's chance in hell that it's going to happen.

I should have couriered the papers over to her. That'll serve me right for calling in. But I'd wanted to finish it, and I thought if I was there when she signed the papers, I could make it clear in person that we were done. I was all prepared for a big argument, but now, after seeing Kora, for some reason my resentment and anger have dissipated, and all I feel is a deep desire to be free.

I might not have said so in as many words, but the fact that I've just turned down Stephanie's dinner proposal has made my position clear. She looks back up at me and her eyes glisten, but I harden my heart. I refuse to give her the power to hurt me anymore.

Kora has been watching us, her sharp eyes missing nothing. Now, she smiles and holds her hand out to her cousin. "Well thank you so much, it's been great to meet you. I'll see you tomorrow at ten?"

Stephanie nods, professional once again. "Yes, I look forward to it."

"I have to go, too," I tell Stephanie.

"Callum..." She hesitates. Then she forces her lips into a smile and holds out the papers to me. "Thank you."

I nod, relieved, and tuck them under my arm. Then I say to Kora, "I'll walk you out," and together we turn and make our way out of the office and along the corridor to the lifts.

We don't say anything while we wait for the doors to open. I do glance at her, though, and she meets my eyes with a warm smile and a touch of pity, as if she can sense what I'm going through.

The lift doors open, and we go inside. I press the button for the ground floor, and the doors slowly close.

Kora turns and leans back on the mirrored wall, her coat folded over her arms in front of her. "Well, well," she says, "it's Callum McDuck."

Her words, and the sense of relief that fills me at the knowledge that my deal with Stephanie is done, make me laugh out loud. "It's been a while," I tell her, flicking back the sides of my coat and sliding my hands into my trousers pockets as I lean on the opposite wall. "It's good to see you."

"What are the chances?" she asks. "Of you being married to my third cousin?"

"Pretty slim, I guess." I didn't even know Kora's last name, so it's not surprising I didn't make the connection.

We study each other as the lift descends smoothly, both smiling. I know she's rich—her clothes and jewelry look expensive, her nails are polished, and her hair is carefully cut to look as if she doesn't care about it. And yet there's something very girl-next-door about her that appeals to me.

"So," she says eventually, "did you do it?"

"Do what?"

"Become a billionaire by the time you were thirty?"

I grin. "I did."

She chuckles. "I knew you would. You had an air of determination about you."

I rarely talk openly about money. Other people are either jealous or resentful of those who have it, even if you've worked your bollocks off to get it. I remember how I felt on the beach when Kora told me about her family, and how they'd grown their business over the past two hundred years, working and investing hard to reach the dizzy heights of their success. I'd been thrilled that someone else understood, and I feel a similar pleasure now that she's not shocked at the discussion of wealth that would make most people's jaws drop.

She pushes off the wall and shakes out her coat to put it on. I move forward, and I hold it up for her so she can slide both arms in together. As I lift it onto her back, my fingers brush her neck, and she shivers.

When she turns, she slides a hand to the nape of her neck and lifts her hair out over her collar, where it lies like a soft scarf. Man, this woman is sexy. She hasn't changed a bit in twelve years.

The lift reaches the ground floor, and, as the doors slide open, a rush of warm air and the chatter of excited children washes over us. We leave the lift and walk toward the exit through the displays of soft toys, and I watch Kora glance at the cabinet containing the old teddy bear and smile. She probably still collects antique toys.

We go through the revolving door and out into the murky twilight. It's freezing cold, and the sky is heavy and gray. A few tiny white flakes dance in the air around us, and Kora holds out a hand to catch some, clearly delighted at the prospect of snow. With her tanned skin, honey-colored hair, and bright blue eyes, she seems to glow amongst the pale, serious faces of those walking around us. I don't know why, but something about her fascinates me now, the same way as it did all those years ago on the beach.

"Have dinner with me," I say.

She lifts her gaze to mine and studies me for a moment. Then she says, "So you don't have a meeting with Japanese investors?"

"No," I admit. "Have dinner with me."

"Does Stephanie want the two of you to get back together?"

I nod. "Have dinner with me."

"And you don't?"

I shake my head. "Have dinner with me. Pretty please. With a cherry on top."

Her lips curve up, but she still hesitates. "I don't want to step on Stephanie's toes."

"That's fair enough, but we're done," I confirm. "The divorce is final. I shouldn't have brought the property papers over personally. She took it as a sign that I wanted to talk. I just wanted to see it finished."

Kora pulls a thin scarlet scarf out of her pocket and winds it around her neck a couple of times, then slides her hands into the pockets of her coat. Her hair bunches up over the scarf, light and fluffy. It reminds me of candy floss, of summer. It makes me want to touch it, to bury my face in it. I bet she smells sweet. I bet she tastes sweet, too.

I can see she's thinking about dinner, weighing up the pros and cons.

"For old times' sake," I tell her. "That's all."

She smiles. "You don't give up easily, do you?"

"It's my superpower. Have dinner with me."

"I'm staying at Claridge's," she says softly. "I'm booked in there for six o'clock. Alone."

"I'm sure they can make space for little old me."

"Little old six-foot-two you," she scoffs. "You've grown a couple of inches over the past twelve years."

"You've been peeking."

"I'm talking about your height," she says with a laugh.

"So am I!" I grin. "It sounds perfect."

Her eyes dance, and she presses her lips together, then gestures with her head to the Mercedes sitting on the curbside. "Want to take my ride?"

"Give me one second to give these to my driver." I jog over to where my car is also waiting on the curbside, and instruct Ralph to take the papers back to the office and give them to my PA. Then I return to Kora's car, walk around to the other side, and get in beside her.

"Back to Claridge's please, Graham," she instructs the driver, and he steers the car smoothly into the traffic. He glances in his rearview mirror at me, but doesn't say anything.

"So," she says as the car weaves through the traffic toward Claridge's. "What have you been up to for the last twelve years? Getting married, obviously. Do you have any children?"

"No."

"Your choice or hers?"

She's as direct as I remember. Usually I hate being asked personal questions, but for some reason I find her frankness appealing, maybe because Stephanie never says what's on her mind.

"We just didn't get around to it. Things started going wrong a couple of years ago, so the topic never really came up. What about you? I don't see any ring."

She lifts her left hand and looks at her bare fingers. Is she wistful? Or thankful to have escaped the matrimonial bond? "No, I haven't been married." She drops her hand back into her lap. "I broke up with my boyfriend, Julian, just before Christmas. I've been a bit flat, which is one reason I decided to come out here." Her voice doesn't hold a lot of emotion, but I can see in her face that she's been through a tough time.

"How long were you with him?"

"We lived together for a couple of years." She looks out of the window. "It's been strange traveling alone. I haven't done that before. I did an OE, I mean an overseas experience—that's what we call the time we spend traveling after university—with a friend, and it's so different doing it by yourself. I am very lucky, though, it's amazing the problems you can sort out when you have a generous bank account."

"Yeah, I agree with that. Things have been a lot easier for me since I started making decent money."

She looks back at me at that, and says, "Stephanie said you were in property, and I know your degree was in property valuation. So do you buy and sell sites?"

"Yes. I seem to have a knack for tracking down a good bargain. I buy buildings nobody else is interested in, divide them into apartments and do them up, and sell them individually. There's a lot of money in that."

"I bet there is. Space is at a premium in London, I'm sure."

"So, did you end up working at an auction house?"

She shakes her head. "I did a placement there, and I really enjoyed it. But I ended up at the family business. I do research into which toys are popular, and come up with ways to build new trends into our business. We also recently opened a theme park just outside Wellington, called the South Pole. It's for the children in the southern hemisphere who'd love to see Santa, but obviously can't afford to get to the North Pole. We have all sorts of rides, as well as a trip to see Santa, and there's a toy exhibition that I helped organize with lots of antiques and displays explaining the development of toys over the years. I really enjoyed that."

"And how is your private collection going?"

She laughs. "I spent far too much money on teddy bears. I'm actually thinking of opening a toy museum in Wellington. We don't have anything like that there at the moment, and I think it could do quite well."

I smile. I love that she's so passionate about the things she loves. If Stephanie had possessed a fraction of her enthusiasm, things might have ended very differently.

"We're here," she states unnecessarily as Graham pulls the car up outside Claridge's hotel.

I'm not quite sure why I asked her to dinner. Obviously, she's only here for another week or two, so there's hardly time for anything to develop, not that I'm in the market for a relationship right now—that's the last thing I need. I just wanted to spend time with her.

Life has been hard lately, like the sky above us, dull, gray, and heavy. Seeing Kora was like the sun coming out from behind the clouds, heating me up from the inside out. Maybe I just want a little bit of that sunshine for myself. Hopefully she'll have some to spare.

Chapter Four

Kora

A porter in a top hat and tails comes over to open the car door, and we go into the hotel and walk through to the Foyer and Reading Room that houses the restaurant. It's still relatively early, so there are plenty of tables available. When I explain I've already booked one for six o'clock but I was wondering whether my friend could join me and we could eat earlier, the waiter smiles and politely says, "Of course, madam, come this way," and he leads us through the restaurant to a table by the window.

Callum and I remove our coats and sit opposite one another. I place my serviette on my knees and smooth it out. My stomach flutters, and my hands are shaking.

I'm not sure why I agreed to his proposal for dinner. Nothing good can come of this. I like the guy, but he was married to Stephanie, and obviously, things went badly wrong there. I don't want to upset Stephanie if she finds out we had dinner when he turned her down, and equally I don't want to give him ideas that I'm interested in anything more. I came here alone, with the full intention of putting men behind me for a while. I need to recharge, to heal, and I can't do that if I continue to put my heart into a man's hands.

But I have to be practical. All he's suggested is that we have dinner together to catch up. There's no harm in that, surely? It's not going to lead to anything else, and I am here alone, so it's nice to go out to dinner with a good-looking guy who seems to like me. I don't have to make an impression, because this isn't a date. I don't have to put on any airs and graces, or watch what I say. I just have to be myself, and that's quite refreshing.

The waiter comes back with a menu for each of us, and asks if we'd like a drink.

"What would you like?" Callum asks. "Do you still prefer champagne?"

"I do." He remembered!

"Do you have any rare bottles?" he asks the waiter.

"Yes sir, we have several. I can recommend a Krug Du Soliste a l'Orchestre, or a Dom Perignon Reserve de L'Abbaye?"

"We'll take the Dom Perignon," Callum says, and the waiter nods and leaves us alone to choose our meals.

"Nice choice," I say. "So you drink alcohol now?"

He smiles. "When the occasion demands. Like now. I feel an urge to celebrate."

"That's a nice thing to say."

"I mean it. It's been a long time, and I've thought about you a lot. Even if you did run off on me." His brown eyes are amused.

I straighten my knife and fork. "Yeah... I'm sorry about that. I knew we were off early and got up to pack the car. I was going to come back but Theo told me we were cutting it fine. And somehow... I didn't know how to say goodbye."

"It's okay."

I lift my gaze and look into his eyes. I've thought about it for years, and I need him to understand. "The thing is... I hadn't done anything like that before. I was recovering from a breakup at the time. I'd been seeing a friend of Ben's, and I was really into this guy, but he wasn't into me, and eventually he walked away without looking back. I was heartbroken. I thought there was something wrong with me. You know what it's like when you're younger—you're so dramatic. And then I met you, and you seemed really into me, and it made me feel... wonderful. But I knew you didn't have long in New Zealand, so it wasn't as if I could ask to see you again. I regretted it all the way back on the plane. When I got home, I rang Mik and asked for Rob's number, and I even rang his Dad's house, but his step-mum said you were out at a cricket match, and when she asked if I'd like to leave a message, I suddenly felt silly. What was I expecting? What could I say? So I said no and hung up. But I've always regretted it. I liked you, Callum. A lot."

He smiles. "You really do wear your heart on your sleeve, don't you?"

I feel a little silly now I've been so open. I'd forgotten he's British and that they tend to keep their feelings to themselves. But I lift my chin and reply, "I believe in saying what's in your heart, yes. Otherwise things go unsaid or can be misconstrued. I'd rather regret something I said than something I didn't say."

"That's very wise."

"I don't know about that. It's gotten me into trouble sometimes."

He chuckles. We study each other for a moment, smiling. I feel a little glow inside at the warmth in his eyes. I'm glad I agreed to come for dinner. If nothing else, it's been nice to be able to put my regret to rest.

He looks around the restaurant. "I've not eaten here before, but I've heard good things about it."

I follow his gaze. Art Deco mirrors shimmer on the walls. Music from the grand piano mingles with the candlelight to make the room warm and welcoming. The round tables are laid with spotless white covers, and the silver cutlery sparkles. White-jacketed waiters weave soundlessly between the tables. It's very English—elegant and beautiful.

"It does look amazing," I agree as I look at the menu. "Jacob, my brother, is a foodie, and he's often taken me to new restaurants across New Zealand and Australia. But I have to say, this menu is exquisite."

"How hungry are you?"

"I'm ravenous."

"Great. Let's go for it then."

We decide to start with the chef's dozen canapes—Cornish crab tartlets with tuna and caviar, duck rolls with peppered blackberry sauce, and tempura prawns with a chili, carrot, and soy dip. Then for a first course I choose Severn and Wye smoked salmon with creme fraiche, pickled mustard seeds, and soda bread, while Callum opts for tuna tartare with tomatoes, lemon, and basil.

We spend ages choosing our mains. There's wood roast Norfolk chicken with girolles—which I know through Jacob are mushrooms—and vegetables with a lemon and tarragon jus. A herb crusted rack of Kentish lamb. Aberdeen Angus beef fillet. Scottish salmon, and much more. In the end, I plump for Claridge's Cornish lobster risotto with truffle sauce, and Callum goes for the beef fillet.

The waiter returns with our champagne, and he pours the sparkling liquid into the glasses before we give him our orders, then withdraws and leaves us alone.

I sip the champagne, and the bubbles burst on my tongue, while my mouth floods with the taste of pear and apple, warming me through as it slides down to my stomach. I hadn't realized how cold I'd become while we were out.

"That's fantastic," Callum states after taking a sip. "I haven't had a drink for a while."

"It's warming me up," I say. "I guess February was a stupid month to visit here. I should have come at Easter, or waited until summer in July, while it was winter back home. But after what happened to Theo, I needed to get away as soon as possible."

Callum's eyebrows rise. "Why, what happened to Theo?"

"You didn't see it in the news? Where Theo was stranded on a desert island? He went missing for ten days."

Callum's jaw drops. "That was your brother, the one I met at the beach party? I had no idea. I saw it on the news, of course, but I didn't make the connection that it was him, obviously, and Stephanie never mentioned being related to him."

"She probably doesn't even know. When I contacted her a few months ago about coming over here, she didn't seem to have much knowledge of the Antipodean side of the family. I guess not everyone is interested in family history."

He leans back, stretching out his long legs, and undoes the buttons of his jacket. "Are you?"

I nod. "In fact, that's part of the reason why I'm here. I'm going to try to track down some of my family."

"Oh? You mean apart from Stephanie?"

"Yes." I sip the champagne again. Already, I can feel it working its magic, loosening my over-tightened nuts and bolts. "Stephanie comes from my father's side of the family. I know a lot about them, because Ben—my older brother—has done some research. He has photos all over his office and at home of Arthur Prince, who opened the first Prince's Toy Store here in Regent Street, and Henry Prince, who was the one who came over to New Zealand."

"I remember you telling me about them at the beach. Stephanie's never mentioned them, so I didn't make the connection that you were related."

"That's weird. We're all so proud of our English heritage over there. We know quite a lot about that side of the family. My mother's family is also from England, but I know hardly anything about them, and she died just over a year ago, so I probably never will."

"I'm sorry," he says. "How did she die?"

"From a brain aneurysm," I reply softly. "It was very sudden, and they assured us she wouldn't have felt any pain. I'm pleased about that, but the suddenness was quite shocking. Literally, one day she had a headache, and the next she was gone. Dad was devastated, and I'm not sure he'll ever recover."

We pause as the waiter brings over our canapes, and tuck into the beautiful little bites.

"Are her parents here in the UK?" Callum asks, sampling one of the tempura prawns.

"No, that's the strange thing. They live in New Zealand, but whenever I've asked them about their family or their background, they've always changed the subject. Eventually I got the hint that they didn't want to talk about it, and I stopped asking. I know they came to New Zealand when Mum was in her twenties, but I don't know why. All I know is that my grandmother's family comes from Hastings. Her brother died a few years ago, but his wife—my great-aunt—is still alive, and her daughter said she'd like to meet me. So I thought I'd go and visit her, and see if she can tell me anything else."

"I hope that works out for you," he says. "Roots are important. They fix us in the present, even though at the same time they lead us back into the past."

I smile, pleased he understands. "It would be nice to feel closer to my mum. I know she loved me. But she was sometimes… I don't know… distant. She'd often get lost in thought, and there would be tears in her eyes. She'd look haunted, and she'd go for long walks. She always came back sort of cleansed, and she'd be all right then until it would start all over again. I'm sure there was something bothering her, but she'd never admit to it. I have a gut feeling it was connected to her past, but Dad didn't seem to know. It would be nice if I could find out what it was."

"I hope it helps you," he says. "The truth can be a double-edged sword sometimes." He doesn't elaborate on that mysterious comment, and instead continues with, "These are magnificent," as he finishes off his last Cornish crab tartlet. "I didn't realize how hungry I was. I was at a meeting and missed lunch."

"Shocking," I reply. "I don't think I've ever skipped a meal in my life."

He chuckles, leaning back as the waiter clears the empty plates. We nod when he returns and offers the champagne bottle, and he pours us both another glass. Just minutes later, he comes back with our first courses, and I tuck into the smoked salmon.

"So," I say, "tell me about your business. What happened after you returned to the UK?"

He explains how he established his property company, Tower Group, with his friend Rob. "He comes from a wealthy family," Callum explains, "and when he was twenty-one he came into some money that he offered to invest in a joint business. I'd saved up a bit from the part-time jobs I'd done too, so we used it to buy a cheap, rundown block in Clapham in South London, and then we hired a building firm to divide it up into apartments. Rob and I worked fourteen hours days, supervising and helping out with the builders to get it just right. And we struck lucky—Clapham was on the up, with lots of new bars and restaurants popping up, and we tripled our money. We used that to buy more property in Peckham. I seem to have a knack for picking out sites in places just before they become popular."

"The Midas touch," I say, remembering that's how I'd described Henry Prince all those years ago, and he nods and grins.

"Maybe, yeah."

The waiter clears our plates again. Callum appears surprised to see his glass empty, looks thoughtful when the waiter offers to refill it, then nods when I say, "Aw, go on."

"You're trying to lead me astray," he scolds as the waiter goes to fetch our mains.

"Maybe. Do you mind?"

"No."

We both laugh and sip the bubbles.

"Have you expanded out of London?" I ask him.

"Yeah, we're all over England now, in most of the major cities."

"So what's next? Europe? The world?"

He gives a wry smile, then sighs. "Honestly? I don't know. Once upon a time, I'd have said there was no limit to my ambition. Now?" He shrugs and turns his glass in his fingers.

"What happened?"

"Life." He doesn't elaborate, and then he changes the subject. "So come on then, tell me more about what you've been up to in New Zealand. How's the toy store going?"

I decide not to push it for the moment. "Brilliant, actually. We have branches in most of the major New Zealand cities now, and we expanded to Australia a few years ago." I pause as the waiter places my lobster risotto before me. "Mmm. That smells amazing." I pick up my fork and dig in. "I've really enjoyed helping set up the theme park. It's been great to see all the children's faces when they visit. This was our first Christmas, and it proved really popular, with people coming from all over New Zealand, Australia, the Pacific Islands, even South Africa, to visit."

"It's a great idea."

"It was Ben's brainchild. He's thrilled it's done so well."

"And your exhibition was popular?"

"Yes, enough to encourage me that the idea of a toy museum might work. I think it would do very well."

"I'm sure it would with you behind the wheel." He smiles.

"Feel free to say more nice things like that," I tell him. "It's been a while since I've had any compliments."

He has a forkful of his Maxine potatoes and studies me thoughtfully. "How long has it been since you broke up with your boyfriend again?"

"Last November. Although it was going wrong months before that. Maybe it had never been right."

"You sound sad."

"Yeah, I guess I am. I'm relieved it's over, but I can't shake the feeling of being a failure. That I should have been able to make it work."

Callum sighs. "Tell me about it. I promised to love someone else until death parted us."

We study each other for a moment, then return to eating our meals in silence for a while.

It's not an awkward silence, though. It feels companionable. We both understand the conflicting emotions involved in a breakup. I'm sad for him that his marriage ended, but it's nice he understands how I feel.

"So do you know much about your family?" I ask him eventually.

He sighs. "More than I care to." His lips twist at my curious look. "Let's just say I'm not proud of my father's side."

I remember his surname is MacDuff. "They're Scottish?"

"Yes, but I've disowned them. I'm one hundred percent English, through and through."

"I can see that." I smile. "Your accent is very English public school."

"I've worked hard on it," he admits, to my surprise. "It wasn't always like this."

"Oh?"

"My mother was from south-east London, and I had quite a Cockney accent when I was young. When I went to the footie wiv me titfer and a packet of fags."

I giggle. "What?"

"When I went to the football with my hat and a packet of cigarettes."

"Titfer means hat?"

"Cockney rhyming slang. Tit-for-tat. Hat. Except you just say the first bit—titfer. It goes on your barnet. Your Barnet Fair—your hair."

"Wow, I'd be totally lost."

"That's kind of the point. It's like a secret code."

I smile. "So you're a Cockney at heart?"

"A true Cockney—born within the sound of Bow Bells. It means born near St. Mary-le-Bow church in Cheapside."

"But you chose to lose the accent."

He places his knife and fork on his plate and pushes it a few inches away, then stretches out his legs with a sigh. "I wanted to go to Oxford, and I didn't want to stand out. When Oxford accepted me on a scholarship, I spent six months having elocution lessons to learn to speak 'properly'." He puts air quotes around the word. "Oxford wasn't all upper class by then, but I wanted to be taken seriously, and I knew they'd always look down on me if I had the Cockney accent."

"I can see that. Where do your parents live?"

He sighs again and studies me for a moment, and I can see he's weighing up how much to tell me.

"You don't have to talk about it if you don't want to," I tell him. "I'm just trying to make conversation. We can talk about the weather. If you like."

"It's okay, I'm not offended or anything. It's a long story, that's all, and not a very interesting one."

"I have all evening."

"Do you want a dessert?"

I blow out a breath. "Actually, I'm pretty full up." I pick up the bottle of champagne, disappointed to find it empty.

"What about a coffee?" Callum suggests. "We could take it through to the bar."

"Ooh yes. That's a great idea." I'm pleased he doesn't want the evening to end yet.

Callum settles the bill, despite my insistence to put it on my room, and then we go through to the Fumoir Bar. The bartender makes our cappuccinos behind a black marble horseshoe bar, while we admire the deep aubergine decor and the black-and-white photos of old Hollywood starlets on the walls, illuminated by the lighting from the Lalique crystal panels. We sit side by side on one of the ruby-red velvet sofas, our arms just a few inches apart.

I don't know if it's my imagination, or possibly the champagne filtering through my system, but I feel the first tinglings of a change between Callum and me. Something chemical is happening; the air is thickening, and it's becoming harder to breathe. My pulse is moving faster, and my mouth is going dry. Goose bumps pop out on my arm as he brushes it reaching for his cup when the waiter brings it. I feel hot all over, even though I'm too young—I hope—to be having hot flushes. I unbutton my suit jacket and lay it on the sofa beside me, glad of the cool air that wafts in over my shirt from the door. Callum looks at me, but he doesn't say anything. He just sips his coffee, his eyes glittering in the subtle lighting. Is he aware of it, too? He's so handsome. I'd forgotten just how gorgeous he was.

I clear my throat and sip my cappuccino. "So… where were we? You were going to tell me about your parents."

He turns his glass slowly around in his fingers again. "Okay, but just remember you asked to hear the sorry tale."

It's a mysterious comment, and now I'm intrigued.

"My father was an alcoholic," he says. The words are blunt, as if he's chopped them up with an axe. Oh… that explains why he didn't drink when he was younger. I also note his use of the past tense. "He wasn't one of those men who become funny when he was drunk," he continues. "He was violent to my mother, and toward me." He has another sip of coffee, this time, I think, to cover his emotion.

"Eventually," he continues, "he also drove my mother to drink. I think it was the only way she felt she could cope. She would drink during the day when he was at work. Even as a young child, I can remember finding empty bottles at the backs of drawers and under the bed."

"Oh, that's not good."

"No. When I was four, she fell pregnant again. My father was angry, because we didn't have much money and he didn't want another child, but she refused to have an abortion. That just made him worse though. So she continued to drink, all the way through the pregnancy. As a result, my brother was born with fetal alcohol syndrome."

"Oh, Callum," I say softly.

"At first, they weren't sure how bad it was, but it soon became clear it had affected him badly. He grew slowly, and he has problems with his hearing. He has ADHD, issues with his memory, and his speech was delayed. He has severe learning difficulties, and now he has a mental age of about fourteen, even though he's only four years younger than me. My mother felt terribly guilty about this. Of course, by then, there was nothing she could do."

He has a big mouthful of coffee. I can see what it's taken him to relate all this.

"Josh found ordinary primary school almost impossible, but Mum had a part-time job and couldn't teach him at home, and they couldn't afford to send him to a special private school. My father was drinking a lot by then, and growing more violent. He put Mum in hospital a couple of times."

"Oh no."

"The police came around to give him a warning, but each time she told them it wasn't him and that she'd walked into a cupboard door or something. There wasn't much they could do if she refused to press charges. I've never understood that."

"You mean how your father could do that to her?"

"Well, yes, of course, that as well, but really I meant how she could stay with him. Why didn't she walk out the first day he hit her? But anyway, things got worse and worse. Then, one day, something tipped her over the edge. He'd bruised her face for the first time, I think, and she'd had enough. I was ten, Josh was six. She took me and Josh to her parents. My grandfather, Jim, saw her face and hit the roof. She just cried. And then my father turned up. He and Jim had a huge argument. He hit Jim, knocked him out cold, stormed into the house, and grabbed Mum and dragged her out."

My jaw drops. Somehow, I know this story isn't going to have a happy ending.

"I ran out with Josh after them, even though my grandmother called me to stay. Dad bundled us in the car and drove off. He and Mum argued. They'd both been drinking. I don't know what happened; I think she pulled his arm, and he lost control of the car. He crashed into the barrier on the motorway."

"Oh Callum, that's just awful. Were you or Josh hurt?"

He slides a hand beneath the hair covering his forehead and lifts it, revealing an old scar. "Apparently there was blood all over my face, but it wasn't a bad cut. Josh wasn't touched. But my parents were both dead by the time they got to the hospital."

My heart fills with sorrow. Clearly, this is an old story, one Callum has gone over in his head repeatedly, but it still hasn't lost its power to hurt him.

"Oh, I'm so sorry. That's just terrible."

He lets out a long sigh, but at the same time it's as if he's released all the tension he's been holding in his body. "I haven't spoken to anyone about it for years."

"Not even Stephanie?"

"Especially not Stephanie." His voice is sour.

I'm really intrigued now as to what went wrong in their marriage, but I don't know him well enough to grill him about that. "So what happened with you and Josh?" I ask instead.

"Jim and Helen—my grandparents—took us in. I know guilt weighed heavily on them for not doing more to help Mum while she was alive. They did try, but you can only do so much for someone when they refuse help. Anyway, we went to live with them until I reached eighteen and got in at Oxford. They taught Josh at home and looked after him. As soon as I was able to afford it, I bought a bigger house for us all. Josh now has a helper with him for several hours a day to give my grandfather a break. Helen died a few years ago, but I think Jim will live forever." He grins. He clearly has lots of affection for the old guy.

"And how is Josh doing now?"

"Pretty good," he says. "I got the best doctor I could find, and they've worked out his medication, so he's a lot more stable than he was. But I don't think he'll ever be self-sufficient. He'll never be able to leave home, get married, and have a house of his own." He gives me a sad smile. "I'm so sorry, I had no intention of blurting all this out. I bet you're regretting agreeing to go to dinner with me now."

"Of course not. I like you, Callum, and it's lovely to find out more about you and your family. I've often wondered about you, over the years, whether you achieved your dream, and what you were up to. It's lovely to be able to fill in the gaps."

"Me too. I thought about you a lot."

We smile at each other. Once again, I feel a flutter deep inside, the sensation of something changing between us. Deepening, warming. It's as if when we met we were wearing suits of armor, but we've gradually unbuckled and removed them plate by plate, until we're standing together, skin to skin.

Ooh, skin. I can smell his body spray, and see the five o'clock shadow on his cheek. It makes me want to run my fingers along his jaw and feel the bristles scrape under my nails.

Callum's eyes darken, his eyelids dropping to half-mast, and his gaze falls to my mouth. He's thinking about kissing me.

"You shouldn't look at me like that," I whisper.

"Why?"

"Because Stephanie wouldn't like it."

"Stephanie and I are divorced," he points out.

"I know…" I'm consumed by curiosity. "What went wrong between the two of you?"

His face darkens, and he looks away.

"I'm sorry." I'm tempted to kick myself. Talk about spoil the mood. "I've put my foot in it again."

He gives me a small smile at that. "No you haven't. It's a fair enough question. It's a sore subject, that's all. I suppose I'm a little embarrassed at revealing all my deep, dark secrets within two hours of seeing you again. There's something about you that wheedles them out of me, though." One corner of his mouth lifts, and then, to my surprise, he reaches out and takes a strand of my hair between two fingers, moving them back so the hair slides through them. I can't suppress a shiver, and the gleam in his eyes tells me he's spotted it.

"I don't mind," I whisper. "I've told you a bit about Vic and Julian. I have plenty more failed relationships in between those two. You could argue my life has been one disaster after another. I'm hardly in a position to pass judgment."

Still, I can't help but be curious about why they broke up. For the first time, I wonder whether he had an affair. I'm not sure how I'd feel if he admitted he cheated on her. Especially after what happened with Julian.

"She had an affair," he says.

I'm so surprised. I can only stare at him. "Seriously?"

"Seriously."

"Why on earth would a woman cheat on a man like you?"

That makes him laugh, and this time his gaze holds affection. "That's a nice thing to say."

"With whom?"

He sighs. "With Rob."

My jaw drops again. "Your business partner?"

"Yup."

"I don't believe it." I remember Rob as a fresh-faced guy with a plummy accent and floppy hair, Hugh Grant style. They'd seemed pretty tight, and of course they set up the company together.

His wife cheated on him with his best friend and business partner. No wonder he's bitter.

"Things weren't going well between us," he says. "Stephanie wanted to move away. She has relatives in France, and she kept pushing me to move to Monaco. But I didn't want to move. My company was here, and of course, although I could attempt to run it all online, I still like to have a hand in searching for property, and physically going there myself to scout it out. Not just that, but my grandfather and brother are here. The thing is, you see, Stephanie wanted to get me away from them. She felt that they had too much of a claim on my time, and if I'm perfectly honest, I don't think she liked Josh at all."

"Oh, that's terrible."

"I can understand it, he's a difficult person to like. He can be aggressive, and I think he frightened her once or twice when he lost his temper and caused a scene in public. But he's my brother, and I'm afraid if you're going to love me, you also have to love my brother."

"Of course."

"So I told her I couldn't go, and things began to sour between us. It was only a few months later that a friend told me he'd seen her and Rob coming out of a hotel room together. She denied it, of course, but when I confronted Rob, he admitted it."

"So you were doubly betrayed," I whisper.

"That's how it feels, yes. I loved Rob like another brother, and in a really strange way, his betrayal hurt more. Does that make sense?"

"Oh yes," I murmur. "Much more sense than you could ever know."

Chapter Five

Callum

I have no idea why I'm telling Kora all this. I can't remember the last time I opened up like this to a woman, to anyone, in fact. I've never spoken about my wife's affair, not to a friend, and not to a therapist. I don't want to go over and over the reasons why it happened. I don't need to analyze how it made me feel. I want to put it behind me and walk away as fast as I can in the opposite direction. So it is surprising that it has all come tumbling out while talking to Kora.

At first, I felt a flicker of regret at opening up so much, not wanting to look weak, and not wanting her to pity me. But her comment about how Rob's betrayal would hurt more has intrigued me.

"Did something similar happen to you?" I ask.

"Julian, my ex, had an affair with my best friend."

Well, she really does understand. I'm shocked we've been through exactly the same thing.

"I'd known Gina since high school," she states. "She was the one who was at the beach with me. We went to the same university, and we were true besties, at least I thought we were. We told each other everything. I had no secrets from her, and I thought she had none from me. Things weren't going great with Julian. He was out a lot, working late, and little things began to make me suspect he was having an affair. You know the signs—indifference, making excuses, strange receipts in his wallet, not that I went looking, but you come across these things, don't you?"

I nod, knowing exactly what she means. "You have this instinct that something isn't right, but when you try to bring it up, they tell you nothing's wrong."

She nods enthusiastically. "That's exactly right. I think they call it gaslighting don't they? Making you question your own sanity. He made me feel as if I was the one in the wrong for even questioning his loyalty. When I tried to talk about it, he got angry and told me I was losing my mind. I'll never forgive him for that."

"How did you find out?"

"Like you, a friend saw them together. At first, I was convinced it wouldn't be Gina, sure she wouldn't do something like that to me. It's so funny, but it's just like you said, I feel her betrayal affected me so much more than his. I don't know why. I mean, he was my partner. She was just my friend."

"I don't know why either, but I feel the same."

"It destroyed me," she states. She takes a shaky breath and blows it out slowly. "We had such terrible rows. He eventually admitted it, and then everything changed. He begged for my forgiveness, and wanted us to stay together. I said that wasn't going to happen, but when you've invested all that time in a relationship, the last thing you want to do is throw it all away. Now, I can't remember why I thought it would be a good idea to try again, but he was so persuasive. And I did love him, I think, and I wanted it to work. There was a period of about two or three months where I went back a couple of times, but I couldn't bring myself to trust him. Every time we parted, I kept wondering where he was going, if he was seeing her. In the end, it drove a wedge between us, and I couldn't get rid of it. He could be extremely unpleasant when he didn't get his own way, and he turned violent—not toward me, but he lost his temper and smashed the TV up. He frightened me, and that was the final straw. I walked out and went to stay with my brother, Ben. He has a lovely house on the edge of the Abel Tasman National Park, and it's so quiet there, and it gave me time to rest and reflect. When Julian did contact me again, and I went back to see him, it was clear to me then that it was over."

I look at this beautiful woman and wonder why we insist on hurting those we love. It's terrible the things people do to each other.

"I'm sorry," she says, giving me a tentative smile. "I try not to talk about it too much because it still upsets me."

"I'm glad I'm not the only one who is cracking open his chest and revealing his heart here," I say wryly.

"I'm just surprised there's any of my heart still left. I thought Julian had destroyed it completely. I feel so empty sometimes."

We smile at each other. It's somewhat sad that we feel brought together by our joint betrayal, but it's also comforting to think Kora understands what I've been through.

"So how have you been since your divorce?" she asks. "Have you started dating again?"

"I haven't even thought about it, to be honest. I still work ten to twelve-hour days, and I've never been a socialite. The women I do meet are normally in a relationship. Maybe one day I'll put myself on the market again, but for now I'm happy to concentrate on my work and my family."

"Put yourself on the market," she repeats. "Trust you to come up with a business analogy."

I chuckle. "What about you? Have you been dating again?"

She also shakes her head. "To be honest, I think I was depressed for a while. I didn't even go out of the house except to fly with Ben straight to the office and then back again. At the end of last year, I moved in with my friend Mollie in Wellington, and I'm still there. I need to get my own place, live on my own for a while, and continue the healing process."

The more she's spoken, the more I can see how badly her relationship has affected her. It's clear her ex's betrayal has run very deep.

"So you're not one of those people who go on Tinder then?" she asks, somewhat mischievously.

My lips curve up at the sudden change in topic. "No, I wouldn't touch that with someone else's bargepole."

"So what you do for, you know, sex?"

"That's what your right hand is for, isn't it?"

Her eyes light up, and she gives an attractive husky chuckle. "Yeah. I have to say it's a lot easier than dating."

My temperature rises at the thought of Kora Prince pleasuring herself. It's the first time our conversation has turned sexual, but I suppose it was inevitable after the way we met last time. A lot of water has flowed under the bridge since then, but the initial spark of attraction I felt for her when I first saw her that day on the beach is still there.

I like her openness, her laid-back attitude, the fact that she has no side, and none of her comments are barbed or spiteful. I feel that what you see is what you get with Kora. She wears her heart on her sleeve, and I like that, after years of living with someone with whom I had to excavate the conversation to discover exactly what she really meant to say.

"I might have a proper drink," I tell her softly. "Would you like one?" I drink so rarely, but I'm really enjoying myself tonight.

She nods. "I'll have a gin and tonic."

I get up and go over to the bar, order hers and a double whiskey for myself, and bring them back to the sofa. The restaurant is a lot busier now, but this corner of the bar is quiet and warm, and we're able to talk without being overheard.

I pass Kora her G&T and sit beside her, a few inches closer than I was before. If she notices, she doesn't comment. We're not touching, but our knees are only an inch apart, and I imagine I can feel the warmth from her body. I rest one arm on the back of the seat, not quite around her, although I could easily pull her into my arms if I wanted.

"I thought a lot about that night on the beach," I say quietly. "I didn't go to the party with the intention of getting laid. It was the furthest thing from my mind when Rob and I went traveling. I've always wanted to tell you that."

"I think I told you the same thing at the time," she replies. "Theo and I had traveled up to be with some friends who then mentioned they were going to Matai Bay that night. We didn't have anything else planned and decided to go along for the ride. I was still getting over Vic, and I certainly didn't mean to sleep with anyone. I've always wanted to say it wasn't as if you were the first port in a storm, if you know what I mean."

"It was a good night," I murmur. "Quite magical in a way. I don't know whether it was the jetlag, but I felt as if I'd stepped through the looking glass. I was on the other side of the world, and it was hot, at Christmastime. Everything was so totally alien, even though New Zealand is very like England in so many ways. Maybe it was because we were in the Northland, which is subtropical, and there's nothing like that here. But everything felt hot and sultry. I remember thinking when you came out of the water that you looked like a mermaid."

Kora chuckles. "And you totally fascinated me. You weren't like any of the other guys I knew back then. As soon as I saw you on the beach, I couldn't take my eyes off you. You were quiet, much more reserved than the men I'm used to. That fascinated me. When we spoke, your accent just blew me away."

"I don't have an accent. You have an accent."

We both grin.

"I seem to remember you had a very hot bikini," I tell her. I'm getting a little more daring now. Maybe it's the whiskey after the champagne, maybe it's the warm, cozy, intimate atmosphere, or maybe it's looking into Kora's eyes, the color of a Bunsen burner turned up to its full heat.

"I was so glad I bought that bikini," she states.

"And your hair was really short." I lift a hand and run a strand of her long blonde hair through my fingers again. "I liked it, but I have to say I prefer it like this."

"I forgot it was short back then," she whispers, and gives a little shiver.

"I'm not normally so forward with strangers," I tell her, "but somehow I don't feel that we are."

She shakes her head. "No, we aren't."

"Thank you for that night."

"Thank *you*." She sips her G&T, not taking her eyes from mine.

I don't know where this is going. When I suggested dinner, I had no intention of taking it any further. All I knew was that I wanted to spend more time with her, and I didn't want to just walk away.

But now... The look in her eyes is stirring my blood. It must be because I haven't had sex for a while, but I find myself picturing undoing her shirt, sliding it off her shoulders, and filling my hands with her breasts. I want to press my lips against her warm skin, and to kiss her. More than anything, I want to kiss her.

Her lips part, and she moistens them with the tip of her tongue. "I thought we were just going to have dinner."

"That's all I had in mind. Originally."

She looks at my mouth. "I don't know what it is about you, I mean, it's been twelve years, but I feel exactly how I did back then."

"How do you feel?" I take the strand of hair between my fingers again, and pull it gently, running my fingers down it.

She swallows. "I haven't had a one-night stand since that night on the beach."

"Me neither."

"So why can't I stop thinking about seeing you naked?"

I imagine how it's going to feel to kiss her again. "I don't know, but there is something between us. That hasn't changed over twelve years." I can feel it stirring, awakening. I'm tingling all over. I want this woman more than I want to breathe.

She clears her throat. "So... do you... want to come upstairs with me?"

A touch of color appears in her cheeks. I can see the courage it's taken her to say those words.

This isn't something she does all the time. She's been badly hurt, and it's taken a lot for her to open up like this. Maybe it's because of what happened between us before, but I believe she feels safe with me. And there's nothing wrong with that.

"I'd love to," I tell her, barely being able to believe it. I was telling the truth when I said I hadn't had a one-night stand since her. I was faithful to Stephanie all the years we were together, and I haven't been with anyone since. Now, though, the thought of taking Kora to bed sets me alight.

We finish our drinks and leave the glasses on the table. Then we rise, pick up our coats, and walk out past the reception desk and over to the lifts.

She presses the button to call the carriage, and we wait silently for the doors to open.

She stands quietly, not looking at me. I'm not sure if she's excited or nervous. Probably both. I feel exhilarated, filled with hope for the first time in a long time. I feel as if I'm twenty-one again, doing something on the spur of the moment, which I very rarely do nowadays.

There are two other couples waiting, so when the doors ding and open, we go into the carriage and stand side by side at the back. Kora presses the button for floor seven, so I know she must be staying in one of the top suites. The doors slide closed, and the lift begins to rise.

The other couples talk quietly. Kora and I don't speak, but I'm acutely conscious of her beside me. I can smell her perfume, and my gaze is drawn to where she's pulled her honey-colored hair around to the other side of her neck, revealing her lightly tanned skin. I want to press my lips to it.

The lift stops and dings at floor five, and the two couples get out. The doors slide shut, and it ascends again.

Kora turns and looks at me, leaning back against the carriage, her hands behind her back. Her eyes are wide, her lips glistening and slightly parted. Her pulse races in her neck.

Without another word, I stride across the carriage, take her face in my hands, and crush my lips to hers.

Chapter Six

Kora

As Callum pushes me up against the wall of the elevator, my whole body bursts into flames.

Okay, maybe not literally, but it does feel as if he's started a fire inside me and thrown lighter fuel onto it. He tilts his head, changing the angle of the kiss, then strokes his tongue across my bottom lip. I'm happy to open my mouth to him, and he delves his tongue inside, raising my thermostat once again.

I lift my arms around his neck, and he slides his hands around me to rest on my lower back. He leans his hard body against me, squashing me up against the wall, but I'm in no position to complain. This was what I wanted. It's been twelve years, but all the feelings I had that night on the beach when we slept together in that tiny tent come rushing back. The cool, calm, and collected Englishman vanishes, no longer in control as his passion sweeps over both of us. When my tongue dances with his, he gives a satisfied growl low in his throat that fires me up.

I haven't been wanted like this for a long time. Sex with Julian had become complicated toward the end, morphing into a power struggle where he attempted to control me. I did my best to fight back, but in the end it was all about him taking his pleasure from me with little regard to my own.

Callum's kisses are demanding, not requesting, and yet it's different in some inexplicable way. Great sex is about being desired, something that Julian never really got to grips with, and Callum makes me feel as if he wants me with every cell in his body.

The elevator dings, and we break apart as the doors open, although there's nobody there. I take his hand, leading him down the corridor to the Empress Eugenie suite.

Outside the door, I pause and turn to face him, resting my hands on his chest. "You're sure about this?" I ask. "This isn't about Stephanie?" Part of me wonders whether he's doing it to hurt her.

"No." He cups my face. "It's all about you." And he kisses me again, taking my breath away as he pushes me up against the door, kissing me until my knees tremble.

It's only when I hear the elevator ding again that I realize someone's about to exit. "Stop," I instruct, and quickly let myself into the suite, pulling him with me.

The door is still swinging shut when his lips find mine again, and then we start tugging off each other's clothes. Coats, shoes and boots, trousers, jackets, shirts, his tie, all drop to the carpet as we make our way to the bedroom, me walking backward, him guiding me so I don't walk into the furniture or the bedroom door.

Soon only our underwear remains, and I feel a surge of relief that I chose to wear a matching cream lace bra and knickers, one of the most exquisite and expensive produced by New Zealand's best lingerie shop—the Four Seasons.

I lean against a chest of drawers, and Callum admires me while his hands skate over my skin. "You look amazing," he murmurs, cupping my breasts and brushing his thumbs over the lace covering my nipples.

"You don't look so bad yourself." I place my hands on his muscular shoulders and brushing down his chest. I grow hot as I glance down at his black boxer briefs and the erection they are barely restraining.

Wanting to speed things up, I reach around behind me, undo my bra, draw the straps down my arms, and toss it away. Callum inhales and fills his palms with my breasts. I moan and arch against him, desire flooding me as my body stirs and awakens.

"Callum... I want you so much. I need you inside me."

That seems to remove his last shred of control, and this time when he kisses me, he doesn't hold back. His mouth is hard and hot over mine, his lips almost bruising me with the intensity of the kiss, but I don't care. I return it hungrily, sliding my hands up into his hair and clutching my fingers there.

He hooks his fingers in the elastic of my knickers and pulls them down my legs. I kick them off, and do the same to him, removing his boxer briefs. Now we're naked, and there's nothing between us to stop this volcano of heat erupting between us.

I begin to walk backwards toward the bed, still kissing him, and then he suddenly bends and lifts me into his arms. It's a four-poster bed, with beautiful white tulle drapes and a crisp white duvet with blue flowers. He peels back the duvet and places me on the mattress, with my head on the soft white pillow, then climbs on and lowers on top of me. He feels magnificent, all that hot skin and hard muscle.

"Do you have a condom?" I whisper, suddenly remembering that I don't have any with me. I hadn't thought I'd need them. I don't really want to have to ring the butler and ask if he could bring me some.

"In my wallet," he states before kissing me again, so deeply it's difficult to catch my breath. Wow, the guy really knows how to kiss. He's making me ache, causing a pressure to build deep inside me that isn't going away anytime soon.

It's not helped when he finally tears his lips from mine and begins to kiss down my neck to my breasts. He takes one of my nipples in his mouth and sucks gently, playing with the other with his fingertips. Darts of pleasure shoot through me, and I moan and squirm beneath him, trying to press my hips against his, although he's too heavy for me to move.

I bear it for as long as I can, but I haven't had sex for a while, and if he continues, I know I'm going to come, and I don't want to, not until he's inside me.

"Where's your wallet?" I ask.

In answer, he gets up, comes back with his trousers, and places his wallet and phone on the bedside table, then retrieves a foil packet. He climbs back on the bed, opens it, and rolls the condom on. Then he leans back over me and looked down into my eyes.

"You're sure?" he asks. In answer, I pull him down on top of me and wrap my legs around his waist, and he gives a throaty chuckle. "Stop rushing me," he scolds. His voice, deep, teasing, makes the hairs on the back of my neck stand on end.

I rock against the base of his erection. "Callum… you're making me ache…"

He kisses me, obviously taking pity on me. "All right." He guides the tip of his erection down, then pushes forward.

We both give a long, heartfelt groan at the sensation of him being buried so deep inside me. I rock my hips, but he murmurs, "Wait," and I still as he pulls his hips back and withdraws until he's almost out, then pushes forward again slowly, coating himself with my moisture. This time he pauses, letting me adjust, before doing it again.

"Nice and slow," he states, continuing to move with long, patient thrusts. "We're in no rush, are we?"

"I guess not." I feel as if I'm floating away on a bed of pleasure, sleepy and lazy with it. I close my eyes and suck my bottom lip as he kisses my neck. "Mmm…"

"Just relax." He trails his tongue over my skin, teasing it until it feels hyper-sensitive, and my whole body is humming. "We'll get there," he promises. "Let's go at my pace, that's all."

"Happy for you to take the reins," I mumble, stroking up his spine. My fingers find the defined muscles in his back and shoulders, and follow the bones across and down to his hips. There I stroke over the large muscles of his bottom that clench and release as he moves. I tighten my fingers on them, trying to get him to thrust harder.

He gives a short laugh, pushes up onto his hands, then withdraws, carefully holding the condom. "I guess I've got to find another way to take charge." And then he flips me over onto my front.

"Callum!" I squeal, breathless and somewhat shocked at how easily he did it, as if I weigh no more than a pillow.

"I told you," he scolds. "Nice and slow." He moves my legs apart, presses the tip of his erection into my folds, then plants his hands on either side of my shoulders and pushes forward.

I groan at this new angle, shuddering as his hips rest against the back of my thighs, and feeling him all the way up inside me as I clench. "Ohhh…"

"Ah, Kora, you're driving me mad…" He slips his arms under mine, his chest resting against my back, his heavy weight pinning me down. I'm unable to move, unable to speed him up, to do anything but lie there and let him slide in and out of me as I grow gradually hotter and hotter. Ohhh… That's so sexy…

Part of me wants him to drive me at breakneck speed toward a climax, but equally I love the way he's taking his time, moving his hips with slow, regular thrusts, stopping occasionally as he turns my face so he can kiss my lips.

I feel decadent and wicked, having sex with a man I hardly know in a country on the other side of the world. This isn't Kora Prince, the well-behaved girl-next-door who doesn't dare step out of place because her brothers will tease her and her father will be disappointed in her. I don't recognize this woman, who's being so open with her sexuality, who's taking risks.

And yet I don't feel as if this is risky, or as if I'm being unsafe. It's not as if I dragged a guy in off the street and forced him to have sex with me.

I can't concentrate anymore; my thoughts are a whirlpool, whipped up with my emotions, which spin around me. Callum's murmuring in my ear… "Do you still moan loudly when you come, Kora? Let's find out, shall we?" And he tugs at my nipple while he fastens his mouth on my neck and sucks.

I can't hold back, and I don't want to, so I let the orgasm sweep over me and carry me away. I clench around him, fiercely, crying out as I bury my face in the pillow. Aahhh… that's so amazing… Ohhh… It's going on forever… and it doesn't stop as he thrusts harder and finally comes himself, shuddering, holding me so tightly I can't breathe.

We lock together for what feels like an ice age, and then all at once our bodies release us, and we collapse together, heaving in great lungfuls of air.

"Fuck," Callum says, and I give a short laugh.

"Yeah."

"Holy shit." He buries his face in my neck. "How come, twelve years later, you're still the best sex I've ever had?"

It's such a nice thing to say, and so surprising, that my eyes prick with tears. I blink them away hurriedly. I'm not supposed to be bringing my emotions into this.

"Skill," I reply, and I feel his answering laugh rumble through him.

He moves back and withdraws, disposes of the condom, then drops back onto the bed beside me and pulls me into his arms. "You do," he states, wrapping his arms around me.

"Do what?" I yawn.

"Moan loudly when you come. Luckily I doubt anyone can hear us here. I'm sure everyone on the beach heard you back then."

I cover my face. "Oh, don't."

"Don't be embarrassed. I love it." He chuckles, lifts up onto an elbow, and pushes me onto my back so he can look at me. He tucks a strand of my hair behind my ear. "You asked earlier, and I don't want you to think this had anything to do with Stephanie. I'm not trying to get back at her, or make her jealous. You and I… we had that amazing night twelve years ago, and when I saw you, I swear I just wanted to catch up and see how you'd been. I didn't expect anything, and it was only as the evening wore on that I couldn't keep away from you…"

I smile, cup his jaw, and brush my thumb against his stubble. "I understand. Me too. It seems we're destined to do this. Shall we make a date for 2033?"

That makes him laugh, and then he bends his head and gives me a long, lingering kiss. When he finally moves back, regret shines in his brown eyes. "I wish you'd been the Prince who owned the Regent Street toy shop."

I think he's saying he wishes he'd married me instead of Stephanie. I'm immensely flattered. "Part of me does, too. Although I would miss New Zealand. I'm a Kiwi through and through, I'm afraid. All the class stuff here would annoy me."

"Yeah. I get that." He kisses my nose. "I think that's what appeals to me so much. You're very open and upfront about things."

He lies back down, and I snuggle up to him again. I'm not sure what time it is—maybe nine, ten o'clock?

Is he going to stay? I'm sure he'll probably want to go home, maybe check on his brother, and I'm sure he has to get up early. But I don't want him to leave. I kind of like having him in my bed.

"Do you want to stay the night?" I ask.

He chuckles. "See? Upfront." He kisses my forehead. "I might stay a while. Make the most of it."

"Okay. I'm glad." I lean across and flick off the bedside light.

"It makes a change," he says, and yawns. "Normally I'm working till ten, eleven o'clock. My PA will wonder what happened to me."

I smile and close my eyes. His chest rises and falls beneath my hand. He smells nice.

Briefly, I wonder whether Princess Eugenie slept with anyone in this bed. And then I fall asleep.

Chapter Seven

Callum

After a while, Kora's slow, regular breathing tells me she's dozed off.

She's warm in my arms, her breasts soft against my chest. Her candy-floss hair is rumpled and fluffy. It looks silver rather than gold in the light from the streetlamp coming through the windows.

There's no moon tonight. The sky is thick and gray. It's definitely going to snow more heavily soon.

I should go. I'm always in the office by seven, and if I walk in wearing the same suit and tie I wore today, my PA will definitely notice. I also don't want Jim to worry about me. I did text him that I was staying with a friend, but he doesn't always remember to check his phone. Josh usually stays up to see me before he goes to bed, and he's probably making a fuss because I didn't appear. Jim is well able to deal with Josh's tantrums, but I feel responsible for my brother, and I don't like leaving the load on Jim's shoulders. He's eighty now, and although he's in good health and fine spirits, he's not as robust as he used to be.

I sigh, and Kora shifts in my arms and murmurs before stilling again. I shouldn't have come up to her room tonight. I don't think either of us will regret it, but I'm going to have to leave, and it won't be any easier than it was twelve years ago. I've never slept around, never had one-night stands. I don't know how people do it.

I could sneak out while she's asleep. It's what she did to me on the beach. But I don't think she did it on purpose. I believe her when she said she was going to come back and say goodbye but her brother stopped her, because that's what Mik saw.

And besides, I'm bigger than that. Sneaking out suggests I'm ashamed of what's happened, and I'm not. I'm thankful, because Kora has proven there's nothing wrong with me. For a long while, I thought there was, because I'd stopped feeling anything.

When I first met Stephanie, she was giving a keynote speech at a conference. There were several hundred attendees, but she didn't look nervous at all, and she spoke confidently and knowledgeably about running a business in the current economic climate. After her speech we split into smaller focus groups, and she happened to be in mine. She was intelligent and even funny at times, completely undaunted by the egos of the men and women who were eager to compete with each other to show their business acumen. If anything, she seemed bored by it all.

I suppose I should have known better, but I was ripe for seduction by this slightly older, knowledgeable woman. I was making a lot of money, and the young women I met seemed to sense that. As a result I'd grown jaded and cynical of women who fell over themselves to get my attention.

Stephanie looked at me with quiet amusement and interest, but made no attempt to engage me. And so I pursued her dutifully, showering her with gifts, determined to find the passionate woman I was convinced lay beneath the disdain she carried for everyone and everything. I had stars in my eyes, and I asked her to marry me within six months of our first date.

Within that first year, I began to realize I'd made a mistake. For Stephanie, I was a status symbol, the younger toy-boy husband, like a flash car or a house in France, a piece of jewelry she donned in public to show everyone how successful she was. She held interviews with the big magazines and photo shoots to show off our house and furniture, which I hated. It wouldn't have been so bad if, when we were alone, she dropped her disdain and became the loving, affectionate woman I'd hoped she was. But she never did.

I told myself I was asking too much, and I had to learn to live with my disappointment. Maybe this happened in most marriages. Perhaps the love and affection I sought was unrealistic.

Then I found out about her affair, and it crushed me. When I confronted her, she declared it was because I'd been too caught up in my work and hadn't paid her enough attention. That shocked me. Was it true? I thought I'd been attentive and loving, as much as I was able, but perhaps I hadn't. I know I work too hard, but I love it, it's my passion, and it wasn't as if she was a housewife sitting there waiting for me—she worked similar hours to me.

Whether it was true or not, having an affair wasn't the way to get my attention. It killed any remaining affection I had for her, and I withdrew, emotionally and physically, leaving her the house she'd made into a show home and purchasing a new property on the other side of London for myself, Jim, and Josh.

Maybe if it had changed her, things would have ended differently. But although she asked me not to leave, insisting she loved me, it was all done with the same cold, bored feeling of disdain she carried with her all the time, and I realized she wasn't capable of feeling any emotion deeper than that. She might love me, in her own way, but she couldn't supply what I needed from a marriage.

So I walked out, and I didn't look back.

I threw myself into my work, but each night when I eventually got home I couldn't sleep, and lay awake into the early hours, trying to numb the pain with whiskey. I yearned for something I was convinced I would never have, and in those dark hours I blamed myself too, thinking maybe I was the same as Stephanie, and unable to feel or express the depth of emotion a true relationship needs. I felt weak and pathetic, and I hated myself for it.

And then I saw Kora, and I felt as if the last twelve years hadn't existed. Maybe I'd been searching for how I felt during that one night of carefree, loving abandon ever since, or maybe I'm just being romantic and seeing something that wasn't there, but the way Kora was with me tonight has gone a little way to sealing the hole in my heart that has been growing since Stephanie and I broke up.

I kiss Kora's hair. I'm tired, and I don't want to go.

Reaching across to the bedside table, I pick up my phone, and set an alarm for five a.m.

Then I turn and wrap my arms around her, and within a minute I fall asleep.

*

When the soft beeping of my alarm wakes me, I turn it off as Kora stirs in my arms.

"What time is it?" she asks, and yawns.

"Five a.m."

"Do you have to go?"

"In a minute." It's still dark outside, and it's cozy beneath the covers. The last thing I want to do is leave.

The two of us have hardly moved all night. She's still pressed up against me, and now she slides her arms around my waist and nuzzles my chest. "Mmm, you're so warm," she murmurs.

I stroke her back, running my fingers up and down her spine. "Thank you for last night."

"I'm so glad we met again. I feel as if we've been able to put things to rights, you know?"

"I do."

"I've just got to think now what I'm going to say when Stephanie asks why I've got a big smile on my face this morning."

"Tell her you had a really good breakfast."

"A warm croissant has been known to be as good as an orgasm in the morning."

I laugh, lift up onto an elbow, and roll her onto her back. She giggles and wraps her arms around my neck. "Almost," she adds.

"Is that a hint?"

"Maybe." Her eyes glitter in the light from the streetlamp outside, and she moistens her lips with the tip of her tongue.

Desire surges through me, even though it's only been six hours or so since we had sex. "You're insatiable," I scold, sliding a hand down her body to cup her mound.

She parts her legs for me and pulls my head down to kiss me. "It's you," she whispers, kissing my cheek, my jaw, then back to my lips. "I can't keep my hands off you."

I feel a flutter of pleasure at the fact that someone wants me. It's such a little thing, but it makes me feel like a king.

I kiss her back, brushing my tongue against hers while I slip my fingers down into her still-moist folds, and I stroke her there for a while, enjoying the lazy spiral staircase of passion we ascend slowly together. I love her perfume that rises to ensnare me, it's fruity and sweet, reminding me of black cherries, and it makes me want to bury my mouth in her and see if she tastes the same.

So I begin to kiss down her body, focusing at first on her nipples, which tighten and turn to hard pebbles in my mouth and I suck them. She moans and clenches her fingers in my hair, and I stay there for a while, continuing to tease her with my fingers as I lick and flick the ends of her nipples with my tongue. Then, after a while, I continue down, shifting on the bed so I can lower myself between her legs under the duvet. She sighs and stretches, unashamedly offering herself to me, and I kiss up her soft thigh before sliding my tongue into her folds and licking all the way up.

"Mmm, Callum…" Her husky, breathless voice turns me on, and I decide to make it my aim to see how loud I can make her moan when she comes. The best way I can think of to achieve this is to keep her teetering on the edge of pleasure for as long as possible.

So I take my time to arouse her slowly, teasing with my tongue and fingers until her breathing quickens and she begins to writhe, and then stopping and kissing her belly and thighs, smiling at her deep groans of frustration. Again and again I do this, until just a brief touch of my lips, a gentle blow across her folds, is enough to make her beg me to let her come.

Then I rise up, roll on a condom, and slide into her in one easy thrust, and ride her hard. I'm so turned on by this point that within thirty seconds we come together in a glorious climax that leaves us gasping and exhausted, and we collapse back into each other's arms.

"You're trying to kill me," she says, still trying to catch her breath. "You're seriously trying to murder me with pleasure."

"What a way to go." I manage to kiss the top of her head as she laughs, then fall back onto the pillows.

As my pulse begins to slow, I think how amazing it would be to lie here for the rest of the day with Kora in my arms. We could get up to eat, then come back to bed and make love until we're like wrung-out rags, sated and satisfied.

But I mustn't fall asleep again. The sun won't stop its determined climb, and the world is already beginning to stir outside, the traffic building as it grows close to six a.m.

"I should go," I murmur, half-expecting her to protest.

She yawns, then sighs and says, "I know. Thank you for a wonderful wakeup call."

"You're very welcome." I lift onto an elbow and look down at her. She looks gorgeous, her fluffy hair lying spread out on the pillow, her lips blurred and her eyes sleepy. "I'm so pleased we met again."

"Me too."

I bend and kiss her, once, twice, three times, then reluctantly roll over and get out of bed.

I dress with her watching me, and meet her gaze in the mirror as I knot my tie. Her lips curve up and return the smile I give before turning and picking up my jacket. I slip it on, retrieve my coat, and slide my wallet back into my trouser pocket.

"Want to exchange phone numbers?" I ask on the spur of the moment. Even though I know it's pointless to stay in touch, I don't want to lose her again. "No worries if not."

"Of course." She reaches for her phone as she tells me hers, and I program it in, and then she does the same with mine.

"Okay. Have a good day."

"I'll try." She purses her lips. I remember then that she's meeting with Stephanie.

"I hope I haven't made things difficult for you," I tell her.

"Likewise."

We smile at each other. On impulse, I go to the bed, lean over her, and kiss her. "I'm so glad we met again," I whisper, cupping her face.

"Me too. I wish…" The words trail off as she hesitates, and she just smiles. "Have a nice day."

I kiss her again. Then I go out of the suite and close the door behind me.

I make my way out of the hotel and stand on the steps for a moment. It's cold, and I pull on my greatcoat, glad of the extra warmth. Tiny flakes of snow flutter around me as if, high above us, someone's sifting flour over the earth.

"Sir? Can I get you a cab?" the porter asks.

I nod, and he goes down the steps and gestures to the next black cab in the rank, who pulls up in front of me. The porter opens the door, and I slide in.

I give the driver my address in Knightsbridge, and he nods and heads into the traffic.

I have an important meeting today, with the group of Japanese investors I pretended I was seeing yesterday. They're looking for cheap offices for their company, and I have my eye on a potential site south of the river that's ripe for development. I've already prepared the documents in case they're interested, which I'm certain they will be, so I don't have a lot of work to do for it, but I still want to look over the paperwork and remind myself of some of the facts and figures.

Despite this, I find it hard to concentrate on business, my mind traveling back instead to that warm bed in the beautiful suite with the gorgeous girl. I'm glad I got her phone number. She was genuine and funny, and I can imagine us exchanging messages from time to time, just keeping in touch. It's a shame it can't be more than that, though.

For a moment, I let my mind dwell on the possibility. She's here for another few days; we could probably meet up a few more times and find out if we get on as well as I think we might when we're out of bed. And if we did? Is a long-distance relationship something that could work?

In the beginning, I can't see why not. It's not like we don't have the money to fly regularly in comfort to see each other. It is a long way—twenty-four hours plus refueling time, and there's no point traveling to the other side of the world for a night or two; you'd have to stay a few weeks to make it worthwhile. That's a substantial chunk of time for me to be away from the office on a regular basis, and I'm sure she'd feel the same.

Would she be open to moving to the UK? It's not like she has kids to worry about. But I know she's close to her family. Her whole life is in New Zealand, and I'm not sure she'd want to let go of that, especially for a guy she's only slept with twice.

So what about me?

I can't deny the thought of moving to New Zealand is strangely attractive. I loved the country when I went there—friendly people, wonderful, varied countryside, relaxed attitude, great coffee… After all the hassle with Rob, I can't deny I haven't considered making a change. At the moment we're officially still working together, even though he works from home now, and we hardly see each other at all, and only communicate by curt emails. We created the company together, and the only way to end it would be for one of us to buy the other out. We both have the money to do that, but Rob is as passionate about the company as I am, and so far we've both been hesitant to let go of the reins.

But I've worked so hard to get where I am, and the thought of walking away and starting again is inconceivable—almost. Briefly, I let myself remember the excitement I felt when we first set up the company, all that hope, the anticipation, the ambition. I'm still ambitious, but I no longer feel the sheer joy I once did when I close a deal, just a kind of grim satisfaction that I know what I'm doing.

I couldn't give it up though. It's a romantic, fanciful notion, but it's completely unrealistic.

When the cab draws up outside the apartment block in Knightsbridge. I pay the driver, get out, and walk up the steps and through the front door.

Stephanie still lives in the nine-bedroomed Italian villa we bought together in Holland Park that cost us thirty million pounds. Now, I live in a six-bedroomed penthouse apartment overlooking Hyde Park. It cost me forty million pounds. I take some perverse satisfaction in knowing it's more expensive than Stephanie's house.

I take the lift up, my rambling thoughts beginning to settle as the carriage rises. How foolish I'm being. Fantasies are one thing, but I can't afford to let them intrude into my daily life. I have responsibilities, both within the company and at home. I might not be married anymore, but Josh and my grandfather rely on me to provide for them and look after them, and I can't up and leave them just because I've had romantic notions about a one-night stand.

The lift dings and opens, and I go out into the corridor.

Even before I open the door to the apartment, I can hear Josh yelling.

I pause in the process of inserting the key, wait for a moment, then go inside.

I stop to remove my coat, hang it by the door, then cross the apartment to stand by the window and look out at the view. The snow still isn't laying, but the flakes are falling more thickly, and the people walking across the park are wearing hats, scarves, and gloves.

It's a glorious view, and a magnificent apartment, with polished dark wood floors and furniture and elegant cream sofas, all organized by an interior decorator. If I'm honest with myself, sometimes I find it a little stark, although I'd never admit that to anyone. A tiny part of me misses my grandparents' home with the thick carpets, colorful decor, and cozy living room. But you can't be a billionaire and live in a two-up, two-down semi. I have an image to keep up.

The noise is coming from the kitchen, so I walk in there. Josh usually isn't up until at least seven, so I'm surprised to see them both there. Jim, always calm, placid, and in control, nevertheless looks slightly harassed as he looks up, relief spreading across his features when he sees me.

"Morning, boy," he says, his name for me even though I'm thirty-three now. "Josh, Callum's home, look."

My brother turns, his face lighting up as he sees me. "Where were you?" he demands. "You've been out all night."

"I stayed with a friend." I go up and give him a hug, then walk around the table to hug my grandfather. I nod as he gestures to the coffee machine.

"What friend?" Josh demands. "Rob?"

I grit my teeth. "No, not Rob. Her name is Kora. I met her a long time ago in New Zealand, and she's visiting London."

Jim glances at me as he slots the capsule into the coffee machine, but he doesn't say anything.

"You should have rung," Josh says somewhat sulkily. "You promised we were going to play Call of Duty on the PlayStation."

"I did, and I'm sorry about that. We'll play later."

"You promise?"

"I promise."

Josh looks appeased and begins eating his Cheerios as he watches a video on his phone.

I move closer to my grandfather, who's steaming the milk for my coffee. "Sorry if I made things harder by not coming home," I murmur.

"You have to have a life, boy." He pours the hot milk over the espresso. "I'm glad you met your friend. Did you have a nice time?"

As he hands me the coffee, his eyes hold a touch of mischievousness. "Yes," I scold, "it was great to catch up."

"You seeing her again?"

I shake my head. "She's only here for a week or so."

"Oh, that's a shame." He leans a hip against the worktop. "Can't remember the last time you stayed overnight anywhere."

I know what he's saying. I haven't had a date since Stephanie and I parted ways.

I give him a wry smile. Although he has many fine lines at the corners of his eyes and mouth, and his hair is white, and he has problems with his sight, he's still a handsome man, as upright and slender as ever. He walks around the park every day, and his mind is as sharp as it's always been. If I look half as good in my eighties, I'll be pleased.

"What's she like?" he asks.

"Beautiful. Warm. Funny. You'd like her."

"Shame I won't get to meet her."

"Yeah." I have a mouthful of coffee, checking the time on my phone. "I'd better have a shower. I've got that meeting with the Japanese investors this morning."

"Oh, by the way, your tux is back from the cleaners."

"My tux?" For a moment I'm puzzled.

"For tonight," he says. "I thought you'd forgotten when you said to Josh about playing Call of Duty."

"Oh, shit, I had forgotten." Tonight is the evening of the NOFAS—the National Organization on Fetal Alcohol Syndrome—charity ball at Leeds Castle in Kent. I'm on the board and I promised I'd be there.

"You can't back out now," Jim says.

I sigh. "Yeah, okay."

"Is the ticket a plus one?" Jim asks.

"Even if it is, I'm not sure how you'd look in a ballgown."

"Haha. I was thinking you could take Kora."

My eyebrows rise. "Eighty-one years old and still playing Cupid?"

"A guy can try."

I laugh and finish off my coffee. "Thanks, but I don't think it'd be a good idea. Better not start something I can't continue, you know?"

"Yeah I guess, although you've worked so hard, Callum, and you've been through a lot." He glances at Josh.

"It's nothing," I say softly. "Some families go through a lot worse."

"Even so. When's the last time you had a day off? Think about it."

Musing on his words, I put the coffee cup in the sink and head off, ruffling Josh's hair as I pass.

Chapter Eight

Kora

"Did you have a good evening, by the way?"

Stephanie asks the question as we reach the end of the fifth floor of her toy store. This floor is targeted at children who love what have always traditionally been 'boys' toys' but are now increasingly also found in girls' homes—action figures, Hot Wheels and Scalextric, Soldiers and Vehicles, and Marvel figures. At the end of the floor is the coffee shop, and she leads me to the counter, having promised me a break after our morning slowly perusing the store. It's nearly midday, and I'm feeling peckish.

I clear my throat and bend to look at the range of sweets and savory options available, remembering the advice given by the lawyer on West Wing—that if someone asks you if you know what time it is, you answer "Yes," and not, "It's eleven a.m."

"Yes, thank you." I tap on the counter. "I'll have one of those chocolate brownies, please."

She gives our orders to the girl behind the desk and orders two coffees. She doesn't order a cake for herself, and I wish I'd passed as well as we take a table to one side.

And now I've got to pick my way through this minefield. I thought I'd gotten away with it as she hadn't asked me about last night. I try not to pick nervously at my nails and instead just give her a cool smile. Callum's announcement that she cheated on him has made me look at her very differently. We're hardly close, but I'm ashamed that any Prince would treat their partner that way.

"What did you get up to? Did you go out and see a show?" She seems determined to press the matter, and for a moment I wonder whether someone saw me with Callum, and she's about to accuse me.

I lift my chin. They're divorced, and I haven't done anything wrong. "No, I just had a meal in the restaurant at Claridge's and then had a quiet evening in." That's not a lie, anyway, as long as you don't count the noise I can't help making during sex. "You?" I ask, a little spitefully.

But I feel a twist of shame as she looks down and rubs at an imagined mark on her spotless skirt. "I was hoping to see Callum again," she says dully, "but he said he was busy. I know he wasn't, though, and I felt a bit depressed after he left." She flicks me a regretful smile. "Sorry, TMI, I'm sure."

"It's okay," I say awkwardly. "It's tough to move on after a breakup. I know I clung on to the hope of getting back with Julian for a while because I didn't want to have failed at the relationship."

"Oh," she says, "Callum and I will get back together eventually. He's making heavy weather of it, that's all. He wants to make me suffer first. And I get that. I just wish I didn't have to spend quite so long in the doghouse."

"Why are you in the doghouse?" My voice is sharp. Why is she so determined they'll get back together?

"I had an affair." She sounds completely unrepentant. "And I don't know why, but it's a completely different thing when the woman does it, isn't it? I mean, it's not like Callum hadn't been unfaithful."

I stare at her. "Callum cheated on you?"

"God, yes. Many times, I'm sure."

"You're sure, or you suspect?"

"I didn't hire a private detective and take photos, but you know when your partner is being unfaithful, don't you? And I thought well, what's sauce for the goose is sauce for the gander. I thought I'd make him understand how it felt." She shrugs. "But he was hypocritical like that. Old fashioned. It was okay for him to cheat, but not me."

For a moment I'm speechless, and I sit back as the waiter brings over a tray with my brownie and our coffees. Callum didn't say anything to me about having cheated on his wife, and his shock at her affair with his business partner suggests to me she's got it completely wrong. Or maybe I'm being the fool. I didn't ask him, so he didn't have to deny it.

My gut tells me she's the one in the wrong, but my gut's been wrong before.

"So why do you want him back if you're sure he's cheated you?" I'm baffled now.

She looks at me as if I'm both an idiot and extremely naive. "You've met him. He's an attractive guy, and he'll always have women falling over themselves to get into his bed. What man wouldn't take advantage of that? I'd be shocked if he didn't. I like that women find him attractive. I just want it to go both ways, that's all."

I understand. He's like a racehorse, a stud she can show off to her friends and colleagues.

I take a bite out of my brownie, no longer caring she's not eating. More fool her. It's delicious. "So what makes you think he'll come back to you eventually? Surely he wouldn't have gone through with the divorce if that was the case?"

"Oh, he knows how to make me squirm. He was always very good at that." Her lips twist as some intimate memory lights her eyes.

I drop my gaze to the brownie, my appetite disappearing, wishing I were anywhere else but here. I shouldn't have slept with him last night. That was a stupid thing to do. Why did I think I wouldn't feel awkward about it?

I need to change the subject. "So… Ben asked me to talk to you about LEGO. How are you finding sales of the architecture range? It's doing really well in our store."

Stephanie twitters away about her bestselling LEGO sets, and I sit back and finish my coffee, happy to let her talk.

How strange to think of her being married to Callum. Even forgetting about her affair and his alleged indiscretions, I'm not at all surprised they got divorced. The first time I met him, I thought he was reserved and very British, but actually he's warm and funny and captivating, and she's so… cold.

In my jacket pocket, my phone vibrates once, announcing the arrival of a text. It's late in New Zealand, but it's not beyond the realms of possibility that one of my brothers is up and wants to know how I'm doing. While Stephanie takes a breath to have a sip of coffee, I pull the phone out, rest it on my thigh, and tap the screen.

It's from Callum. I inhale, and my heart bangs on my ribs. The whole message won't appear until I unlock the phone, but I can see the first few lines. *Hey! How are you today? I have something to ask you…*

I lift my gaze to see Stephanie watching me. She looks away and waves at someone behind the counter who raises a hand to greet her.

I look back at the phone, swipe up, and bring up the text.

Hey! How are you today? I have something to ask you. Feel free to say no! I'm sure you're busy. And it's very very late notice. But I have to go to a charity ball tonight at Leeds Castle. And I wondered if you would like to be my plus one? Text or call if you'd like to discuss further. Otherwise, take care! C x

I turn off the phone as Stephanie looks back at me. "Shall we move on?" she asks.

"Yes, of course." I finish off my coffee, rise, and follow her out of the coffee shop.

She takes me up to the next floor, which is all about board games, and I follow her around, but I'm hardly listening to anything she's saying. All I can think about is Callum's message.

I shouldn't. I was planning to go to a show. And besides, it's a bad idea. I've already been plagued with memories all morning of what happened last night, and the more I see him, the harder it's going to be when I leave.

There's also the issue of what Stephanie told me about him having multiple affairs. Is it true? And if it is, do I really want to get involved with another man who cheats on his partner?

This was supposed to be a man-free vacation, a chance to get back on my feet, mentally and emotionally. How do I land myself in these positions?

But even as I think that, I know why it happens. I told Callum: *I'd rather regret something I said than something I didn't say*, and equally I'd rather regret something I did than something I didn't do. If I've ever had a choice of whether to do something, I've always taken the risk. Sometimes it hasn't worked. But I've never had to look back and regret that I didn't take the opportunity.

It will make it more difficult to say goodbye to him. But is that a good enough reason to say no?

I decide to talk to him about Stephanie's accusation and see what he says. I consider myself a pretty good judge of character, and I think I'll be able to tell if he's being honest or not.

While Stephanie stops to talk to an employee, I quickly bring up the text, hit reply, and type, *Thanks for the offer! The answer is probably. Will ring shortly to discuss.*

My thumb hovers over the send button, then, as she turns back to me, I press it and slide the phone back into my pocket.

"Nearly done," she says. "I hope this has been helpful."

"Very. I have a lot to report back on." I follow her dutifully to the end of the floor, pretending to pay attention to the way they've organized the different versions of Monopoly, while inside, my mind is a whirl with thoughts about tonight.

What am I going to wear? I need to source myself a ballgown quickly. I'm sure Claridge's will be able to help with that. I can do my hair and makeup myself. And I presume Callum will pick me up and take me there. I just need to pack an overnight bag. The sooner I get back to the hotel, the better.

Luckily, Stephanie is obviously eager to get back to work, and it's not long before we're making our way up to her office. I am due to have a meeting with her financial director this afternoon, but as we go in, I announce, "Steph, I'm really sorry to be so awkward but I have a migraine starting. Would it be an imposition to cancel the meeting?"

"Of course." She frowns in concern. "Can I get you anything?"

"No, I just need to lie down in a dark room." I cross my fingers behind my back. I do suffer from migraines so it's not a complete lie. Well, it is, but what the hell… "Thank you so much for your time today."

"No problem at all, anything for family." She smiles and leans in so we can touch cheeks as we kiss.

I stifle the wave of guilt, say goodbye, and make my way back to the elevator, phoning Graham as I go to ask him to come and pick me up. I only have to wait a few minutes before he turns up, and before long I'm back in the car. It's less than five minutes to Claridge's, so I'll be there by one o'clock.

My pulse picking up speed, I bring out my phone and dial Callum's number.

"Hello, Kora," he answers.

His deep voice makes all the hairs rise on the back of my neck. "Hey. Are you able to talk?"

"Yes, I'm in my office, between meetings. How are you?"

"Good, thanks. So… you're off to a charity ball tonight?"

"Yes, at Leeds Castle. I'm on the board of trustees for NOFAS—that's the National Organization for Fetal Alcohol Syndrome. There'll be a two-course meal, entertainment, a live auction, a silent auction, raffles, that kind of thing, with all proceeds going to the charity. There will be a live band too, if you like dancing."

"I love dancing."

"I knew you would." I can hear the smile in his voice. "So you're not busy?"

"I can cancel what I'm doing." I hesitate. I have to get it out in the open. "I have to ask you something."

"Fire away."

"I've just been with Stephanie."

"Ah."

"Yeah. Um… Can you hold on a minute? I'm pulling up outside the hotel."

"Sure."

Graham stops outside Claridge's, and a porter comes over to open the door. I smile at him as I get out, go up the steps, and pass through the revolving door. I walk across the black-and-white tiles to a quiet corner of the entrance hall and sink onto one of the armchairs.

I clear my throat. "Are you still there?"

"Ready and waiting."

"Okay. Callum… she told me the reason she had an affair was to get back at you because of the affairs you'd had."

He's silent on the other end of the phone.

"I don't believe her," I say honestly. "But I hope you understand that I need to ask you about it."

"She accused me of having an affair several times," he replies. His tone is clipped, angry. "She thought it explained why I'd withdrawn from her. She never understood it was because of what was happening between us. I fell out of love with her, Kora, because she was cold and heartless, and she hated my family. I never cheated on her. It was one of the reasons why our divorce took time to come through; I stated her adultery as the reason, and she contested it at first, saying it should state we were both unfaithful. I refused to agree. I wasn't going to admit to something I hadn't done. In the end, her solicitor convinced her to go ahead, even though I'm sure he was convinced I'd been unfaithful. I hated her for that." He stops, a little breathless from his passionate outburst.

"All right," I say softly. "I'm sorry I asked."

"It's perfectly understandable after what she said."

"Even so. I didn't believe her, Callum, I swear. The man she was describing didn't match the guy I'd met."

"I'm glad," he murmurs.

"So... I'm guessing I need to get a ballgown? How much time do I have?"

"It'll take us about an hour and a half to get to Leeds Castle," he states. "It's in Kent. It's a beautiful setting. We're supposed to be there by six. Can Claridge's help you find a gown? The ball has a Valentine's Day theme."

Oh, of course! I'd totally forgotten it was Valentine's Day. Not having a partner this year, I haven't had to worry about buying a card or present—or receiving one.

"I'm sure they can," I reply. "Will you pick me up?"

"Of course, at four thirty."

"And... are we staying overnight or coming back here afterward?"

"Sorry, I should have said. I have a room there for the night. You are welcome to stay with me, but I'd be happy to see if I can get you your own room, if you'd rather."

"I'd like to stay with you." I feel a warm glow. He doesn't just want a date for the night. He wants to see me again.

"There's one more thing," he says. "I was thinking... you mentioned going to see your great-aunt. Hastings is about another hour south from Leeds Castle. I wondered whether I could drive you there the next day?"

My eyebrows rise. "Seriously? Don't you have to work?"

"Nothing I can't push back. I was talking to Jim—my grandfather—this morning, and he said I deserve to have some time off, and I was thinking that I haven't had a holiday in... well, I can't remember the last time. And honestly, I could do with a break. It's tough at the office at the moment. Rob's still technically part of the company, and even though he's working from home, he has to come in from time to time for meetings. Jim's right: I could do with some time away with a beautiful woman."

I smile. "Smooth talker."

"So that's a yes?"

"Yes," I say happily. "Thank you."

"Later, then?"

"Four thirty. I'll be ready."

Chapter Nine

Callum

When I pull up outside Claridge's at 4:25 p.m., Kora is standing there talking to the porter, her overnight bag at her feet.

She's wearing a faux-fur wrap over a full-length gown that sparkles in the light spilling out from the hotel. It looks as if it has a skin-colored lining, making it seem as if she's naked beneath the sequin-covered lace over the top. She's piled her blonde hair on the top of her head, leaving a few tendrils to curl around her pale, slender neck.

Wow. She's driving me crazy, and we haven't even said hello yet.

She looks down at the car and her features light with surprise as she sees me behind the wheel. She says something to the porter, who picks up her case, brings it down, and places it in the boot for her while she comes around to the passenger side.

She slides into the seat beside me and closes the door. "Hello."

"Hey." I inhale as her perfume washes over me. Cherry again. It makes my mouth water. "Happy Valentine's Day."

She laughs and buckles herself in. "You're driving."

"Well, aren't you the observant one?" I wave to the porter and pull away into the traffic.

"I'm just saying, I would have thought you'd have had a chauffeur."

"I do normally. I hate wasting time sitting in traffic when I could be working. But I like driving. And this car doesn't often get a chance to stretch its legs."

She looks around the Aston Martin, admiring the black leather and red carbon fiber interior. The Vantage is beautiful and sleek. Not unlike Kora herself.

"It's gorgeous," she says.

"Mmm."

She meets my eyes and laughs. "I'm talking about the car."

"Me too. But you do look amazing." It's the truth. I tear my gaze away from her and try to concentrate on the road. Maybe I should have taken a chauffeur.

"Thank you. You don't look so bad yourself, Mr. Bond."

I chuckle. "Every guy looks good in a tux."

"Oh Callum, I think we both know that's not true. That's a quality suit and you fill it rather splendidly."

"Why thank you." We both smile at each other.

"I'm glad you're coming with me," I tell her.

"I was flattered you asked me out of all the women you must know."

"You were the only candidate," I scoff. "If you'd have said no, I'd be sitting here alone." I don't want her to think I had a list, because that's far from the case.

"Good." She snuggles down in the seat, pulling her wrap around her neck with a satisfied smile.

I grin, taking the road past Berkeley Square and heading for Green Park. From there we'll go around St. James's Park, cross the Thames at Westminster Bridge, and then head southeast toward Lewisham on the A20 and then take the M20 all the way to Leeds Castle.

It's started snowing again, and although the flakes aren't yet settling, the weather forecaster promised they would by morning. It's icy outside, but I've had the heater on in the car for a while, so hopefully she's not too cold.

"I'm sorry for mentioning what Stephanie said," Kora declares. "I just want to get that out of the way. I shouldn't have said anything."

"It's okay. It was fair enough of you to want clarification." I don't express the searing anger that my ex-wife's words caused me to feel. I never even looked at another woman while I was with her. The fact that she's now telling people I was repeatedly unfaithful makes me feel sick with fury.

"It's not okay, and I can see how much it upset you. I can tell when you're annoyed. You get a knot at the corner of your jaw here." She reaches out and touches beneath my ear. "You're gritting your teeth."

I inhale as she strokes my skin, then exhale, long and slow, as she lowers her hand. "I admit it annoyed me. Mainly because I don't want you to think badly of me." With some surprise, I realize it's true.

"Well, hopefully it'll please you to know that my first emotion was confusion. It didn't fit with the Callum I'd met. You strike me as an honorable guy. It's one of the things that really attracts me to you."

Her compliment warms me, and I hold out my hand. She slides hers into it, and I close my fingers around hers, resting hers on the gearstick so I can hold her hand and change gear.

"So enough about that," she says. "Tell me about the ball tonight, and about NOFAS."

I rub my thumb across the backs of her fingers. Tonight, I'll have her all to myself again. I'll be able to strip off her ballgown and kiss her all over; or maybe I'll leave the gown on, and make love to her surrounded by all those sequins. Hmm.

"Ah… NOFAS." Stop thinking about her naked, Callum. Plenty of time for that. "Yeah. They asked me to be on the board of trustees after I gave them a donation. I didn't say yes immediately as it's a significant call on your time, but they needed someone with business skills, and that person also needed to be dedicated to the charity's mission. They've done a lot for Josh, so in the end I agreed to do it for a trial period of six months. I'm really glad I did. It's been rewarding. I've been on the board for seven years now."

"That's very admirable; I'm impressed."

"It's the least I can do. You have to give back somehow, don't you? Unless you're incredibly self-centered." It then occurs to me that she might not agree. Lots of rich people prefer to keep their money to themselves. I can't imagine that Kora is like that, but you never know. "Do you… uh… have any connection with a charity?"

"Oh yes. On my father's side of the family, I'm related to a family called the Kings. Yeah, I know, Kings and Princes. It's a standing joke. Anyway, they make medical equipment for children who have respiratory illnesses."

"Not the Three Wise Men?"

"Yes!" She looks delighted that I've heard of them.

"The kid of a work colleague had an asthma attack," I explain. "In hospital they gave him a brand-new kind of nebulizer, and I remember thinking the company name was interesting. The nebulizer had a toy attached to it from the Ward Seven series of books."

"Yeah, my Uncle Matt wrote them."

"Seriously?" I laugh. What a small world. They were made into a TV show some time ago. Practically every kid in the UK has one of the soft toys at home.

Kora continues, "They also run a foundation called We Three Kings where they grant wishes for sick children. At first they just had a couple of offices, but now they're spread all across New Zealand. We've all raised money for them in different ways. Dad's now in the process of organizing trips around the South Pole—our theme park—for sick kids."

"How did you raise money?" I ask.

"I jumped out of a plane."

"Wow, really?"

She chuckles. "It was super scary, but I'm really glad I did it. I could have just donated the money, of course, but then you don't bring the attention the charity needs."

"Yeah, that's right. It's about getting the charity into the public eye."

"I'd like to do more. Do you..." She hesitates.

"Do I what?"

"I don't want to offend you."

"I promise I won't be offended."

"All right. I just wondered... do you ever feel guilty for having money?"

"Why would that offend me?"

"I know you've worked extremely hard to get where you have. Unlike me, who was born into money."

I squeeze her fingers. "I do and I don't. Feel guilty, I mean. I don't because, like you said, I've worked extremely hard to get where I am. Ten-to-twelve hour days, often more, six days a week, sometimes seven, ever since I was eighteen. There aren't many people who can say that."

"But sometimes you do feel guilty?"

"This car cost over a hundred thousand pounds. Do I ever think maybe I should get myself an old banger and give the money to charity? Live in a one-bedroomed flat instead of a luxury apartment? Eat fish and chips every night instead of dining in the finest restaurants? Wear an off-the-peg suit instead of a bespoke one from Savile Row? And give all that extra cash away? Of course I do. Maybe coming from no money makes that worse, I don't know. But I donate plenty. I'm not going to crucify myself for enjoying a fraction of what I earn." I glance at her. "What about you?"

"I've done nothing to earn the money I have. I mean, now I do a bit, but the division of wealth is so unfair isn't it?"

"Yes, it is, but I'm sure your ancestors worked their socks off to make sure their children didn't have to go through what they did. If you gave it all away, you'd be dismissing all their hard work."

"That's a good point."

"I'm sure you do plenty," I tell her.

"It's never enough," she says. "There's so much suffering out there. So much unhappiness."

"True. But there's not enough money in the world to cure every problem that exists."

She makes a non-committal noise and looks out of the window. I look back at the road. I made my peace with having money long ago. I refuse to feel guilty after having worked myself into the ground to make my family comfortable.

I change the subject and ask her about her ballgown, and she brightens and tells me about how Claridge's contacted a local store and asked them to bring her a dozen gowns to try in her room.

"It's gorgeous," she says. "And I love the wrap."

"I saw the plans for how they were going to decorate the castle. It's going to be amazing."

"I'm excited." She glows with enthusiasm. "But mostly because I'm going to be able to spend time with you."

I laugh. "You really say what's on your mind, don't you?"

"I don't know any other way. I'm guessing Stephanie wasn't so open."

"God, no. I used to need an Enigma machine to decode our conversations."

Kora giggles, but I feel a stab of guilt. I dislike bitchiness in other people, and deplore it in myself. I make a mental note that I'm not going to mention Stephanie again during our time away. We're done, and I need to move on. It's tough when Stephanie continues to hang onto the hope of us being together—she sent me a text after Kora left her today, asking what I was up to tonight. But hopefully she'll eventually get the message and leave me alone.

We continue to chat as the Aston Martin eats up the miles, and it's not long before the houses turn to fields that become shrouded in darkness as the sun sets. When we eventually take the turnoff and emerge through the trees to see Leeds Castle in front of us, it glows like a jewel in the dusk, light spilling out from its many windows to guide us there.

"It's a real castle," Kora says, astonished.

"What did you expect?"

"Some kind of Disney-like fabrication, I suppose."

"Well, this castle is mostly nineteenth century, although there has been one here since the early twelfth."

"The early twelfth?" Her eyes nearly fall out of her head. "I love this country."

I laugh. "I'm glad."

"We're really going to spend the night here?"

"Absolutely. Looks great, doesn't it?"

"Like something out of a fairytale." Her eyes catch the light pouring from the castle as we approach it, and they sparkle with excitement. I hadn't given much thought to how the place would look to guests as they arrive, but I can see now how it's going to transform the evening for Kora from a standard charity gala to a magical night of fantasy.

I like seeing the world through Kora's eyes. If I was here alone, I would probably have been lost in thought, going over facts and figures in my head, and I wouldn't have appreciated the beauty of the place.

Skirting the moat, I pull up outside the front of the castle. "Wait here," I tell Kora, and I get out and hand the car keys to the parking attendant. A porter comes up, and I tell him my name, and he promises to take our bags and clothes up to our room. Then I open the passenger door and offer my hand to my date.

Kora slides her hand into mine and swings her legs out of the car. Only then do I see her sexy high-heeled sandals.

"I got them a few days ago," she admits as she sees me looking at them. "They just happen to go with the gown."

"What luck."

"I know, right?" She gets to her feet and looks up. She's nowhere near as tall as me, but the heels have given her a little height, and if I were to lean forward, my lips would brush her eyebrows. She's wearing false eyelashes, long and black with little sparkling gems near the base. Hmm, they're sexy too. Everything about this girl is telling me to take her to bed right now.

But we have a whole evening to get through, so I sigh and offer her my arm, and she slides her hand into the crook of my elbow.

Guided by a trail of small white solar lights, we walk through the inner barbican and into the castle's inner bailey with a line of other guests. Ahead of us are the main castle buildings where the dinner will take place, and as we walk down, we're treated to an array of old-fashioned entertainers like jugglers, stilt walkers, and acrobats, who tumble and spin in their bright colored costumes, breathing fire and tossing balls impossibly high in the air.

We stop for a few minutes beneath one of the outdoor heaters to watch the display, Kora clapping her hands as one of the entertainers stops right before us and breathes a long flame that reflects in the sequins of her dress, making it look as if she's on fire. Then we continue on toward the buildings, the front doors of which are open to welcome us in.

We're shown through the library for pre-dinner drinks and hors d'oeuvres. We accept a glass of champagne each, and together we walk through the room, admiring the tall bookcases and stopping occasionally to talk to someone I recognize.

And it's now that I really see the difference between her and Stephanie. Even though I promised myself I would stop comparing them, it's impossible not to. Part of the reason Stephanie and I got together was out of a mutual desire for a partner to accompany us to events like this. I know we made an elegant couple, and she also has a head for business that means she's able to hold her own in any working conversation. She exudes a cool beauty, not unlike the moon I compared her to yesterday, something to be worshipped and admired from a distance.

But she lacks Kora's natural charisma. This evening, Kora is lit up from the inside out, practically glowing with excitement and enjoyment of her surroundings. When I introduce her to someone, she greets them warmly, occasionally touching them on the shoulder, and making them feel as if they're the only person in the room. She compliments the women on their clothes or hair and, despite her beauty, they turn toward her as if they're flowers and she's the sun, keen to be her best friend. And I swear every guy she talks to falls immediately in love with her, as they crowd around her, trying to catch her attention and be the one to whom she grants her dazzling smile.

I watch her laughing at something one of the older members of the board says, and I feel a strange mixture of attraction, affection, and desire, all swirled up inside me. I want to stay here and watch her, and have all the men here know they can't have her, because she's here with me. The surge of jealous possession, of smug satisfaction that she's mine—for tonight at least—takes me by surprise, because I've never felt that way before.

Holy fuck. I think I'm in love.

Chapter Ten

Kora

I'm having a whale of a time. I feel like a million dollars in the dress and Jimmy Choo sandals. The champagne is amazing, and the setting is beyond belief.

I'm chatting away to a group of people, telling them a bit about New Zealand, when I realize Callum isn't beside me, which is odd because he's been glued to my side for the past half an hour. I look over my shoulder and see him standing to one side. He's sipping from his own glass of champagne. He's also watching me.

He looks a bit cross. He isn't smiling, and there's a slight frown on his brow. Puzzled as to what I could have done, I extricate myself politely from the conversation and wander over to him.

He's so handsome, and he looks amazing in his bespoke dinner jacket, wing-collared shirt, and black bow tie. He told me he buys his suits from Savile Row, where I know they're taught to measure within a sixteenth of an inch. It explains the exquisite cut, the beautiful fabric. The cut is typically British, the jacket having a narrow waist and high armholes. It wouldn't surprise me if it cost him around five thousand pounds.

The fairy lights they've strung around the room make his eyes glitter. My heart skips a beat as he looks down at me, unsmiling.

"You okay?" I ask. "Something wrong?"

"No."

"What's on your mind?" I wonder whether he's thinking about Stephanie. Maybe he came here before with her, and someone asked him where she was.

He bends his head so his lips are near to my ear. "I'm thinking about how I'm going to make love to you when I eventually get you back to our room."

Whoa, I didn't expect that. I look up at him, my eyes widening, and moisten my lips with the tip of my tongue. His gaze drops to them for a moment, then returns to mine. Ooh, the desire in his eyes makes a shiver run down my back.

"What options have you come up with?" I murmur, my heart banging against my ribs.

His lips brush the shell of my ear. "You want me to talk dirty to you? Right here?"

"If you're brave enough."

His breath warms my ear as he chuckles. "My imagination is pretty vivid. You seem like a nice girl. I might shock you."

"I want you to," I whisper. The thought of this man describing what he wants to do to me makes me ache.

He touches his lips to the sensitive skin behind my ear. "I can't decide between stripping you naked and torturing you slowly with my mouth, or just lifting up your gown, throwing you on the bed, and fucking you hard until you scream."

I close my eyes, turning to caramel inside. And there was me thinking he just wanted me here for eye candy. Both times we've had sex, he's set me alight, but this is the first time he's hinted at the deep seam of passion running within him.

The Ice King? I almost laugh out loud at Stephanie's description of him. Clearly, she didn't know him at all.

"Maybe both," I whisper. I open my eyes and look up into his. He's staring at me as if he wants to eat me alive. Ooh. Perhaps he will, if I'm lucky.

"Goodness me, you two, get a room! You're going to set us all alight if you keep on staring at each other like that." The woman approaching us with a smile is in her fifties, tall and slim, her long black curly hair threaded with silver. Her gold-colored gown compliments her warm-brown skin. Her eyes are creased at the corners, so she obviously smiles a lot.

"Jasmine," Callum says, and he leans forward to kiss her cheek. "You look amazing."

"I should hope so, darling, the amount of makeup I'm wearing. I had to apply it with a trowel." She's fibbing—her makeup is artfully applied, so she's being self-deprecating. I like her already. "Aren't you going to introduce me?" she asks him, smiling at me.

"Kora, this is Jasmine Spencer, Chair of NOFAS' Board of Trustees. Jasmine, this is Kora Prince, all the way from New Zealand."

"A Kiwi!" Jasmine beams with delight. "Oh, I adore your country. I made James take me there after we watched *The Lord of the Rings*. I couldn't find Mount Doom, but the rest of the country was as beautiful as in Peter Jackson's movies."

I laugh and shake her hand. "It is an amazing country, and very diverse in appearance, I know."

"Yes, jungles in the north and mountains in the south! I loved it to bits. Where are you from?"

"Wellington."

"A gorgeous little city. Oh, wait… Prince? Don't tell me you're Theo Prince's sister?"

I smile. "His twin sister, yes."

Her mouth forms an O. "I'm so glad he was found! We were all watching the news with bated breath. Imagine being stranded on a desert island for ten days! I bet he was absolutely terrified, poor dear."

"It helped that it was with the love of his life," I say lightly, determined not to think about how slowly those ten days passed, and how petrified I was that I'd never see him again. Callum's hand slides into mine, though, and I know he's picked up on my emotion.

"Yes, of course, Victoria Sullivan. I follow her yoga channel on YouTube. Such an amazing love story. Oh look, they're calling us in for dinner. We should be on the same table—Callum, darling, if we're not, can you switch some nameplates so we're sitting together? I couldn't bear it if I was stuck next to that nincompoop Roger Green and his stuffy wife."

Callum chuckles as he offers me his arm. "Will do. Where is James, by the way?"

"Oh yes, I'd better find my husband, I suppose. He had his head stuck in one of the books he found on the shelves. Only my husband would come to a ball with all these fascinating people and be more excited about a first edition of Darwin's *On the Origin of Species*."

We both laugh as she wanders off to retrieve her errant husband. "She's a character," I tell him.

"She's one of my favorite people in the world," he announces, surprising me as we follow those in front of us into the hall. "Her niece has fetal alcohol syndrome, and she's very active in the charity, and holds all kinds of events. And even though they both act as if he's a mad professor, her husband isn't as scatterbrained as he makes out. He's a lead scientist in the field of biological engineering."

"Wow. Now I feel inadequate."

He gives me a wry smile. "You're as smart as they come, Kora. Intelligent, sexy, gorgeous, and a nice person. I'd say that's a pretty perfect package."

"I'm far from perfect," I mumble, thinking about how terrible I look in the morning before I've done my hair, but still, I appreciate the compliment.

We walk into the hall, and I stop and stare around us as my jaw drops. Two long tables run the length of the hall. The walls are hung with old tapestries and beautiful paintings, including one of Henry VIII. The ebony-wood ceiling is decorated with fairy lights, so it looks like a fairytale grotto, and there are red hearts everywhere. There's a magnificent stone fireplace in the center of the wall with a leaping log fire. The tables are covered with white cloths and bear silver cutlery and white candles. The waiter Callum gives our names to is wearing a white jacket with a red pocket square.

"They've done well," Callum remarks as the waiter shows us to our seats. "When we discussed themes for the ball, I wasn't sure about the Valentine's Day idea because I thought it would make anyone on their own feel lonely, but now I'm convinced."

"Did Henry VIII actually come here?" I slide into the chair the waiter holds out for me.

Callum checks the nameplates around us, maybe making sure they bear Jasmine and James Spencer's names, then takes the chair opposite me. "Scholars think he might have stopped here on the way to France in 1520. You see that painting?" I follow his gaze to a huge painting on the wall which shows ships at sea behind a fort at the bottom. "It's called The Embarkation of Henry VIII at Dover. It shows the king crossing the English Channel to go to a summit with King Francois I of France at the Field of the Cloth of Gold."

"Oh, I've heard of that."

"He had an entourage of about six thousand people with him, and supposedly they stopped here on the way."

"And emptied all the castle larders, no doubt. I can't imagine having six thousand people turn up on your doorstep for dinner."

He laughs. "No, me neither."

"It's beautiful," I say with feeling. "Thank you so much for inviting me. I'm so glad I came."

"I'm pleased." He smiles then as Jasmine appears beside him, while an elegant older black gentleman introduces himself as James and sits next to me.

"I understand you're a biological engineer," I say to him as a waiter pours champagne into our glasses. "That sounds interesting."

"It's very boring," he tells me. "Jasmine always asks about my day when she's having trouble sleeping."

We all laugh. "I don't believe that," I scoff. "I think it's a fascinating field of study. What's your area of expertise? Kinetics? Biomechanics? Thermodynamics?"

He looks delighted. "You have an interest in the field?"

"I'm afraid I don't know much about it, but yes, I find it fascinating."

"Oh Lord," Jasmine says, "now we'll never shut him up." But her smile is warm and genuine.

"I work in the medical profession," James says. "Developing portable and rapid disease diagnostic devices."

"Well, you'd get on like a house on fire with my… well, I'm not sure what relative he is, actually. First cousin once removed, something like that," I tell him.

"Why? Who's he?"

"His name is Charlie King. He designs medical equipment for children with respiratory illnesses."

"From the Three Wise Men?" James laughs. "I met him last year at a conference in Australia. He's a genius."

"He is, in the science world. In the real world he can't tie his own shoelaces." I'm teasing, of course; Charlie King is an absolute darling.

"Sounds like it's a profession-wide trait," Jasmine comments. "James works with biological machines I can't even spell, and yet he has no idea how to turn the DVD player on."

I meet Callum's eyes and find his gaze fixed on me. He's smiling, but the fire in his eyes has only intensified. I think I'm going to be in real trouble when he eventually gets me back to our room.

Oh my.

But first we have a whole evening to get through. It's not an onerous task. To get everyone relaxed and talking, magicians make their way around the tables, performing tricks for donations and making people's reading glasses and other items disappear before magically producing them again. There are several jars along the table and a list of banned Valentine words like 'love', 'loving', 'romance', 'red', and 'heart', and every time someone mentions one of them, they have to put a pound coin in the jar. As we've all had a couple of glasses of champagne already, the atmosphere is very merry by the time the dinner arrives.

We have roasted lamb leg with thyme sauce or a vegetarian lasagna, with ratatouille vegetables and sauté potatoes, and a Baileys Irish cheesecake or a deep-dish apple pie for dessert. The champagne continues to flow, along with a variety of other wines. There's lots of entertainment while we eat, and after the meal, the auctions and raffles take place. I win a huge box of luxury chocolates in the raffle, which is a bonus.

Afterward, we're asked to move back into the library, where we watch a wonderful, condensed performance of A Midsummer Night's Dream by a theater group. Then we return to the hall to find the tables have been cleared and a band has set up, and soon they're playing all the old favorites, while heart-shaped lights move across the floor.

"What a glorious evening." I have to raise my voice for Callum to hear me. We've found a table not far from the bar. James is getting us all a drink, and Jasmine is up dancing with a friend. I'd like to join her, but I want to spend time with Callum, too.

"Would you like to dance?" he asks. "Your feet seem to be saying yes."

I look down at where my toes are tapping on the carpet, then up at him in surprise. "You're offering?" In my experience, guys rarely like dancing, unless it's a slow song and they can get to grope the girl.

"Of course. I love a bit of disco."

"That's a pound in the jar," I tell him, my mouth close to his ear.

He chuckles and pops a coin in the jar on the table, then stands and holds out a hand. "Come on. I want to see how you move in that dress."

I take his hand, leaving my bag and wrap behind as it's warm in the room now, and let him lead me onto the dance floor. My heels are extremely high so it's tough to do more than wiggle my hips, but Callum doesn't seem to mind. Wow, the man has rhythm, and the two of us move together as if we were born to it, never more than a few inches apart as the beat takes hold of us and refuses to let go.

One song leads to another, and we dance for several hours, barely stopping except to get a drink and for Callum to shed his dinner jacket as the room grows even warmer. Jasmine and James join us, and the four of us joke and laugh and just have a great time as we dance the night away.

I'm several glasses of champagne down by now, but it's only when the music changes to a slow song and Callum pulls me into his arms that I feel the effects of the alcohol. My face flushes, and although the room isn't going around exactly, I feel as if all my rough edges have been filed off. I'm like a piece of ancient oak, chopped and planed and sanded until I'm as smooth as silk.

I'd forgotten what Callum said to me in the library when we first arrived, but it all comes flooding back to me as he slides his hand down my back to rest at the base of my spine, and pulls me close so I have to look up to see his eyes.

"I love this dress," he murmurs. "You look like you're not wearing anything beneath all that lace and sequins."

"You owe the jar a pound," I say, a little breathless from the heat in his gaze. "And you're right. I'm not wearing anything beneath it."

His eyes widen. "You mean…"

"Totally commando."

His jaw drops. "Holy fuck."

I chuckle as he brushes up my back to confirm there's no bra strap.

"You must have guessed," I scoff. "The dress has spaghetti straps."

"I assumed you were wearing a strapless bra. You have very firm breasts."

My gaze drops to his mouth. "You think so?"

"I know so. I'm an expert, you see."

"Are you now?"

"Most men are, even though usually we're polite enough to hide it." He slides his hand down to examine for the line of my knickers and frowns as he finds something.

"A garter belt," I tell him.

"Stockings?"

I nod, and his eyes darken. Ooh, he likes that idea.

We move slowly to the music, as the singer's smooth caramel voice sends shivers down my spine.

"Thank you for a wonderful evening," I whisper. "I've had such a good time."

"I'm so glad you came with me. It wouldn't have been the same without you."

He implied he wouldn't have asked anyone else to come if I'd said no, and I believe him, although surely someone would have made a move on him if he'd been alone. I glance around, not surprised to see some of the single women watching him. He looks very handsome in the tux, and it's also clear he has money. He's a great catch.

What a shame my net won't stretch this far.

But I mustn't feel sad about it. I knew what I was getting into, and I made the decision to come with him anyway. I have to enjoy the time we have together, and not grow too morose over what could have been in another world.

I moisten my lips. "I think maybe it's time we went to bed, don't you?"

His gaze drops to my mouth. "Oh yeah."

"Have you made your mind up which option you're going for?"

"I've been watching you all evening. Thinking about kissing you, being inside you. All I know is that right now I want you more than anything I've ever wanted in my entire life, and that's something considering I'm the most ambitious guy I know."

Tears prick my eyes. "I think that's the nicest thing anyone's ever said to me."

He kisses my nose. "Come on. Time to get you to bed."

Chapter Eleven

Callum

It takes a frustratingly long time to get up to our room. It feels as if everyone in the room wants to say goodnight to us, and to thank me for coming. It's great that my work at the charity is appreciated, but tonight part of me wishes I was a nobody, and that we could walk straight out.

But Kora takes her time to congratulate the organizers on their splendid event, to chat to some of the entertainers and compliment them on their work, and to shake Jasmine and James's hands and promise to keep in touch when she gets back to New Zealand. In the end it takes us about fifteen minutes to make our way out through the stone archway. They've remade the spiral staircase out of wood, and we mount the twisting stairs slowly, as Kora is still wearing her high heels.

She's in front of me, but we're holding hands, and I brush my thumb across the backs of her fingers. "I thought we'd never get away," I murmur.

"Aw. It'll be worth the wait, I promise."

I chuckle, then as we reach the landing, I pull her over to the window. We peer through the tiny panes of glass and both inhale as we see the snow has started to settle, covering the grounds in a white carpet.

"It's so beautiful," she whispers.

She's right, but I only have eyes for her. The long lashes with their diamonds at the base make her eyes look sultry, and I can imagine them fluttering as I arouse her. She's painted her lips a deep pink, and I can't help but picture them closing over the tip of my erection. I want to brush back the loose curls of her hair that hang around her neck and kiss her there, and move down to the soft skin of her shoulder and breasts. I want to part her thighs and taste her and slide inside her. She's classy and elegant but she oozes sexual appeal, and I don't care how many pound coins I have to put in the tin, I'm happy to say it over and over again—she's made for loving.

"If you keep looking at me like that, the snow will never lay," she says. "It'll melt as soon as it touches the earth anywhere near us."

"If you insist on setting me on fire, what can you expect?"

She laughs and lifts her arms around my neck, and we exchange a long, passionate kiss, only breaking apart when we hear someone else's feet on the wooden steps behind us.

"Come on." I take her hand, checking the number on the key I was given, and lead her along the corridor to number fifteen. I unlock it—it's a real key, not a card you have to wave in front of the lock—open the door, and then lock it behind us.

It's a beautiful bedroom, all decorated in blue, with white-and-blue bedding and deep blue drapes, but they're open at the moment, no doubt giving a view across the moat. There's no time to examine the room in detail though, because my blood is up, and all I can think about is Kora Prince and kissing her soft mouth.

I take her wrap from her shoulders and place it over one of the chairs. Luckily someone has banked up the real wood fire and the room is pleasantly warm, so she shouldn't feel the cold. I hope she doesn't anyway, because soon she won't even have the flimsy dress to keep her warm. I considered letting her keep it on, but now I have her here, I want to take my time, and I want her naked beneath me.

"It's so beautiful," she says, looking around the room.

"Is it?" I move closer to her and slide a hand beneath her chin to lift her gaze to mine. "I know it sounds corny, but I only have eyes for you." I lower my lips to hers. They're soft and slightly sticky from her lip gloss. Wow, I've only been kissing her for, like, two seconds, and I'm already hard as oak.

I touch my tongue to her bottom lip, requesting permission, and she parts her lips and allows me in. I tilt my head a little to the right, changing the angle of the kiss, slip my hand to the back of her head to hold her there, and then kiss her deeply, delving my tongue into her mouth.

Kora arches against me, her hands splaying on my chest, and darts her tongue against mine, the slick slide of it making me groan. I kiss her while she undoes my bow tie, enjoying the feel of her silky hair beneath my fingers. She removes the tie from beneath my wing collar, then begins unbuttoning my shirt. I help her out with the tight button at the top, then let her slide off my jacket and shirt.

"Your hair," I murmur as she returns after placing them over a chair. "Can you take it down?"

Obediently, she begins to remove the tiny silver clips holding up her locks. While she's doing that, I move behind her, take hold of the zipper of her dress, and slide it down her spine, being careful not to catch the delicate fabric. Slowly, I reveal the golden skin of her bare back, and then right at the bottom the cream lace of her garter belt.

Her hair tumbles around her shoulders as she finishes removing the clips, and she turns in my arms, lowering her own to let the straps of the gown slide down. I hold her as she steps out of it, and we drape it over the chair.

Now she's naked except for her stockings and high heels. I circle my finger in the air, and she does a twirl for me, then poses, hands on her hips. "I'm guessing you want me to keep these on?"

"Definitely." Her stocking-covered legs have a beautiful sheen in the firelight, and look long and slender in the sexy sandals. Her legs will look great wrapped around my waist.

It's too much for me to bear, and I pull her into my arms and crush my lips to hers. Kora moans and lifts her arms around my neck, her soft breasts pressing against my bare chest. I cup them, groaning at the feel of their weight in my palms, and brush my thumbs over her nipples. They're soft and swollen in the warmth of the room, but they tighten as I tease them, and when I tug them gently, they extend and harden until they're like two small pebbles in my fingers.

"Ohhh…" she says helplessly, her teeth tearing at her bottom lips as I arouse her. Her cheeks are flushed pink, and I've already kissed off most of her lipstick, leaving her lips looking blurred and bruised. How does this girl look so made for sex?

After toeing off my shoes, I bend and lift her, and she wraps her legs around my waist, kissing me with such joy that it makes my heart swell. I carry her over to the huge bed and bend to let her pull the duvet back. I lower her onto the edge of the mattress, then drop down onto my knees in front of her. As I part her legs, she falls backward and covers her face, letting out a low moan when I brush my thumb through her folds. She's already moist, glistening in the firelight, like a juicy peach, ripe for me to consume. Moving my thumb down, I slip it inside her to gather some moisture, then slide it back up through her folds to tease her clit. Finally, I lower my head and lick all the way up.

Kora groans and buries her hand in my hair, urging me on, and so I dedicate myself to making her come with mouth, using my tongue, lips, teeth, and fingers to slowly bring her to the edge. It doesn't take long; less than five minutes and her breathing quickens, and her hips rock against my mouth, searching for the release she knows is there. This time I take her all the way, feeling the powerful pulses claim her, and true to form she cries out loud, informing the snow-filled night of her pleasure.

When she's done, I stand and rid myself of my trousers and underwear, retrieve a condom from my wallet, and join her on the bed. I roll the condom on, then lie back on the pillows, pulling her down into my arms.

Her cheeks are a beautiful rosy-pink, her hair is mussed, and her eyes are sleepy with desire. "I don't know what you're doing to me," she whispers, "but I like it."

I cup her face. "I'm not doing anything. You're the one setting me alight." I pull her head down to kiss her.

We exchange a slow, languorous kiss, our tongue engaging in a dance that soon has me hard as a rock again. I could easily toss her on her back and thrust myself to a climax in seconds, but I'm more of a gentleman than that, and besides, as pitiful as it sounds, I don't want the evening to come to an end. I want to stay like this forever, locked in this old bedroom, with the snow falling silently outside, caught in the magical bubble of sensual lovemaking forever.

So I take my time arousing her again, sliding my hands over her beautiful body, kissing her mouth, her neck, behind her ears, down her arms, the inside of her elbows and wrists, over her breasts, and dipping my tongue into her belly button. Then I turn her over and kiss all the way down to her ankles and up to the backs of her knees. I kiss over her bottom, running my tongue across the creases at the top of her thighs, then follow the curve of her spine up to her neck.

By this point we're both breathing heavily, and when I slide my fingers beneath her I find her more than ready for me. I push one of her knees up, position myself beneath her, then slide into her from behind in one smooth thrust.

She exclaims, her fingers clutching at the pillow, so I wait and let her adjust, closing my eyes and reveling at the sensation of being encased in her soft heat.

"Callum…" she murmurs, burying her face in the pillow. "Ohhh…"

When I'm sure she's relaxed, I begin to move with slow, steady thrusts, pulling back until I'm almost out of her, then pushing forward again until my hips meet her bottom. I sit back on my heels so I can watch myself slide in and out of her, and fuck, that's sexy, seeing myself glistening with her moisture.

"You're killing me here," she says with a groan, tipping her head back, her hair tumbling across her shoulders. "Please…"

"What's the rush?" I slide a hand beneath her and play with her nipple. "We've got all night to play. Why get it all over with in minutes?"

"I can't… I'm going to come…"

Chuckling, I withdraw from her, and she buries her face back in the pillow. "Argh, Callum!" She looks over her shoulder and glares at me.

I bend and kiss her, and she sighs, opening her mouth to my tongue and moaning as I kiss her deeply. When I eventually lift my head, her pupils have dilated, and the look in her eyes is dark and sultry. She pushes up onto her hands and knees and looks back at me again, moving her hips from side to side.

"Come on," she teases. "Ride me hard and fast, cowboy. You know you want to."

I cup her breasts, sliding my erection beneath her, through her folds. "Hard and fast?"

She moans, pushing back against me. "Yes. Please…"

I give in. What's a guy to do when his girl is begging him like that?

I press the tip of my erection into her, and in one smooth push, bury myself in her, balls deep.

Kora squeals, moans, then drops onto her elbows so her bottom is high in the air. I put one hand on her back, keeping her there, and begin to thrust, hard and fast as she requested, slamming into her and driving us both at speed to the finish line. It takes less than thirty seconds before she cries out and clamps around me, and I only need five or six more thrusts before I'm coming too.

We collapse onto the pillows in a tangle of hair and limbs, our chests heaving, still locked together as our bodies finish their blissful union.

Beneath me, Kora shudders, then goes limp, moaning slightly into the pillow.

Our skin is damp and sticking together, and the fire still glows in the grate, but it won't be long before the evening air cools, and I don't want her to get cold.

Carefully, so as not to hurt her, I withdraw, dispose of the condom, then pull the big, thick duvet over us and snuggle back up to her.

"Are you okay?" I murmur. "I didn't hurt you?"

"No, no, of course not." She turns over to face me. I wrap my arms around her, tucking the duvet behind her to make sure Jack Frost can't slide his icy fingers down her spine.

"That was amazing," she whispers, and gives a big sigh. "That's the best sex I've ever had."

"Me too."

She turns her face and rests her chin on my chest so she can look at me. "You needn't say things like that, Callum. I know you're more experienced than I am."

I tuck an arm under my head. "Probably not. I had a couple of girlfriends before you. One other and Stephanie after I met you. And that's it."

Her lips curve up. "That surprises me. I'd have thought you'd have had lots of girlfriends. You're a great catch."

"You mean the money?"

"Well, that as well, but I meant more that you're tall, dark, and gorgeous. You dress well. You're funny and warm. Intelligent. Sophisticated. What's not to like? I'm surprised women aren't around you like bees around a honeypot."

I can't help but smile back as I run a strand of her hair through my fingers. "Are you saying I look like Pooh Bear?"

"There are worse things in the world, I assure you."

I laugh and kiss her forehead. "I could say the same about you. Not that you look like Pooh Bear, but about you having lots of partners. You're clever, gorgeous, sexy. How come men aren't lining up to get you into bed?"

"I could have had more partners if I'd wanted, I suppose. It's a good time to be a woman, sexual freedom and all that. But the thought of just jumping into bed with a guy doesn't appeal to me." Her eyes meet mine. "Well, apart from you."

"I suppose I should be flattered by that."

"You should. I haven't had any other one-night stands. That evening on the beach totally took me by surprise. As have the last few days."

"Me too." I curl the strand of hair around my finger. "I wish we lived closer."

"The same hemisphere would be a start."

I chuckle. "Yeah."

She yawns. "I guess some things aren't meant to be."

Sadness settles over me the same way the blanket of snow is settling over the grounds outside. "No, I guess not."

"Be back in a minute." She leaves the bed and goes into the bathroom. A few minutes later, she comes out *sans* makeup and false eyelashes, her hair in a loose braid, climbs back into bed, and snuggles up to me again. She turns her head and rests her cheek on my shoulder. "Goodnight."

"Sleep well."

"No worries there. I could sleep for a fortnight."

Sure enough, within a minute or two her breathing deepens, and I know she's dozed off.

I lie awake for a lot longer, though, watching the snow falling outside the window.

Chapter Twelve

Kora

When I wake the next morning, the room is filled with a strange light. I blink and rub my eyes.

"It's been snowing all night," Callum says, and I turn my head to see him lying on his back, looking at the window. We didn't close the curtains last night, and that's where the strange light is coming from.

The fire has gone out, and the central heating has kicked in, but it's still a little chilly. I rise and go over to the window, shivering and wrapping my arms around me as I peer out of the window. Sure enough, the grounds are covered in thick snow. Strange bumps indicate where rocks, bushes, and benches lie. Occasionally clumps of snow fall from the trees. Thankfully someone has gritted the drive so we should be able to reach the main road. It's beautiful, though; a magical end to a fantastic adventure.

I turn and scurry back to the bed, thankful when Callum pulls the duvet over us. "Have you been awake long?" I ask.

"A while. It seemed a shame to sleep and waste the time we have."

"I know what you mean." I think he enjoyed the evening as much as I did. I don't think he's been out much since he broke up with Stephanie. It's a lovely thing to say, though. I kiss his nose, then his lips, and we exchange a long, leisurely embrace.

"So," he says when we eventually come up for air, "off to Hastings today. Are you excited?"

"Yes. And nervous. I can't shake the feeling that I'm going to discover something unusual. I have no idea what, though."

"What time did you say you'd be there?"

"Between ten and eleven, so no hurry."

"Time for breakfast first, then?"

"Oh, definitely!"

Part of me wants to make love again, and I'm sure if I said so, Callum would happily oblige. This will probably be the last time we'll spend together, and it seems a real pity to waste it. But even though he was gentle, most of the time, I'm a little tender from last night's loving, and so in the end we just lie there and kiss and chat for a while, and it's lovely finding comfort in his arms, just being with him.

All good things come to an end, though, and eventually we get up, shower, dress, and go down for breakfast. Jasmine and James are already there, tucking into eggs and bacon, and we join them at the table and delve into a full English breakfast, which is so scrumptious that I finish it all. By the time we're done, I'm bursting at the seams.

"It was lovely to meet you," Jasmine tells me as she kisses me on the cheek when we go to part. She glances over at Callum, who's laughing at something James is saying. "You're good for him, my dear. I haven't seen him laugh like that for a long time. And he's obviously crazy about you."

"Oh, I don't know about that…"

"It's written all over his face. Is there really no chance of the two of you making a go of it?"

"Unfortunately not. I can't move to England," I tell her. "All my family is in New Zealand, and I'd miss them terribly. And obviously Callum has responsibilities here, as well as his company. It's just one of those things."

"Such a shame. You're obviously made for each other." She sighs. "Well, I hope you have a good flight back. And make sure you keep in touch!"

"I will." She's already sent me a friend request on Facebook, so I know I'll be hearing from her.

I say goodbye to James, and then Callum and I head outside. Ooh, it's cold! I'm glad of the thick coat and scarf I brought with me, and my boots. Callum is also wearing his long black coat, and he holds my hand as we walk through the inner bailey and out to the front drive.

It's still snowing, although only lightly now. We stand for a while and watch a group of kids making a snowman and throwing snowballs at each other, laughing as they squeal and try to dodge. Then, as the porter brings our bags out and the driver pulls up in the Aston Martin in front of us, we load it up, get in, and head out toward the main road.

"It was such a beautiful setting for a party." I look over my shoulder one more time at the fairytale castle that glows like a jewel in the middle of the winter wonderland, before settling back in my seat.

"It was a real success," Callum admits. "And it raised huge amounts for the charity, which is the best thing."

"Of course." I look out of the window, thinking about Jasmine's niece and Callum's brother. "It's such a shame when babies are born with a condition that could so easily be avoided."

"Well, if the mother doesn't drink then this condition, at least, wouldn't occur. But it's a bigger picture thing, isn't it? Helping people with alcoholism."

"Yes, of course. I didn't think about that. If the mother has alcoholism, it's not as simple as just saying 'don't drink while you're pregnant.'"

"Exactly."

"I think it's hard for people who don't suffer from addiction to understand it."

"Yeah, definitely."

"Is it hereditary?"

"Scientists think there can be a genetic predisposition to substance abuse. With alcoholism and other addictions, it's unclear, but my guess is that yes, it does run in families."

"Is that why you didn't drink when you were younger?"

He nods, indicating and pulling out onto the main road, heading south toward Hastings. "If I'm honest, I was terrified I'd end up like my parents, so I didn't touch a drop until I met Stephanie. One night, I was stressed out of my head because I had a big meeting the next day. I've never taken drugs, and I didn't really have any way of dealing with it. Sometimes exercise helps, but that night it didn't. So Stephanie suggested I have a small whiskey with her and promised just the one would help me relax. I gave in because I was so tense. I didn't like it particularly, but she was right—afterward I felt it threading through my system, and I did feel better. And once I realized I could have just one, and I didn't have to drink every night, I felt better."

"So in your case, you don't take after them."

"Oh, I do," he says, surprising me. "Just in another way. I know I'm addicted to working."

"You think so?"

"I know so. I always have been."

"Isn't addiction about compulsive engagement in rewarding stimuli despite adverse consequences?"

His eyebrows rise and he gives a short laugh. "I guess that's an apt definition."

"But surely your work doesn't have adverse consequences?"

"Not in the sense that the harder I work, the more money I make. But I find it impossible to stop. I have to set myself an alarm each evening, and it takes huge willpower for me to close my laptop and go to bed."

"You were all right last night."

He grins. "I had something to distract me."

"But what about today? Wouldn't you normally be at work now?"

"Yes. I get up at six and I'm in the office by seven. I usually work through until seven or eight, then go home and often do another couple of hours. And I can't remember the last time I had a day off. Seriously, it's very rare."

"You never go on holiday?"

"Nope. My honeymoon was the last time. And before that, my trip around the world when I met you. So, you see, only something very special could have convinced me to take a day out of the office." He glances at me and smiles.

"I'm flattered," I say softly, holding out my hand, and he covers it with his big bear paw. "Can I ask you something?"

"Of course," he says. "Fire away."

"Do you want kids?"

He thinks about it. "I don't *not* want them. At the moment, though, I can't see it happening. After I broke up with Stephanie, I had no desire to meet anyone else. I don't know that forever and kids are on the cards for me."

"Of course they are," I scold. "You're far too gorgeous not to be snapped up by some amazing girl." The thought gives me a strange twist in my stomach. I don't want some other girl to snap him up. But that's being a dog in the manger, and that's not fair.

"I wouldn't enter another relationship unless I was sure I could commit to it a hundred percent," he advises, "and I don't think I could at the moment. My work is everything, and I spend any spare time I do have with Jim and Josh. I can't imagine a woman understanding that."

"They would, if they loved you. I understand, don't I?"

He looks at me again, then turns his gaze back to the road. Oh, oops, does he think I'm saying I love him? Because I'm not. I can't. I've only been with him two days. Love is something that needs time to grow and develop.

I am in lust, though. I acknowledge that. I'm already regretting not taking advantage of him this morning. What an idiot. I should have shagged him senseless, even if it meant I couldn't walk for a fortnight.

"What about you?" he asks. "Do you want kids?"

I look back out of the window, at the snow-covered rooftops, the white trees and fields. "I don't know. I guess so. I'm thirty, and I know a lot of women begin to feel their body clock ticking at my age, but I don't feel broody or anything. I like kids. But I'm not sure I'm ready for that kind of responsibility. And anyway, I need to get my own life sorted out before I'm ready to make another one."

"Yeah," he says, "I guess that does help."

He changes the subject, and we chat away about movies and gaming for a while. He plays a lot of games with Josh, and I've always played with my brothers, so I'm able to discuss Call of Duty and The Witcher and Last of Us in great detail, to his delight.

It seems like no time at all before we pass a signpost that announces Hastings is only three miles away, and points in the other direction to a place called Battle.

"Is that where the Battle of Hastings was?" I ask, astonished.

Callum continues on to Hastings, but nods. "An abbey was built on the site and the town grew up around it."

"Wow, that's amazing! I've read about it since I was a child, but I never thought I'd actually visit the place."

"We can go there if you like, after we visit your family."

"Don't you have to get back to work?"

"Another couple of hours won't be the end of the world."

I don't say anything, but I feel slightly smug at the thought that he wants to take time off to be with me.

I put the location of Seagulls Care Home into the GPS, and Callum follows the directions past Hastings Castle toward the Old Town. We take a road to the left, and then suddenly there's the sea in front of us, iron-gray and icy cold.

Callum points out The Stade—which is an Old Saxon word that means 'landing place', and is probably where William the Conqueror landed back in 1066.

"I wonder if the sea looked as uninviting back then?" I ask.

"I wish you could have been here on May Day," he tells me. "They hold a pagan festival with maypole dancing and a Jack in the Green."

"I can't imagine you dancing around a maypole."

"Not since I was a kid. I was chosen as the May King when I was fourteen."

I stare at him as something clicks. "You grew up here?"

"I did. This is where Jim and Helen lived, and where I came to stay when Mum and Dad died. He only moved to London when Helen died."

"And you were the May King. I'm not surprised."

He chuckles. "My name is engraved on the stone by the school. There for all eternity."

He continues to the end of the Old Town and follows the road inland a little, finally turning off and heading up a long drive to what looks like a large manor house fronted by a huge lawn that's now completely white. He pulls up out the front, and we get out and stretch, looking up at the home.

"Nice place to see your days out," he says.

I have to agree. The house has a large central building and a wing on each side. I'm sure the view from the numerous windows is usually a lot more colorful than it is at the moment. No doubt the lawn is manicured and there are pathways for the residents to walk down and admire the flowers.

Callum goes to climb the steps to the front door, but I hesitate, feeling a sudden flurry of nerves.

"Hey." He turns and comes back down to take my hands in his. "What's up?"

"I don't know. I feel so nervous. Maybe I shouldn't have come, Callum. What if I discover something here, and I wish I hadn't?"

"You're just looking for the truth, aren't you? What could you possibly discover that might make you wish you hadn't come?" He pulls me into his arms and gives me a hug. "I know you miss your Mum, and you'd like to understand more about her and your family. Even if you find out something that comes as a shock, in the end it's got to be a good thing. Your roots are what ground you. Maybe it'll be what you've been looking for all this time."

That night at Claridge's, I told him I felt empty. I thought it was because of what Julian did to me, but maybe Callum's right, and it goes a lot deeper than that. I miss Mum a lot. I try not to think about it too much because it makes me so sad, but that doesn't mean that loss isn't there, inside me. I know I'll never see her again, and that has had a huge impact on me ever since she died.

Perhaps finding a few more pieces of the family jigsaw will go a small way to mending some of my broken heart.

I move back and take his hand, and together we walk up the steps and go inside.

Chapter Thirteen

Callum

We go up to the front desk, and Kora informs the receptionist that we're here to see Violet Johnson, her great-aunt. We sign in and receive a visitor sticker, and we take a seat while the receptionist finds a member of staff to take us to her room.

Kora's knee bounces up and down while she's sitting. She's obviously nervous. I find it strange that she's expecting to discover some bad news. I wonder whether that's connected to her mother's death. Theo's disappearance must also have had a huge impact on her. I keep forgetting she's a twin. I'm sure when you've had a couple of phone calls in the night bearing bad news, it takes a long time to get over the fear that everything's going to go wrong.

My phone vibrates, and I pull it out and check the screen. A text message, from Stephanie. My thumb hovers over it. I wish she'd stop contacting me. My fault for continuing with the property sale for her, but it's done now, and there's no reason for her to keep in touch. Part of me wants to delete the message unread, but that's just childish, so I tap the screen and bring it up.

I hear the charity ball went well, Stephanie says. *I hope Kora enjoyed herself.*

So someone told her I was there with Kora. I bet that stung. I feel a twinge of regret. I don't want to hurt Stephanie. I also don't want to make things difficult for Kora while she's here.

But I don't owe Stephanie anything. She cheated on me, not the other way around. And I'm not going to feel guilty for spending time with a woman who makes me feel good, no matter who she is. Anyway, it's not like she's Stephanie's sister. She's a—what—third cousin? They're hardly close. And it's none of Stephanie's business who either of us chooses to date.

I quickly thumb through my other messages. There's nothing there that can't wait. With some surprise, I realize I haven't thought about work once this morning. I can't honestly remember the last time that happened. Even on the morning I got married, I was still taking phone calls and answering emails.

"Ms. Prince?" A woman walks up to us, smiling hesitantly. She's not wearing the white jacket that a couple of staff members who've passed us have worn. She's about sixty, I'd say, with brown hair flecked with gray, cut short in a practical style, and wearing jeans and a blue sweater.

Kora stands. "Yes, hello."

"I'm Fiona Richardson," the woman replies, holding out her hand.

I try to get the family tree organized in my head. Kora told me that her mum was called Olivia, and her grandmother, who lives in New Zealand, is Carol. Violet, who lives here, was married to Carol's brother. And Fiona is their daughter. So Fiona and Kora's mum were cousins. I think I've got that right.

"How lovely to meet you." Kora looks delighted. I love the way she's so genuine and open about everything. "I'm Kora, and this is Callum MacDuff, my… friend." Her pause is imperceptible, but I can tell she was suddenly confused as to how to introduce me.

"Pleased to meet you." I shake Fiona's hand.

"I thought it would be a good idea if I was here as well while you spoke to Mum." Fiona turns and leads us across the foyer toward the east wing of the building. "She suffers from dementia, and I thought it might make things easier if I helped out."

"Oh, I'm sorry," Kora says softly. "Are you sure it's not too much for her, seeing us?"

"No, no. Just be prepared that she might get confused. It's so lovely to meet you! All the way from New Zealand. I've always wanted to go, but have never got around to it."

Still chatting, she leads us past a large room where some of the residents are watching TV and sitting at tables playing cards or doing crafts, then along a hallway with doors leading off either side. Halfway down, she stops and opens one of them, standing back to let us enter.

It's a pleasant room, with a bed in the center against the wall, and a couple of armchairs facing a TV. Sliding doors lead onto a small area with an outdoor table and chairs—a nice place to sit in the sun in the summer, although now they're all covered with snow. A partially open door to one side leads to a small bathroom. The place is light and airy, and I can smell the rose-scented potpourri on the bedside table.

An elderly woman sits in one of the armchairs, and she looks up as we enter. Her white hair is neatly curled, and she's wearing fawn trousers and a cream sweater over a white blouse.

"Thank you, Jason," Fiona says from behind me, and I move aside as one of the orderlies brings in a couple of plastic chairs and puts them next to the armchairs, so we all have a place to sit.

"All right, Mrs. Johnson?" he asks Violet cheerfully. "Nice to have guests on such a cold, snowy day!"

"Yes, lovely," she replies, although she clearly has no idea who we are.

He meets my gaze and smiles, then leaves the room, closing the door behind him. Fiona gestures for us to sit, and I indicate for Kora to take the other armchair next to Violet, while I sit in one of the plastic chairs, and Fiona takes the other.

"Mum, this is Kora Prince," Fiona says, raising her voice a little. "She's Carol's granddaughter. And this is her friend, Callum. I told you they were coming, remember?"

"Of course I remember," Violet says, her eyes clearing. "From New Zealand."

"That's right," Kora replies brightly. "It's so lovely to meet you and Fiona. I hope you don't mind me coming to see you. I don't know much about Mum's side of the family, and I really wanted to meet you and find out about you all."

"We were thrilled to hear from you," Fiona says. "It's not often you get to meet family from the other side of the world. We're all big fans of *The Lord of the Rings*, and the scenery looks absolutely amazing."

"It's not CGI either," Kora explains. "It's all real. I went to Weta Workshop, too, where they make all the models, and last year I visited the site where they filmed Hobbiton. I had my photo taken in front of Bilbo and Frodo's hobbit hole, and saw the tree where Bilbo had his eleventy-first birthday party. It's well worth a visit if you ever get to go there." She presses her lips together and glances at me. She's worried she's babbling. I give her what I hope is a reassuring smile.

"How do you two know each other?" Fiona asks.

"We met in New Zealand twelve years ago when Callum was on holiday." A touch of color appears in Kora's cheeks. She still doesn't know how to describe our relationship. "And I bumped into him a couple of days ago."

"It's been great catching up again," I say easily, and she smiles.

"So, tell us all about your family," Kora says to Violet. "Your husband's name was Richard, wasn't it?"

Violet nods. "He died two years ago."

"I'm very sorry to hear that. I'd like to have met him."

"He was a lovely man, bossy and grumpy sometimes, but honest and loyal."

"We miss him a lot," Fiona says, her voice husky.

"And do you have brothers and sisters?" Kora asks her.

"Yes, two brothers. They couldn't make it today, which is a shame. They would have loved to meet you."

"And you?" Kora asks Fiona. "Do you have children?"

"Yes, a couple, for my sins!"

We all smile.

"I'm sorry," Violet says to Kora, "but who are you again?"

Kora glances at Fiona, who gives her an apologetic smile. "I'm Carol's granddaughter," Kora says to Violet. "Olivia's girl."

Violet frowns. "I don't understand. Carol couldn't have children."

"No, Mum," Fiona says patiently, "she adopted, don't you remember the twins?"

"Oh yes." Violet's eyes clear again. "I'd forgotten."

I glance at Kora. She blinks and looks at me. I can see the truth reflected in her eyes.

She didn't know her mother was adopted.

"What?" she says.

Fiona also looks at her, and her jaw drops. "Oh no. Don't tell me you didn't know?"

Kora has gone completely white. "My mother was adopted?"

Fiona nods slowly, looking contrite. "I'm so sorry. I assumed you knew. Carol couldn't have children."

"And what did you mean by 'the twins'? Mum was a twin?"

Fiona looks at me and blows out a long breath before returning her gaze to Kora. "Yes. Carol and Alan adopted them when I was eight. The twins were six. We spent quite a lot of time together when we were kids."

I reach out and take Kora's hand. I don't think she even notices. "The twin," she asks, "what was her name?"

"Margaret. We all called her Maggie."

"Were they identical?"

"No, they were fraternal."

"Like me and Theo," Kora whispers.

"Olivia was fair, but Maggie had brown hair. She was a little taller, too. They looked more like sisters than twins."

"Where is she now?" Kora asks.

Fiona's face creases with pity. "I'm very sorry—she died."

Kora swallows. "When?"

"It was on the girls' twenty-first birthday. Maggie was dating a guy called Alex, and he had a motorbike. Carol hated Maggie going on it, but you know what young people are like, they never listen to their mothers. She'd gone out with Alex for a ride, and they were on their way back to their birthday party, and a lorry pulled out of a side road. Alex tried to turn the bike, but it tipped and skidded, and they went right under the wheels. She was killed immediately—Alex died on the way to the hospital. It was very tragic."

Kora presses her fingers to her lips, obviously fighting against her emotions.

"Carol and Alan were devastated," Fiona continues. "And Olivia, obviously, was distraught. She…" Fiona pauses and glances at me. "I'm not sure if I should say."

"Please," Kora says, her voice husky with emotion. "I want to know everything."

"Well, a few months later, Olivia tried to take her own life with pills."

A tear runs down Kora's cheek. "Oh no."

"Luckily, her dad found her and got to her hospital, and she recovered. But after that, all three of them decided they wanted a new start. The paper company he worked for had a branch in Christchurch, and he applied for a job there and got it. So the three of them emigrated. We were all devastated to see them go, but we understood."

"I never knew," Kora whispers. "Mum never spoke of any of it. And Gran and Grandpa didn't either. They all refused to talk about the past and their family. Now I know why."

"They cut themselves off from us when they moved," Fiona says. "It wasn't as easy to stay in touch back then anyway—we didn't have Facebook or anything. I was very upset about it all, but they'd been through a lot, so I did my best to understand."

"Do you remember Olivia and Maggie?" I ask Violet, as Kora searches for a tissue in her handbag.

Violet nods slowly. "Yes. I'd forgotten that Maggie died, but I remember now. I am sorry. My memory isn't what it used to be."

"It's okay." Kora leans across and holds Violet's hand. "I'm so sorry to come here and stir up old emotions."

"It's nice to talk about them after so long," Fiona says. "I'm the one who's sorry to drop that bombshell on you. It didn't occur to me that you might not know."

"Do you think maybe your mum didn't know she was adopted?" I ask Kora. "And that's why she never told you?"

Fiona shakes her head. "I'm sorry, but they definitely both knew. I remember asking them once if they wanted to find their birth parents when they grew up. Maggie said she might. Olivia said she wouldn't, though. She loved Carol and Alan, and said they were her parents, and she didn't want to know about the woman who gave them up."

So Olivia chose not to tell her own family she was adopted. I wonder whether Kora's father knows? And Ben, and Kora's other brothers? Surely it's not just Kora who's in the dark?

"So… do you know who Mum's birth mother was?" Kora asks quietly.

"I'm afraid not. I'm guessing Carol and Alan knew, but they never told us." Fiona looks at Violet. "Did she ever tell you, Mum?"

"It was during the war," Violet says. "She came on a train to Devon."

Fiona frowns. "Who did?"

Violet blinks. "Who did what?"

Fiona gives us an apologetic smile. "She's talking about herself. She lived in London, and she was evacuated to Devon during the Second World War." She glances at Violet. "I think she's getting a bit tired. Do you have any other questions?"

"No, you've already told us far more than I could have hoped for." Kora gets to her feet, and I follow. "Thank you so much," Kora says, shaking Violet's hand. "It was lovely to meet you."

I say goodbye as well, and then follow Fiona to the door. She accompanies us down the hallway, and back out into the foyer.

"I just want to say sorry again," she says as we get to the front door. "I really didn't mean to pull that grenade on you. I can't imagine what a shock it was."

"It was a bit," Kora admits. "But I came here to learn the truth, and you've certainly helped with that. Thank you for meeting with us."

They kiss on the cheek, and I shake Fiona's hand, and then we sign out and head back to the car.

We get in, and I start it going so the heater comes on. I sit there for a minute, though, letting the windscreen demist, and hold Kora's cold hand in mine.

"Are you okay?" I ask softly. "You're ever so pale."

"It was such a shock," she says. "I just didn't expect it. I can't believe Mum never told us she was a twin, or that she was adopted." She looks out at the snow-covered grounds. "I feel… I don't know… hurt, I think, as if she lied to me. Although she didn't lie, she just omitted to tell the truth, I suppose. But why? Why not tell her family?"

"Do you think your father knows?"

She inhales, then exhales slowly. "I don't know. I hope not. Because if he does, it means he withheld the truth, too."

"If he did, I'm sure it would have been because your mum asked him not to tell you."

"Probably." She looks down at our hands, then finally up at me and gives me a shaky smile. "I'm sorry, I'm sure this is the last thing you expected when you agreed to come with me today."

"No. Don't be sorry. It's odd, but I feel sort of honored to be here. I'm glad you weren't alone."

"Me too." She looks up into my eyes. Hers are a beautiful deep blue, the color of a summer sky. They remind me of my holiday in New Zealand, that sultry December and January.

"I wish you could stay." I didn't mean to say it. I don't want to get all deep and meaningful. It's pointless, because our lives are at the opposite ends of the world. We both have commitments and other lives.

But Kora says what's in her heart, and so I thought I might as well, too.

Her lips part, and I lower mine to them and kiss her. They're cool, so I kiss her for a while to warm them up. It's a good excuse.

Chapter Fourteen

Kora

"What would you like to do now?" Callum asks me as he heads north out of Hastings. "It's a cold day to be traipsing around historical sites. Would you rather go back to London?"

"No. This will probably be my only chance to be able to see it. I'm okay. If you're sure you have time."

"Of course," he says. "All right. I haven't been there for a long time."

I'm surprised that he doesn't want to head straight back to work, but I don't say anything, and look out of the window at the snow-covered walls and gardens of the houses. The roads have all been gritted so they're clear, and the pavements are turning to slush. It's like all the magic that was in the world yesterday has rotted away. I don't realize I've said the words aloud until Callum sighs.

"I'm sorry you feel as if your trip has been spoiled," he says. "I know it must have come as an awful shock. But still, maybe try and take from it the positive things, too. Perhaps when you think about it a bit more, it'll help you understand your mum, like for example how she was a twin, and that's probably why she also had twins. I guess it means you're more likely to have twins?"

"I suppose. It's really shocked me that she was a twin. Theo and I do have a different relationship than the one we have with our brothers. Of course I'd be devastated to lose any of them, but it would be different if something happened to Theo—that's why it was so hard when he went missing. No wonder she tried to take her own life. And she had to spend all that time without Maggie. Now I understand why she used to have those quiet times, and why she took those long walks. She must have felt as if half of her was missing."

"I wonder if it made it worse, being adopted," Callum asks. "If she felt Maggie was her last connection to her birth parents."

I swallow hard as tears prick my eyes. "I don't know why I feel so upset. It doesn't really make any difference to me, does it? What does it matter who her birth parents were? Gran and Grandpa loved her, so that should be all that matters."

Callum curls his fingers around mine. "Honestly, I think you're still grieving for your mum. Hot on the heels of her passing came your breakup with Julian, and then Theo's disappearance."

"My grandfather died, too, in December."

"Jesus, Kora, really?"

I nod. "And there was Rebecca's death."

"Rebecca?"

I tell him about Ben's first wife, about their poisonous relationship, and what a shock it was when we found out she'd been killed in a car crash. "Of course it was horrible, and I felt sorry for little Estella, who lost her mum. But it was a very confusing time. Ben was so unhappy with her, and I think it was such a relief that she'd gone from his life, and then he had terrible guilt for feeling that. He was really mixed up until he met Heloise, and even now they can't be open about their relationship, because publicly he has to be seen to be mourning his wife."

"And all that around the time of your own breakup," Callum says. "No wonder your first thought is that everything's going to fall apart again."

I muse on that as he navigates a roundabout. We were talking about addiction on the way down here this morning. Is it possible that I'm somehow addicted to misery? That I focus on the worst that could happen? What do they call it, catastrophizing?

When Fiona told us about Mum being adopted and having a twin sister, my first emotion was hurt that Mum hadn't told me the truth. As her only daughter, we were close when she was alive, closer than she was with my brothers, or so I thought. It gives me a funny feeling in my stomach to think of the evenings we spent painting our toenails and listening to music while we talked about boys and going to university, and all the while she had this huge secret she didn't share with me.

But the thing is, I didn't own my mother. She had a life before she met my father, before she had me. The fact that she didn't share it doesn't mean she loved me any less. I get that. But it still stings.

Did Dad know? My fingers itch to pull out my phone and ring him, but it's past midnight there, and he'll probably be in bed. I'll have to wait until I know he's up.

Callum takes the turnoff for the town of Battle, and shortly after signals at the signpost for Battle Abbey. He parks in a public car park, which is brave of him considering people stare at the Aston Martin as we drive by, locks it, and we walk up the paved path toward the gatehouse.

I try to put this morning's revelation out of my mind. It's not easy, but the fact that I'm walking around the site of the Battle of Hastings is fascinating enough to distract me for a while. Callum tells me a few facts about the battle, and we pass a pleasant hour looking around the abbey buildings and snow-covered ruins. I especially like the plaque on the ground that commemorates the spot where King Harold—he of the arrow in the eye—purportedly died, which also marks the original church's high altar.

We go to the visitor center and the gatehouse exhibition, and to the shop, where I treat myself to a beautiful scarf printed with a scene from the Bayeux Tapestry, and Callum buys Josh a Norman knight figure on horseback that he says his brother will love.

"Funny to think of all the people who've lived and died before us." I shiver as we walk back through the walled garden, currently covered in snow. It sure is cold today. "Puts it all in perspective, doesn't it?"

Callum studies me for a moment, then takes my hand. "I think it's time for a hot coffee and some lunch, don't you?"

I'm still fairly full from my full breakfast this morning, but a coffee and a cake sound attractive, so I nod and let him lead me to Battle Abbey café. It looks like the sort of tearoom I've seen on English TV shows—small and cozy, with round tables covered with blue-and-white-checked cloths, menus written on chalkboards, serving Devonshire-style cream teas and a variety of baked goods made on the premises. We find a table by the window and order two coffees, and I choose a piece of fruitcake, while Callum goes for a chocolate muffin.

"This is nice." I slip off my coat and hang it over the back of the chair. The smell of coffee and fresh baking grounds me, and I feel warmer and less shivery than I did in the abbey grounds. "And lovely of you to suggest. I thought you would have wanted to get back to work."

"Now I'm AWOL, I'm quite enjoying myself." He grins and leans back in his chair. He looks so handsome today. He's wearing black jeans and a cream fisherman-style sweater over a white T-shirt. He didn't shave this morning, and so he has a fine stubble on his cheeks and jaw that give him a bit of a rakish look compared to his normal suave appearance. I like rough Callum. But then I like smooth Callum too. I pretty much like Callum in any form he chooses to appear.

"So what do you want to do after this?" he asks.

"I don't know. I guess I'm in your hands."

"Hmm." He surveys me for a moment, his eyelids dropping to half-mast. My instincts tell me he's thinking of something naughty.

"Stop it," I scold.

His lips curve up. "Can you read my mind now?"

"It's not difficult. You've got a wicked gleam in your eye. Tell me you weren't thinking of something rude."

He chuckles. "Maybe. It's hard not to when you're sitting there like that."

"Like what?" I look down at myself. I'm wearing black pants and a bright blue sweater that matches my eyes, with my favorite shimmering green scarf.

"You look beautiful," he says, surprising me. "Like a flower pushing through the snow. Everyone here is so pale and drab. You still remind me of a mermaid in those blue and green colors. You make me think of summer and the sea, barbecued food, and the sun on my skin."

I'm so taken aback by his poetic description that I can't think what to say. In the end, I just sit back as the waitress brings over our coffees and cakes, placing them before us.

"Thank you." I wait until she's gone, then meet his eyes. "These last few days have been special in so many ways. I hope you don't think I've spoilt our time together by being down about what I've found out."

"Not at all. Of course it was a shock. You just need time to process it, that's all."

"I thought I might ring Gran tonight." I break off a piece of the fruitcake and eat it. Ooh, that's nice—moist and full of plump dried fruit. "I want to see if she knows who Mum's birth parents were.

Because if she did, maybe I could get in contact with them while I'm here?"

Callum takes a big bite of his muffin and chews thoughtfully. "You'd have to be prepared for the fact that they might not want you to get in touch. Not every birth parent is happy to meet the child they gave away."

"That's true." I'd have to prepare myself for rejection. But would I be able to forgive myself if I came all this way and didn't try?

"So do you want to go back now and try to ring?" he asks.

"It's late there. Gran and Grandpa go to bed early, so I'd better not wake them. I was thinking... is there anywhere else near here we could go and see? I know it's cold and snowy, but it seems a shame to waste the day while I have you."

He smiles. "There are lots of historical sites, if that's what you mean."

"Anything Roman? I'd love to see something Roman."

"We could go to Pevensey Castle. It's mainly medieval—it's the place where William the Conqueror landed—but the Roman curtain wall still survives. It was one of the Saxon Shore Forts, built to keep the invaders out."

"I'd love to see that."

"Then that's sorted." He takes a big bite of muffin. "Eat your cake. I think we'll need the calories on a day like this."

He's right; it's brisk and breezy, and it continues to snow, whipping the flakes around the south-east countryside. After we finish our coffee and cake, we call in at a clothes shop and treat ourselves to two beanies and two pairs of gloves. At Pevensey Castle, the snow lays thickly on the old stones and the grass between them, but there's something magical about the sparkling snow that lifts my spirits.

Or maybe it's just being close to Callum, who keeps his arm around me in an attempt to keep us both from freezing, his breath warming my ear as he tells me the story of the Conqueror landing here and building his temporary fort within the Roman walls. I find it so odd to think that to William, the Roman site was already ancient. This country is built in layers that go back so far it makes my head spin.

When we're done, we finally decide it's time we went home, and Callum drives us back to London. We both fall quiet on the way, lost in thought. I wonder whether the proximity to the city is getting him back in the frame of mind for work and his family. I'm sort of doing the same, beginning to think about ringing my Gran tonight, and what I'm going to say.

It's snowing more thickly here, slowing down the traffic, and it's nearly five o'clock by the time he finally draws up outside Claridge's. "I suppose you need to go home," I say, "get back to Josh and Jim."

"Yeah, I don't like to leave them for too long," he says. "Alice—our assistant—comes in today, so at least that's given Jim a break, but even so…"

I smile at him. "Have a nice evening with them."

"Thanks." He puts the handbrake on but leaves the engine running. The porter comes down to open the door, but I signal for him to wait a moment, and he steps back.

"Callum…" Suddenly there's so much to say, and no time to say it. "I've had such a lovely couple of days."

"Me too." His light-brown eyes shine in the light of the lamps hanging outside the hotel. He's so incredibly handsome. I feel a stab of resentment that he lives here, and I live so far away. Yet again, Fate intervenes to thrust a knife between my ribs.

"I wish…" I begin.

"I know." He leans forward and presses his lips to mine. He holds the kiss for a few seconds, then moves back. "Take care of yourself, won't you?"

"I will. Keep in touch?"

He nods.

I get out of the car, wave one last time, and run up the steps to the hotel.

Inside, I pause for a moment, tears pricking my eyes. It's pointless to get upset. I knew nothing could come of this. I need to take it for what it was and move on.

I'm getting hungry, and I could go into the restaurant and book myself a table. But suddenly I just want my own company. So instead I go up to my suite, have a hot shower to warm myself up, then order some room service. When it comes, I curl up in bed and eat the burger and fries I felt like ordering, while I watch a British quiz show on TV.

I try not to feel sorry for myself, but it's hard. I miss Callum, more than I would have imagined. I love the way he looks at me, with that sparkle in his eyes that suggests he's remembering naughty things we've done together, and planning a few more. I feel incredibly flattered that he spent all that time with me, time he would normally have devoted to his all-important work. I can't help but think about making love with him, and how it felt to have his hands on my skin, to have him inside me. I want more of that. But I can't have it. And it makes me want to cry.

But I'm a big girl now, not a lovesick teenager, and it's time to move on. As the clock ticks and I decide Gran will now be up, I text her, asking her if she'd be around for a chat on Zoom. Then I wait for her to reply.

Chapter Fifteen

Callum

I should go to the office, but I'm tired after my day with Kora, and a little emotionally wrung out. So instead, calling my PA on the way and answering a couple of urgent queries, I drive straight home.

I discover Josh in the kitchen with Alice, making cookies.

"Chocolate chip," he announces cheerfully, rolling the dough between his hands and then flattening it on a baking tray. "For after dinner."

"I look forward to them. They look amazing." I give him a hug and smile at Alice. "Something smells nice."

"A casserole in the crockpot," she advises.

"Mmm. Where's Jim?"

"Out for a walk."

"Okay, I'm going to change." I leave them to it, go through to my room, and close the door.

I take off my jeans, pull on a comfy pair of jogging bottoms, then pick up my phone. I check for messages. Several—including one from Stephanie. But nothing from Kora.

Leaving the one from Stephanie unread, I go back into the kitchen and pour myself a whiskey.

"Can I have one?" Josh asks.

"Sure." I pour a splash into another tumbler, tip in half a dozen ice cubes, and top it up with plenty of water from the fridge.

My brother isn't a child, and the last thing I ever want him to feel is that I'm treating him like one. Legally he's old enough to go into the army, to get married, to drink alcohol in a pub, and to have children of his own. I've always tried to give him the freedom to live his own life and make his own decisions.

But the reality is that he's like a fourteen-year-old boy trapped in a twenty-nine-year-old's body, and most of the time he's just not able to rationalize situations in a logical way. It would be irresponsible of me to let him go out and roam the streets, or to have access to unlimited drink and drugs. So I try to let him explore the world in a safe way, so that he doesn't feel as if he's being policed every minute of the day.

For example, when he told me he wanted to learn to drive, instead of giving him a straight no, I took him out of town after hours to a quiet industrial estate and let him drive around the empty streets for a while. He enjoyed roaring up and down the straight roads, but as soon as he came to a junction and had to navigate oncoming traffic—albeit only two other cars—he put the handbrake on and got out, declaring he didn't want to drive anymore, and he hasn't asked to go out again since.

Both Jim and Alice take him to the park to play football with friends, or to the local sports club because he likes to swim and play table tennis. He's also part of a group run by NOFAS that helps people with learning disabilities find jobs in the community, and three times a week he works at the local supermarket, stacking shelves and packing bags.

But the truth is that he'd rather be at home, and he hasn't shown any great ambition to strike out on his own. It's not impossible, but it's unlikely he'll get a high-paying job, marry, and have his own home. And that's fine by me. It's just sometimes I feel guilty for not spending more time with him.

"Come on," I say as he puts the baking trays in the oven, "let's wash up, and then we'll do some Call of Duty, eh?"

His eagerness to play makes cleaning the bowls and utensils extra speedy, and it doesn't take long before we take our drinks into the living room, leaving Alice to get started on dinner, and pick up where we left off with our PlayStation game.

Twenty minutes later, Jim comes in, the shoulders of his coat and his woolly hat covered with a layer of snow.

"You look like a snowman," Josh comments, complaining when Jim bends to kiss his forehead and shoots a handful of snow onto Josh's lap.

"Cold out there," Jim says. "Roll on summer." He blows on his hands. "What's for dinner? I need thawing out."

"Lamb casserole with dumplings," Alice announces, coming out and wiping her hands, "and it's nearly ready, so you'd better get changed!"

Jim goes off to shed his coat and hat, and Josh and I finish the level we're doing and then join Jim at the dining table. Alice puts the crockpot full of steaming lamb casserole before us, advises us there's a jam roly poly in the oven, then blows us a kiss and heads out for the night. I've asked her many times to join us for dinner, but she has a husband and a couple of teenage kids, so I know she likes to get home and have dinner with them.

While we eat, I tell Jim and Josh about my day, and give Josh his present of the Norman knight on horseback. He collects model soldiers and is thrilled at this new addition to his collection, and places it on the table so he can study it while we eat.

"It's nice to have you home for dinner." Jim eyes me as he tucks into a dumpling.

I don't meet his gaze and focus on spearing a piece of lamb from the delicious stew. I understand his surprise. I can't remember the last time I sat down and had dinner with them. Usually I roll in about eight o'clock, long after they've finished.

"Yeah, well, I was late getting back and thought I might as well come home than go back to work."

Josh finishes off his last mouthful and picks up his soldier. "I'm going to put him on the shelf."

"Don't you want any jam roly poly?" Jim asks.

"Later." He dashes off.

We smile at each other and continue our dinner.

"That was a nice thing to do," Jim says. "Buying him that knight. Nice of you to think of him when you were busy." His eyes twinkle.

I give him a wry look. "You might as well ask. I know you're dying to."

"I'm curious, yes. I don't think I've ever known you to blow off work. Ever. She must be special."

I finish off the last mouthful of stew, sigh, and push the plate away. "She is. But nothing can come of it."

"She wouldn't consider moving here?"

"I don't think so. We've only spent a couple of nights together. I mean, yeah, it's been fun, but that's not enough to make the huge change of emigrating to the other side of the world."

"No, I suppose not." Jim looks sad. "It would be nice to see you settled and happy, though, before I pop my clogs."

I give a short laugh and get up from the table. "Want a glass of wine, you miserable old codger?"

"Yeah, why not? Have to make the most of my last days on earth."

I grin, take my plate out into the kitchen, and find us both a wine glass. Then I choose a Merlot from the rack and pour us both a glass.

I carry them back to the dining table, and we sit and sip the wine while we look out over the view of snow-covered Hyde Park.

"I am partly serious," Jim says. "I am eighty-two this year."

"You're going to live forever," I scoff. "You're strong as an ox."

"Callum," he says softly. "We should talk about this. One day I won't be around, and then it's just going to be you and Josh."

"We'll manage."

"I know you will. But it's not all about managing. It's about quality of life."

"You don't think Josh has that?" I can't help but bristle.

But he shakes his head. "I'm not talking about Josh. The lad's happy enough and you've done well by him. I'm worried about you."

I raise my eyebrows, astonished. He's never expressed any concerns like this before. "Why?"

"Don't get me wrong. You've been incredibly successful at work. I mean, exceeding any expectations I could ever dream of having. The money you've earned has made both Josh and I very comfortable. I would never have imagined I'd live in a place like this, in such luxury." He leans forward earnestly. "But it's not all about money, Callum."

"Isn't it?"

"You know it's not, and you know what I'm saying."

I stare moodily into my wine. "It's not my fault my wife had an affair." Jim is the only other person I've told about what happened.

To my surprise, he doesn't answer with, "Of course not," as I'd expected. Instead, he remains silent, and eventually I look up at him.

"You think it was my fault?" I ask.

"Let's just say I think it's rare for a person to play away if they're one hundred percent happy at home," he replies softly.

I'm so shocked, I just stare at him. He's always been my biggest supporter, the one person I know I can rely on to be on my side.

Jim frowns. "I'm not saying what she did was justified. Of course it wasn't. But I do think it was a cry for help. I think she'd been trying to tell you she was unhappy, and you hadn't listened. So she tried to get your attention another way. She was wrong to do that, but I do kind of understand why she did it. She knew she was second to your obsession with work, and that's gotta hurt."

I get up and go over to the window. We've never talked about my marriage ending, other than the practical details. I want to yell at him that it's private, and that he shouldn't stick his nose into stuff that has nothing to do with him. But I don't.

"Don't be angry with me," Jim murmurs. "I shouldn't have said anything. It's none of my business."

There's a gap in the snow clouds, and as they move across the sky, for a moment the nearly full moon shows her face. Hyde Park glitters in the silvery light, a winter wonderland, just like last night, when Kora and I walked into Leeds Castle.

"I'm angry because I know you're right." I watch a couple walking through the park, hand in hand, laughing away at something. Was I ever that young? That happy and carefree? "Both of us thought the other person was someone different. And we were both disappointed. I know I let her down. Maybe if she'd been different, if she'd been more…" Like Kora? I don't say it, but I think it. "I might have changed." Jim sighs and leans back, and my lips twist. "I know what you're thinking. I'm putting the blame on Stephanie again, for not being my perfect woman. And you're right. She was my wife. I should have been more attentive. Spent more time with her. But there was more to it than that."

"I'm sure there was."

"She wanted me to ask you to move out." The words are blunt, as if I'm chipping at a stone statue with a chisel. "You and Josh. She asked me to choose."

Jim stares at me. "And you chose us over your wife? Ah, Callum…"

"I don't want to be married to any woman who asks me to make that decision."

His expression softens. "Yeah."

"You'll always come first," I say fiercely. "I know it might not seem like it when I work all the hours under the sun, but my family is everything."

"I know. Come 'ere, you silly arse." Jim rises, and I walk up to him and give him a hug. "I'm sorry," he whispers. "I shouldn't have said anything. I just want to know that when it's my time to go, you're happy. Because otherwise, what's the point?"

I muse on that as he claps me on the back and goes into the living room, where Josh is now watching an action movie. I pick up my wine glass and go back to the window to look out at the view. The moon has gone back behind the clouds, and it's snowing again, light flakes drifting across the park.

Otherwise, what's the point?

I've dedicated my life to my work. It began as a need to provide for my family, but if I'm honest, my inner ambition and drive to succeed soon took over. I'm addicted to the dopamine high I get when I make a deal. There's nothing like it. But it's fleeting. And afterward, what's left?

I can't sniff at the money. I like being rich. I can buy practically anything I want. A new house, new car, a private plane or a yacht if I was into such things. My family is comfortable and safe, and never wants for anything.

But are any of us happy? I'm not even sure what the word means anymore.

And then I think of Kora. I think she could make me happy. But it's not meant to be. Probably the best I can get out of our brief relationship is the proof that I am still capable of love, and my heart isn't as frozen as I thought it was.

I sip the fine Merlot, watch the snowflakes fall, and think about the way Kora makes me feel warm from the inside out.

I could give it all up. Leave everything behind and run off Down Under with her.

But I can't leave Jim and Josh here. I just can't. And anyway, I'll be fucked if I sell the company I worked so hard to create to the man who pretended to be my best friend, and then stole my wife.

Chapter Sixteen

Kora

I get a text back from Grandma almost immediately, saying she'll be happy to do a Zoom call in five minutes to give her time to put on a bit of lipstick. Smiling, I set my laptop up on the desk, then put on a shirt, although I keep my pajama bottoms on. Zoom is a wonderful thing.

At that moment, my butler arrives with the gin and tonic I ordered. I sit in front of the laptop and take a few sips. I should be thinking about what I'm going to say to Grandma, but instead my mind wanders to the night Callum and I had dinner in this hotel, when I also ordered a G&T. Will I ever see him again? I feel a wave of sadness at having to say goodbye to him. I know what we had was just a seed, but it could have grown into something magnificent. Still, some things just aren't meant to be, I guess.

If I think about it anymore, I'm going to cry, so I check the time, then press the dial button.

Grandma answers within a couple of rings. "Hello!"

"Hey, Grandma." I wait for her picture to pop up, and smile as she appears. It's nine in the morning there, and she looks fresh and ready for the day. She's put on her pink lipstick, which compliments her English-rose complexion and silver hair.

It's funny, but I've always thought that she doesn't look much like Mum or me. Mum had blonde hair and a heart-shaped face like me, whereas Grandma's is round. Now I know why.

"Goodness, is that snow behind you?" She peers at the screen.

I glance over my shoulder, where the open curtains reveal flakes of snow drifting past the window in the light from the streetlamp. "Yes. It's been snowing for the last couple of days."

"Oh how lovely. Have you been out in it?"

I tell her briefly about the ball at Leeds Castle, and my trip to Battle and Pevensey Castle. "It was freezing," I admit, "but it's an experience I'll never forget."

"And who's this Callum?" she asks, her eyes twinkling.

"Just an old friend, Grandma. I bumped into him while I was here, and we spent a bit of time catching up."

She knows better than to push me, so she just nods and smiles. "Well that was nice."

"How's Grandpa?"

"He's good, thank you. Out in the garage at the moment. I asked him to make some shelves for the spare room. I'm turning it into a craft room. I've always wanted one, and I thought it was time I did something for myself."

She looks down for a moment, squaring her laptop on the table.

"Are you thinking about Mum?" I ask gently.

She gives a little shrug. "I miss her a lot. Every day. Sometimes, I've felt like I don't want to go on." She looks embarrassed to have admitted it. "But I have to, for Grandpa, for Nick, for the sake of all you kids, and for me."

"It must be very hard to lose a daughter," I reply. I take a deep breath. "Especially when you've already lost her twin."

Grandma blinks, and then realization spreads across her expression like the sun coming out from behind a cloud. Her eyebrows lift, her jaw drops, and she inhales sharply. "What... how..."

"I met with Violet," I explain. "And Fiona. I wanted to find out more about Mum's side of the family, and she and you never seemed to want to talk about it. Now, of course, I know why."

Tears fill her eyes, and she clamps a hand over her mouth.

"Oh no." Pity and guilt stab me fiercely. "I'm sorry. I didn't mean to upset you."

"Carol?" Behind her, Grandpa comes into the room and stops, startled. "What's the matter."

"I can't..." Tears streaming down her face, she gets up and rushes off, out of shot.

Grandpa stares after her, then bends and looks at the screen. "Kora?"

"Grandpa... I'm so sorry, I didn't mean to upset her..." Tears prick my own eyes.

"Hey, it's okay. Look, give me a minute to check on her, then I'll come back and talk to you, all right?"

I nod, and he walks off out of shot to find his wife.

I should have expected this, I think, as I try to compose myself hastily. Of course it would be a shock for her. She's spent over thirty years keeping the information about Maggie and Mum being adopted to herself. Realizing I know must have been a real surprise.

It's only another thirty seconds or so before Grandpa returns and slides into the seat at the table. He's in his eighties now. He has heavy lines around his eyes and nose, and a tonsure on the top of his head, but he's always been a big man, and it means he doesn't show any signs of frailty.

"Is she okay?" I whisper.

"She's fine. She apologizes. It was just a shock for her. So… I understand that you went to see Violet and Fiona."

"Yes. I am sorry I didn't run it by you guys, but I really wanted to find out more about Mum's side of the family."

"And we don't like to talk about it. I understand." He sighs. "What did they tell you?"

"That you and Grandma adopted Mum and Maggie when they were six years old. And that Maggie died on their twenty-first birthday. I know it must have been very hard for you all. Fiona said that Mum tried to take her own life." I swallow hard. I still don't like to think about how bad Mum must have felt to do that. "And that's obviously why you moved to New Zealand."

Grandpa nods. "Olivia took her sister's death very hard. After she made that attempt on her life, we took her away for a holiday to Cornwall, and we spent a long time walking on the beach with her and talking. She said that she wanted to make a big change, and get away from all the places that reminded her of Maggie. She wanted a fresh start. She was adamant, and I know she would have left the country without us if we hadn't gone along with it. So we decided we'd all move away."

"Why did you choose New Zealand?"

"I had a work colleague whose son had moved there, and he'd just been to visit him. He was full of how wonderful the country was—how it was so like England, with a few different twists. And I said to Grandma and your mum, well, how do you fancy moving across the other side of the world? They both immediately said yes. Grandma also had an old school friend who'd moved here, and she was able to help us out with Immigration and finding a house. We went home and applied for residency, and within six months we were on our way."

"You hadn't actually been there?"

"Nope. We just got on a plane and left."

"That must have taken some courage," I say softly.

"It was a huge adventure," he admits, "and yes, it was scary, but it was the best thing we could have done for Olivia. She loved it here, and of course she met your dad within months of landing. Then she had Ben and the rest of you, and she never really looked back. Thoughts of the old country, and Maggie, did plague her from time to time, but she never regretted moving."

I can remember Mum going through quiet periods, where she'd take herself off for long walks by the sea, or sit in her bedroom by the window, gazing out at the fields, lost in thought. Sometimes I'd catch her crying. But when I asked what was wrong, she'd always say it was her hormones and not to worry, and I'm ashamed to say I didn't give it much thought. Some women cry a lot, including me—it's a chemical thing, and it makes us feel better afterward, so I didn't think there was anything strange about it.

"I'm so sorry you had to find out like that," Grandpa says. "It must have been such a shock for you."

"It was. I couldn't believe I didn't know. It explains why Theo and I are fraternal twins."

"Yes, your mum knew there was a relatively high chance of having twins."

"And I guess there's a chance I might, too."

"Yes, I suppose."

A silence falls between us for a moment. I look over my shoulder at the snow, thinking how different it is here to the beautiful summer day back home. New Zealand is my home. I've never thought of myself as English, and neither did Mum, as far as I know.

"You never came back here, did you?" I ask him.

He shakes his head.

"Not even for a holiday?"

Another shake. "You have to understand what a huge change it was for us, moving here," he tries to explain. "The rest of the family were heartbroken, and some even said quite nasty things about us not caring about their feelings. At the time, we were hurt that they couldn't seem to understand why we needed to move. It was all very awkward, and emotions were running very high. When we came here, we just gradually lost touch with everyone in the UK. It was partly our fault, partly theirs. We were making new lives here, and our days were full of creating a home and finding jobs and just learning to be happy again. We didn't want to go back."

"Grandpa, why didn't you tell us—Ben and me and the others?"

"Your mum didn't want us to," he says simply. "Her life was with us and Nick and her kids. She loved New Zealand, and she didn't want anything to do with her past life."

"I understand," I say, trying to suppress my hurt. "But it is important to know about your past." I think about what Callum told me: *Your roots are what ground you. Maybe it'll be what you've been looking for all this time.* He understood.

"Yes, I agree. But we all do what we can to get through the days. All Grandma and I can do is ask for your forgiveness and understanding."

"You have it," I say without hesitation. "Of course. I'm upset and a bit hurt, but I do understand."

"Well that's good to know."

"Does Dad know everything?"

He hesitates, then nods slowly. "She told him when he asked her to marry him."

So he chose to keep it from us, too. In an odd way, I find that the most shocking thing of all. Although I loved my mum, and I considered us close, I always felt there was a little piece of her she kept to herself, a part of her I couldn't reach. I somehow knew she had secrets, and I accepted that about her. But I never thought my father would keep anything from me. He's always been so open and loving. He gives every one of his kids a hundred percent of his love and affection. To discover that he's kept this from me is like a punch to my stomach.

"And Ben and the others?" I ask. If everyone knows except me, I think I'm going to lose it.

But Grandpa shakes his head. "As far as I know, they don't know any of it."

Well, that's something, although I know it's going to be a shock to all of my siblings.

I have a big mouthful of my G&T, feeling the need for some Dutch courage. "So... what I really wanted to ask was... do you know who Mum's birth parents were?"

Grandpa sighs. "I suppose now your Mum's gone, you might as well know it all. You probably know by now that Grandma and I couldn't have children, and we'd decided we were going to adopt. It was 1968. We found out there were twin girls available, six years old. They were living with a couple called Simon and Harriet on a farm in Devon. I can't remember the surname... Oh, yes I can—Rowe! That was it—R, O, W, E. We went to visit them to see the girls. They were both a bit... abrupt, I suppose."

I scribble down their names. "Abrupt? Why?"

"They weren't unpleasant. But they had three kids of their own around the same age as the twins, and I think maybe they saw the twins as a burden. Simon told us that his parents had adopted the twins' mother after the Second World War. I think his dad's name was George. Don't remember his mum's."

"Do you remember the twins' mother's name?"

"I do. It was Rachel Hoffman."

I muse on that for a moment. "She sounds Jewish."

"Yes, I agree. She'd died a few months before. She wasn't married. On the twins' birth certificate, the space for the father's name just said 'unknown'. Simon said he didn't know who the father was. He said they didn't have the time and money to devote to bringing them up. It was clear to us that they'd been landed with these two girls and they wanted someone to take them off their hands as soon as possible. That's all I know. We adopted the girls and picked them up soon after. We never saw Simon or Harriet again, and never heard from them."

"And neither of the girls tried to contact them?"

"No. Maggie sometimes said she was thinking about it, but Olivia flatly said no. She said if they didn't want her, she had no interest in seeing them either. I think she felt rejected by them, and rightly so."

"I understand that. But wasn't she interested in finding out more about her birth mother? Rachel? And who her birth father was?"

"Maybe in private she wondered, but your mother was very keen not to hurt our feelings. She said not every parent got to choose their children, and it made us extra special parents." He stops, his voice turning husky, and he clears his throat.

"Sorry," I murmur, touched by his emotion.

"It's okay. I miss her, that's all. And Maggie too, of course. Losing her was very hard, but of course we had another thirty years with your mother. She was our daughter. It didn't matter that Grandma didn't give birth to her. And I think part of us was pleased when she didn't want to tell her own children about her past. It wasn't important to any of us. Our future was what mattered."

It was a selfish decision, and they weren't taking the feelings of their grandchildren into account, but I understand why he and Grandma, and Mum, made that decision.

"Is there anything else you can tell me?" I ask him.

He shakes his head. "I can't think of anything. I'll have a word with Grandma, and I'll let you know if she comes up with anything."

"Okay. Well, thank you so much. I'm sure you'd probably rather have kept it secret, but it's helped me a lot. I feel a bit closer to Mum now. Is that weird?"

"Not at all."

"I feel as if I understand her a bit more. Now I get why she had those quiet periods, and why she'd sometimes be lost in thought." I sigh. "Please tell Grandma I'm sorry for shocking her like that."

"She'll be okay. She'll probably ring you soon."

"Yeah. I'd better leave you to it now. I'll be going to bed soon."

"Okay honey. Take care of yourself, won't you? Come back to us safe."

"Will do. 'Bye, Grandpa."

I stop the call and close my laptop. Then I turn in my chair and look out at the snowy night.

Well, what a series of revelations. It's a lot to process!

I'll need to think about it all for a while, but it's done. The End. I should be glad I've discovered what I have, and get back to sightseeing during the days I have remaining, before I go home.

But part of me is more intrigued than ever. There are still things I want to know. Rachel Hoffman, for example. What was her story? Was she Jewish? What happened to her during the war, and why was she adopted? Who was the man who fathered her children? Was he famous or something? Is that why she didn't want to tell anyone? It's a puzzle, and there are still pieces missing.

I still have two days here in the UK. That's plenty of time to do research and some exploring. I wonder what else I can find out before I have to go home?

Chapter Seventeen

Callum

Sitting in the chair by the window, I fall into a half-doze, tired from all the walking and the emotions that are whirling inside me like the weather outside. I'm still aware of Jim and Josh in the living room, talking occasionally while trucks explode and the good and bad guys trade gunshots. But my mind drifts, chasing my memories of the day like a dog catching snowflakes.

I'm not sure why Kora haunts me in this way. She's not the most beautiful woman I've ever met. Or the most intelligent, or the wittiest, or the most charismatic. In fact, on the surface she's fairly ordinary, a girl-next-door, like your best mate's sister, the kind you wouldn't mind taking home for your mother to meet because you know she'd approve.

And yet there's something about her that's woven a ribbon around my heart and has pulled it tight.

It's not love. In two days? Of course it isn't. But there is a deep-rooted, unusual attraction between us I don't think either of us suspected would happen. We caught a glimpse of it back in New Zealand all those years ago, and although the flame died when we parted, it didn't go out completely. It turned to embers, and when I saw her in the toy store, it was as if someone blew on those embers softly, causing them to leap into life all over again.

She dances in my mind, her summer-blue eyes fixed on mine, and I can smell her cherry perfume, and feel the press of her lips. I miss her. I want her. Why can't I have her?

I jerk awake. It's dark, the only light from the lamp on the table. There's no sound from the living room—I think Jim and Josh have gone to bed. Why didn't they wake me? I sit up and see the note on the table and pick it up—It's in Josh's looped handwriting. *We thought we'd let you sleep. Goodnight bro. See you tomoz!*

It's cool in the apartment; it's still snowing, and the temperature has dropped outside. I check my phone—it's nearly eleven. I'm normally in bed by now as I rise early, but I don't feel like retiring yet. My mind is buzzing, but for once it's not focused on a business deal.

I go into my bedroom, retrieve a sweater, and pull it on. Coming back out, I pour myself another whiskey, then go into the living room. Jim has left the gas fire on, and the flames leap in the fake grate. I turn it up a little, sit in the armchair, and prop my feet on the coffee table.

I could put on the TV and watch something, but I quite like the cool, quiet darkness, and being alone with my thoughts. It's very unusual for me to sit alone and do nothing; normally I feel restless if I'm not engaged in a task. But tonight I feel the need for solitude.

In the window I can see my reflection, the leaping flames, and beyond them the silent, swirling flakes. Something's changed. I think about that as I sip the whiskey, enjoying the slide of the firewater down into my stomach. My analytical brain wants to refine the statement, so I try again.

Kora has changed something in me. I don't know what yet, but I feel different. Or maybe it's not Kora; maybe it's what Jim said earlier, suggesting at least part of the blame for the failure of my marriage lies with me.

I'm not stupid or blind. Of course it does. I do think that even if I had been the most attentive husband on earth, it wouldn't have worked out between us. We're two completely different people who want different things from life, and that would have eventually forced us apart. Or maybe I'm just making excuses. I don't know. Whatever, it's done. It's over. All I can do is learn from it and move forward.

I just want to know that when it's my time to go, you're happy. Because otherwise, what's the point?

I lose myself in the flames for a long, long while, until my phone rattles on the table, announcing the arrival of a text.

My heart sinks. Stephanie has been known to contact me late at night, hoping to start a conversation. That's the last thing I want right now. I'm tempted to leave it, but something makes me pick the phone up and glance at the screen.

Are you awake? It's Kora.

My heart skips a beat. It's an unusual feeling, enough for me to notice it.

I open the text and reply, *I'm here! You're up late.* She told me earlier that the jetlag means she gets tired early but she's up early, too.

Can't sleep, she replies. *I spoke to my grandma earlier this evening.*

Oh, what did you find out?

Do you have time for a chat?

This time my heart leaps, which is again unusual enough that I take notice of the feeling. I smile and bring up her number, then press dial.

She answers immediately. "Hey! I wasn't sure if you'd still be up."

"Normally I'm in bed by now, but I dozed off earlier, and I thought I'd sit up for a bit."

"Dozed off?" she teases. "Doesn't sound very high-powered."

"I honestly don't know if I've ever done it," I admit.

"You've never had a nanna nap?"

"Never. Afternoons are always the busiest times for me."

"What about with Stephanie? Never had some afternoon delight?"

I stretch out my legs, the heat from the fire beginning to warm my outside, while the whiskey heats me internally. "Maybe on our honeymoon."

"Oh, Callum. That makes me sad. Everyone should partake in some Sunday afternoon nookie."

My lips curve up. "So tell me what your Grandma said."

She sighs and relates the details. I listen with growing surprise at her revelation. "Oh… that is intriguing," I say when she finishes relating the details.

"I know, right? Rachel Hoffman. She's got to be Jewish, hasn't she?"

"From a Jewish family, at least. So this family adopted her? I wonder if she came over from Germany during the war?"

"I was wondering that. I've been doing some research. Apparently before war broke out, the UK took in close to ten thousand Jewish children from Nazi Germany, as well as Austria, Poland, and Czechoslovakia. They went to foster homes, and places like schools and farms, which matches Grandpa's story that this family lived on a farm in Devon. It was an organized program, and it's sometimes called the Kindertransport."

"Children's transport," I muse.

"Yes, meaning children who were brought here on the train without their parents. I was thinking about what Violet said: 'She came on a train to Devon.' Fiona assumed she was confused, but what if she was right? Often these kids were the only survivors of their families after the Holocaust. Can you imagine how frightening it must have been for those children traveling all across Europe, and coming to the UK? It must have been so hard for them to learn the language and the customs."

"Yeah, they must have had a difficult time fitting in."

"Interesting, isn't it? There are still pieces of the puzzle that are missing. Who was my birth grandfather? Why didn't Rachel marry him? How did she die? She must have been relatively young, surely? My mum was only six. She was born in 1962. If Rachel did come over on the Kindertransport, presumably she was, what, less than ten years old? So she must only have been in her thirties when she died."

"Yes, true."

She sighs. "I wish I hadn't upset my grandma."

"I'm sure it was just the fact that it came out of the blue."

"Yeah, but maybe I should have been a bit gentler. I honestly didn't expect it to affect her the way it did."

"And your father did know about it?"

"Yes. I'm going to have to talk to him about that." Her voice is hard.

"So what now? Is that it?"

"Well, I've been thinking that I still have two days left here, and I could try to do some more research. So I was wondering whether you have any ideas how I might find out where Simon and Harriet Rowe are?"

I stare into the flames, my heart sinking. She just wants to find out more about her family. She didn't contact me because she missed me.

Even as the thought enters my head, she continues, "Well, anyway, it was a good excuse to call you. The truth is that I haven't been able to stop thinking about you since we parted." Her soft voice is like a finger stroking up my spine.

"Me too." I slide down in the armchair. "I've been thinking about you all evening."

"I know you're a very busy man." Her voice has turned a tad husky. "But I wonder whether you'd have any time to meet up over the next few days?" I hesitate, and she immediately picks up on it. "But of course, I'm sure you've got lots of catching up to do," she says smoothly. "No worries at all if you're super busy."

"It's not that." I decide it's best to be honest. I'm done keeping my feelings to myself. Burying my head in the sand hasn't worked out for me in the past. "I'm concerned about falling too hard for you, Kora."

"Oh…" I can almost feel her exhalation of pleasure brush across my ear, and it makes me shiver.

"I like you," I tell her. "A lot. I'm already half in love with you. I know that's a crazy thing to say, because it's only been a couple of days, and it can't possibly be true. But how else do you define being in love, except by saying it's when you can't stop thinking about someone? When you wish you were with them all the time?"

I stop, embarrassed by my outburst. Maybe she just wanted to be with me because I was good company while she's in a strange country, and her feelings don't run that deep.

But she says, "I thought it was just me…"

I run my hand through my hair, feeling as if I'm sixteen years old. "I didn't know whether to say anything, because I know it's pointless. But I wanted you to know how I feel."

"I'm so glad you said something. I wasn't brave enough to."

A silence falls between us, but it's not uncomfortable. I can tell she's thinking about what I said.

While I let her process it, something occurs to me. I lean across to the table and pick up my iPad, open it, and type something in.

"So…" When she eventually speaks, she draws out the word. "Bearing what you said in mind, do you think we shouldn't meet again?"

"The more we see each other, the more it's going to hurt when we do have to part," I reply gently.

"Yeah. I guess."

"But is that a good enough excuse to stay away? I don't know. Better to have loved and lost… Isn't that the saying?"

"Yeah. And Callum… I never thought I'd say this after what happened with Julian, but I think I'd rather be with you for a few days and miss you terribly than not be with you at all."

I smile. "Me too."

"So can I see you maybe after work?"

"Yeah. Why don't we go out for dinner again?"

"That would be lovely."

"Okay. First, though, I've got my iPad open and I'm pulling up a family tree site."

"Oh!"

"I joined it ages ago. Jim was doing some research into his family tree—he reckons one of our ancestors was a highwayman with Dick Turpin."

That makes her laugh. "I can see the family resemblance."

"Thank you. Anyway, I have a membership, so I'm just logging in. There you go. Now, I can look up deceased people if we know their year of birth or death or marriage. Any ideas?"

"I'm guessing Rachel was born around 1930."

"So, Rachel Hoffman, born 1930. Let's put Devon and see what that throws up." I press search and wait. "Okay, it's given me a list of names. Nothing's jumping out at me.'

"Hold on, she wasn't born in Devon, was she?"

"Oh, of course not." I'm being an idiot. Her birth wouldn't have been registered in the UK. "Okay, what year do you think she died?"

"Grandpa said she died a few months before he met the twins, and he told me that was in 1968."

"Right." I choose date of death and type 1968. This time, I strike gold. "Right. At the top of the list is Rachel Hoffman, died 1968. No spouse mentioned. Possible children, Olivia and Margaret."

"That's her! Does it say where she was born?"

"No. It would only mention it if she was born in the UK, so that confirms our suspicions that she came from Germany or somewhere else in Europe."

"It doesn't give an address where she died?"

"No, but it says her death was registered in the civil parish of Tiverton, in Devon."

"Hmm. That's not a lot to go on."

"We're not done yet. I've got a hunch." I type in another name. "I'm looking up Simon. If he's still alive, it might not show for privacy reasons, but it's a possibility he's passed away by now. He would presumably have been around Rachel's age, as your grandpa said he had three kids the same age as the twins, so I'll put in 1930 for his year of birth. Hold on."

This time, it takes me a while. I play with the date of birth, moving it forward a year at a time. I'm just about to assume he's still alive, and then he pops up.

"Here he is! Simon George Rowe, born 1942. Died in 2010, in the civil parish of Tiverton. Father was George Rowe."

"That's him! Grandpa said his dad was called George, so that would fit."

"Simon had three children—Guy, Emily, and Pamela."

"Can you look them up?"

I try. "No, so they're still living apparently."

"I wonder if they're still in the town of Tiverton?"

"The civil parish will include some of the surrounding towns, which makes it quite a big area. Okay, the first thing is to look up Simon's obituary." I try a few sites and eventually find what I was looking for. "Here it is, dated August 2010. Simon Rowe, born 1942, late of the town of Bradninch. That's a small town near Tiverton."

"Brilliant!"

"I can look up his kids in the online BT phone book. Hold on." I pull up the site. "Right. Here we go. Guy Rowe." I press search. "There are five Guy Rowes in Devon. And yes, there's one in Bradninch."

"Oh wow, do you think that's him?"

"I would say it's quite likely."

"He might remember Rachel and the twins."

"He'd have been young when they left, but yes, he might. I wonder if he can shed any light on what happened?"

"Does it have a phone number?"

"Yes." I read it out to her. "Are you going to call?"

"Definitely. Oh, Callum, thank you so much. I'm so excited!"

"It might not lead to anything," I warn.

"I know, but then again it might. I don't know why it feels so important, but it does. It makes me feel closer to my mum."

"I can understand that."

"Okay, well I'd better let you go, I guess." She sounds reluctant. "I'll text you in the morning and let you know how the call goes."

"Yes, please do. And then we'll go out for dinner in the evening."

"I look forward to it. You take care."

"You too. 'Bye." I hang up and put the phone on the coffee table.

I know it's madness to see her again. But I feel happier than I've felt for such a long time, and that can't be a bad thing, can it?

I just want to know that when it's my time to go, you're happy. Because otherwise, what's the point?

SERENITY WOODS

Jim's words continue to whirl in my head, like the snowflakes out in the cold night.

Chapter Eighteen

Kora

When I eventually fall asleep, I have strange, confusing dreams about my mum and dad, Rachel Hoffman, Simon Rowe, and Callum, all mixed up in a kind of Greek play. I jerk awake at five a.m., relieved to discover it wasn't real. Not wanting to go back to sleep, I get up and make myself a coffee, then go back to bed to read for a couple of hours.

At seven, I take a shower and get ready for the day. Then the butler brings me breakfast on a tray—yoghurt with fresh fruit, croissants, and jam. I eat a little, but I'm too nervous to really enjoy the food.

Finally, at nine a.m., which seems like a decent hour, I telephone Guy Rowe's number.

A woman answers the phone after a dozen rings. She sounds brisk. "Hello?"

"Oh, good morning. I was looking for Guy Rowe."

"He's at work. Who's calling?"

Now I'm flummoxed and tempted to hang up, but I force my trembling hand to keep hold of the phone. "Um… he doesn't know me. My name is Kora Prince. Um… it's a bit complicated to explain…"

"I've got, like, a thousand things to do," the woman says. "And I've never heard Guy mention a Kora Prince." Now she sounds hostile. I'm not surprised. I might be suspicious if a strange woman rang me at home asking for my husband.

"No, like I said, he doesn't know me. But he might remember my grandmother." It feels strange to call Rachel that. "Guy's grandparents adopted her. Her name was Rachel Hoffman."

"Oh…" Her tone tells me the penny has dropped. "Oh, right."

"I'm very sorry to bother you, I'm sure you're very busy, but I've traveled all the way from New Zealand, and I was hoping to find out more about Rachel and my mother. Do you think Guy might be willing to talk to me?"

"I'm sure he will." Her voice is gentler now. "I'm Susie, by the way. I'm Guy's wife. Look, he'll be out on the farm all day. But he'll be home tonight. I will say, though, I don't think he'll be keen to discuss it over the phone. Can I suggest you come and see him?"

My eyes widen. "In Devon?"

"Yes. Where are you?"

"I'm in London."

"There's a train from Paddington to Exeter St. David's, or to Tiverton Parkway, which is a bit closer. It's up to you, of course, but I know Guy, and it's… a delicate matter, and I don't think he's going to want to blurt out his family history to a stranger over the phone."

"I understand," I say softly. "I'm happy to come down. What's the best time for you?"

"Well, he's off looking at new equipment today, so he won't be as late as he sometimes is later in the year. He's a farmer, you see. Would six o'clock be too late for you? I'm not sure when the last train is back to Paddington."

"Oh, that's okay, I'll find somewhere to stay the night. Yes, six will be fine."

She tells me their address, which I already know, and how to find them, and then hangs up.

I sit there for a moment, my head spinning. I wonder what she meant by it being a 'delicate matter'. There's definitely a strange mystery going on, and I can't wait to uncover it.

I look at my phone. Going away does mean I won't be able to meet Callum for dinner. I'm disappointed about that, especially as he was the one to suggest it, but I really want to meet Guy. I'm sure Callum will understand.

I send him a text. *Hey! Just got off the phone with Guy Rowe's wife. He's at work now but she suggested I go down to meet him tonight. I'm so sorry to blow you off but it sounds as if he knows the whole story. Can we take a rain check and meet tomorrow? xx*

After adding the kisses, I press send. Then I start looking up train tickets from London Paddington to Tiverton Parkway.

I'm just calculating which one will be the best to catch when my phone rings. Looking at the screen, I see that it says Callum, and answer it with a smile. "Hello?"

"Hey, it's me," he says.

"Hey, you. You got my text?"

"Yeah."

"I'm so sorry to cancel our plans. I really wanted to see you tonight, but I just have to do this."

"It's okay, I understand completely. What I rang to ask was, would you like some company on the journey?"

I blink. "Pardon?"

"I'll take the afternoon off and drive you down if you like."

My jaw drops. "Another day off? You're serious?"

"I'm starting to like playing hooky. It's addictive."

My lips curve up. "I feel as if I'm leading you astray."

"You totally are, and I love it. So what do you think? Unless you want to go on your own, which is fine of course, although I will sulk."

I laugh. "I'd love to have company. But you're sure Tower can do without you?"

"My PA will have a heart attack. But Rob can fill in for me with any important meetings." His voice is suddenly steely.

"Okay," I murmur. "I said I'd be there for six p.m. What time do you think we should leave?"

"Probably two-ish would get us there in plenty of time, although we could leave a bit earlier and see some sights on the way."

"What sort of sights?" I ask happily.

"Stonehenge? We'll pass right by that."

I breathe in sharply, excited at the thought of seeing the ancient monument. "Really? Oh yes."

"Okay. How about I pick you up at midday?"

"Sounds great. And… what about tonight? Will we drive back afterward, or shall I book us a place to stay over?"

"Oh, let's stay over. Somewhere in Exeter—it's a beautiful city."

"Okay. And Jim and Josh will be okay?"

There's a brief pause, and then he replies with a smile in his voice, "They'll be fine, and thank you for thinking of them."

"Of course. They have to come first."

"You're a lovely girl, Kora Prince. I'll see you at midday."

I hang up, touched by his words, and a little puzzled by them. Family has always come first for me. I find it strange that it doesn't for everyone.

I'm excited at the thought of the upcoming trip. Not only am I one step closer to solving the puzzle, but I have another whole day and night with him!

I only have a couple of hours to wait. I decide to do a little work—I have emails to answer and I want to put together a few ideas for a proposal for a toy museum. So I make myself another coffee, then sit up at the table with my laptop to work.

It's difficult to concentrate, though. I have so many thoughts whizzing around in my head. After sitting there for ages with my fingers resting on the keys, I close my laptop, pick up a pen and paper, and resort to doodling as I let my mind wander.

*

When Callum pulls up outside at twelve, I'm standing on the steps chatting to the porter, who's holding my overnight bag. The porter places the bag in the boot, then opens the door for me, and I slide in and wave goodbye.

"Hey." Callum smiles at me. Wowza. Today he's wearing faded jeans and a black sweater. He looks good enough to eat. In fact, maybe I'll try that later on. "What?" he asks as my eyes glaze over.

"Just thinking how gorgeous you look." I lean forward and kiss him, and he slides a hand to the back of my neck and holds me there so he can make the kiss last longer.

When he finally releases me, he chuckles, puts the car into gear, and pulls away. "That'll give the porters something to talk about."

"You've kissed off my lipstick," I tell him, looking in the mirror.

"Is that a complaint?"

"No."

We exchange a smile, and the spark that flared inside me when he first mentioned driving me turns into a warm glow.

He said it would take us three to four hours to drive down today. I feel inordinately excited at spending so long with him, just the two of us. Is that crazy? I hope we don't run out of conversation. It's not like we have a huge amount in common, after all.

But we don't even come close to exhausting topics to talk about, as the smooth Aston eats up the miles. The motorways gradually turn into smaller roads, and the countryside morphs from the big city to large towns, and then fields begin to pop up between the houses. It's slow going, because it's still snowing, but we're in no hurry, and I enjoy getting a chance to look around the English countryside.

"We're in Wiltshire now," Callum explains about halfway through our journey, as the A303 snakes through a wide, snow-covered landscape. "This is Salisbury Plain."

"What are those bumps?" I point at the low mounds that rise out of the open fields to either side.

"Burial mounds."

"Wow, really?"

"This is an ancient landscape, dating back to Anglo-Saxon, Roman, and prehistoric times. There are chalk carvings on the hillsides, and of course, the mighty Stonehenge."

He points ahead, and there it is in the distance on the right side of the road—the magnificent stone monument.

I stare, open-mouthed, as we draw closer, and Callum indicates to take the turn-off. "I know this sounds crazy," I murmur, "but it's smaller than I thought it'd be."

"Yeah, I know what you mean. We're told all our lives about these massive stones, and somehow we imagine they're going to be like skyscrapers. The sarsen stones are only thirteen feet high. But they weigh twenty-five tons. Even the bluestones weigh four to five tons, and they apparently came all the way from Wales."

"Wales?" I blink.

"Yeah. Nobody knows how, but it's thought maybe they were transported on rollers."

I can't imagine the effort that would have taken. It makes me look at the monument very differently, as Callum pulls up in the car park. It's freezing, and although the road has been gritted, the fields are thick with snow. Flakes drift across us, giving the monument an ethereal, ghostly feel as it looms in the distance.

We go into the visitor's center, where we learn about the history of the site. As it's so cold, we decide to take the shuttle bus rather than do the half hour walk. It drops us off at the start of the circular path, and finally we're able to circumnavigate the stone circle.

It looks much bigger up close, and extremely imposing. How on earth did they move the stones so far? I'm caught up in the magic of the henge. This country feels so old compared to New Zealand. There, the oldest stone building in Kerikeri dates from 1832. I've always been aware that's relatively new compared to so many other parts of the world, but it's only now that I realize how my country is so young, only seven or eight generations old. Here, some old families trace their lineage back to the Conqueror, and there's evidence of human occupation going back 900,000 years. Hundreds of thousands of people have trodden this very earth I'm standing on. Just like at Battle, I can almost feel them. So many people living and dying… It brings tears to my eyes and chokes me up.

"Kora?" Callum, who has been taking a few photos of me in front of the henge with his phone, comes up and puts his arm around me. "Are you okay?"

"I didn't expect it to affect me so much," I whisper, tears freezing on my lashes. "In New Zealand we're not bothered much by the past, but here, it's all around us. Layers of it. It's so ancient, Callum. Doesn't it bother you?"

"I don't tend to think about it," he says, a little amused.

"How can you not? I feel like I can see ghosts all around us."

He takes one of my hands in his and rubs it. "You're freezing. Come on, I think we need to get you back to the café for a hot drink."

I let him lead me back to the bus, disappointed to say goodbye to the stones, and yet oddly relieved, too. It's not long before I'm sitting in the café, nursing a hot chocolate and eating one of their famous rock cakes, finally feeling a bit more grounded.

"I'm so sorry," I tell him as he sits back, sipping his tea and watching me with his warm brown eyes. "I keep having funny turns. I don't know why. I'm not normally like this. It's as if these historical sites are really high off the ground, and I come over all dizzy when we're there."

"It's okay, it makes sense." He pinches a piece of my rock cake. "It's not something the Brits think of because we're surrounded by it all the time, but I can see how it would be weird if you're not used to it."

"So much of our land is untouched by humans." I think of the plane flight I've taken so many times from Wellington to the Bay of Islands, across high hills and valleys filled with forests. "But I doubt there's anywhere here that a human foot hasn't trod. I keep thinking about those generations stretching back into the past. All parents and grandparents and great-grandparents. In New Zealand, Maori say that going to a *marae* or meeting house is a way of staying connected to their ancestors. I had a Maori friend at school who said he was told to imagine his father standing behind him with his hand on his shoulder, and his grandfather's hand on his shoulder, and his father's on his, all the way back. I don't think I ever really took that in until now."

"It's all the family research you're doing," Callum says. "Before, your history stopped with your grandparents, but now you're realizing how far back it actually goes. Those genes being handed down through the millennia. Whether we like it or not, we're connected to our ancestors, all the way back to Mitochondrial Eve."

Whether we like it or not... I realize what he's referring to. "Callum, I am sorry, I didn't think. All this talk about family and ancestors... Has it been making you think about your own father?"

"A bit, yes." He blows out a long breath. "I guess I've tried to disassociate myself from him over the years. Pretend we weren't related, and that I'm nothing like him. But the truth is that those genes are inside me. He's a part of me. And maybe shutting myself off from him hasn't been healthy in the long run."

I reach out a hand, and he slides his into it. "That doesn't mean you're going to turn into him," I say, knowing what's on his mind.

"I hope not." He gives me a crooked smile.

"You won't, because you're aware of it, and that means you'll take steps to avoid it. Besides, you're too lovely to end up like him, Callum. Far too sexy and warm-hearted and gorgeous."

He chuckles, but I can see the compliment has pleased him. "How are you doing?" he asks softly. "Ready to go?"

I breathe in deeply, then exhale slowly. "Yeah, I'm ready."

After a quick look around the shop, where Callum treats Josh to another figurine, we make our way out to the car, and the blustery wind blows loose flakes across my face. I'm close now, I can feel it, to solving the puzzle. And maybe then I can finally let my mum's ghost rest.

Chapter Nineteen

Callum

Once again, I surprise myself by not thinking about work once, while I chat away to Kora, the car eats up the miles, and the sun slowly heads toward the horizon. I'd have thought that taking time away from the office would have meant I'd be constantly checking my phone for texts and emails. But I'm shocked to find I don't care.

Is this how far I've fallen? Am I so disillusioned with the business that I can't bring myself to summon up any enthusiasm for it?

From an outsider's point of view, I'd probably say I was burned out, and I just need a break, a few days off. But that's not normal for me. I've never needed recharging. I've always had the next goal in mind; I've always reached up for the next rung of the ladder.

I know I've been this way for a while, but it's the first time I've actually acknowledged it.

"Penny for them?" Kora's voice cuts through my musings.

"I was just thinking the turnoff is coming up soon." It's not a convincing lie as the GPS will inform me where to go, but Kora doesn't question it, although she studies me for a moment before she returns her gaze to the road.

There's no point in expressing my current dissatisfaction to her. I don't want her to think it's her fault, and there's no way she can help. All I can do is take comfort from her presence while she's here, and hope she helps me refill the well of inspiration so that when she eventually leaves, I feel refreshed enough to get stuck into the business again.

Sure enough, the polite voice on the GPS announces it's time to come off the motorway, and I take the slip road toward Cullompton. Kora looks out of the window, lost in thought. The scenery is now shrouded in darkness, so I'm guessing she's thinking about what Guy Rowe might be able to reveal.

I leave her to her thoughts, and head for the small town of Bradninch. Here the main roads have been gritted, but some of the smaller roads have yet to be done, and the snow is piled up on the verges where people have come out of their houses and dug it with shovels. It's quite dicey in the darkness. The Aston crawls along the narrow lanes, its headlights revealing the way, until eventually the GPS announces we've reached our destination.

I park outside a pub, not far from the church, and turn off the engine. We're a little early, but I'd rather be that than late.

"Shall we have a walk around the church?" I ask.

She nods, so we get out, lock the car, and head up the tiny lane, past the small, white-washed cottages, to the iron gate. It's open, although I suspect the church will be locked.

It's cold, and Kora pulls the collar of her coat up around her neck. The building is well lit outside, and surprisingly big for such a small place.

"When do you reckon it was built?" Kora asks as we walk slowly through the churchyard.

"Don't know... maybe fifteenth, sixteenth century? Some of it looks later. There might well be earlier remains beneath the later walls."

Sure enough, the door is locked, so we content ourselves with walking around it, our boots scuffing up the virgin snow, eventually ending up back where we started.

"I do love these old churches," Kora murmurs, "but they make me sad, too." She looks around at the graves. The newer ones bear fresh flowers, but the gravestones of some of the older ones are worn, moss-covered, and unreadable.

"It's what happens," I reply. "Everything fades in time." I wonder then if I'm talking about myself—my passion and *joie de vivre*.

She nods, but turns for the gate, and we walk back along the cottages to the main street. We're still a bit early, but Kora heads up toward the house, and I follow.

She knocks on the door, and it's only a few seconds before it opens. A man stands there, dressed in jeans and a thick blue sweater. His brown hair is threaded with gray and his face is weather-beaten and confirms his outdoor day job. I suspect he's in his late fifties.

"Kora?" he asks.

She nods. "I'm early, I'm sorry, would you like us to come back in a little while?"

"No, it's fine. Come in. I'm Guy." He shakes her hand, then steps back and lets her pass him.

I introduce myself and we shake hands, and I follow her in. It's a tiny cottage, the same kind that can be found all over Devon, probably made from cobb—a mixture of clay-based subsoil, straw, and water—with small windows and dark oak beams inside. It's well lit, though, and a log fire dances in the grate, so Kora and I remove our coats as he gestures toward the sofa and says, "Have a seat, please. Can I get you a tea or coffee?"

Kora asks for coffee, I ask for tea, and he goes through to the kitchen, where I hear him relaying the order, presumably to his wife.

I glance at Kora as we sit. She's pale and quiet. She sits perched on the edge of the sofa, her spine stiff.

Guy comes back into the room and sits in the armchair nearest the fire.

"Thank you for agreeing to see me," Kora says. "I appreciate it."

"I have to be honest, I didn't want to," he admits. "If Susie had taken your number, I'd have rung and ask you not to come, but she didn't, and it seemed rude to turn you away at the door."

Surprised by his admission, I wait for Kora to get embarrassed or flustered. But she just says smoothly, "That's fair enough, and I'm sorry you didn't get the opportunity to do that." It reminds me that she's a businesswoman who's used to dealing with all kinds of people. I forget that sometimes.

"So." He shifts in the chair, clearly uncomfortable. "What do you want to know?"

"Well, anything you can tell us about my mother, and her mother, Rachel." Kora takes a deep breath. "Let me give you a bit of background." She goes on to explain that she's from New Zealand, that her mother passed away a year ago, and that she didn't know anything about Olivia's life before she emigrated. Then she tells him how she met with Violet and Fiona, who revealed Olivia had had a twin, and how they'd both been adopted.

"It came as a real shock," she admits. "I didn't know. I spoke to my grandfather about it. He said their birth mother was called Rachel Hoffman, but the father was unknown. He said your grandfather adopted her."

Guy nods slowly. "She was a Jewish refugee. She came to England on the Kindertransport in 1938."

Kora glances at me—we guessed right.

"She was from an orphanage that had been destroyed on Kristallnacht," he states. "Two hundred children came over to England. On the way, SS members boarded the train carrying the children, and they went through the children's luggage."

"It must have been terrifying for them," Kora says, horrified.

"A lot of children came over," Guy states. "Some of them were placed with friends or family members. But newspaper adverts also asked for people to house them and pay for their upkeep because the government refused to use state funds to pay for them. At the time, my grandparents—George and Win—owned Bluebird Farm, and they didn't have any kids, so they offered to have one of the children with them."

He stops as his wife comes in with a tray bearing our drinks. "Hello," she says, placing it on the coffee table in front of us. "I'm Susie." She shakes our hands as we introduce ourselves, and then sits in the other armchair. "How are you doing?"

"Guy was just explaining about how many Jewish children came over before war broke out," Kora says.

"Yes, there were ten thousand or so that were saved," Guy says. "The kids were supposed to return to their own country when the refugee crisis was over, but of course by the end of war it was discovered that most of the Jewish population had been murdered."

"Did all the kids stay in England?" I ask.

"About a thousand of the children were classified as enemy aliens," Susie says. "They were incarcerated on the Isle of Man, or sent to Canada or Australia."

"Oh, that's awful," Kora exclaims.

"Some were reunited with family members," Guy says. "But many of them stayed. Some of the older ones ended up fighting for Britain against the Nazis."

"And Rachel?"

"Because she was an orphan," Guy says, "my grandparents were able to apply for adoption. Then in 1942 my father was born, and my grandparents went on to have two other boys."

"How did they get on with Rachel?" Kora asks.

Guy hesitates, and I know we're starting to get to the bottom of the matter. "Not well. Rachel was a difficult child, by all accounts. I don't think my dad and his brothers liked her at all. It didn't help that she was the apple of my grandparents' eye, even though she was the adopted child. Maybe it was because she was the only girl in the house, but I know they favored her and spoiled her, while they were quite strict on the others. It made my dad and his brothers very resentful."

"Things only got worse when George died," Susie says. "Win had already passed away a few years before. Simon—Guy's father—had met Harriet and they had their own farm by then, and his brothers had also left home. Rachel was still living at Bluebird Farm though. And it turned out that George had left the farm to her and not his boys."

"It was understandable," Guy says. "Rachel apparently worked hard on the farm and was as good as any of the boys. And of course, if you're adopted you have every right to be treated the same as the others. But my father didn't see it like that. In his eyes, he was his father's heir."

"I can see how that must have been difficult," Kora says quietly. "Do you remember how she died?"

He nods. "She had a brain aneurysm."

Kora's jaw drops. Of course—that's how her own mother died.

"It was sudden," Susie says. "Apparently she'd been complaining of a bad headache for a couple of days, then one evening it got much worse. They rushed her to hospital, but she died just a few hours later."

Kora swallows hard. I can only imagine how difficult this must be for her.

"My parents had three kids under six at the time," Guy explains. "And neither of them wanted to have to bring up Rachel's twins, so they put them up for adoption."

"So… do you know who the father was?" Kora asks.

Guy exchanges a glance with his wife. Susie gives a small nod.

"This is difficult for me," Guy states. His voice is very quiet. "And I probably wouldn't tell you, except that my father passed away a few years ago, and mum's gone now, too, so there's nobody left to hurt. My dad was the father of Rachel's girls."

We both stare at him. "Simon Rowe?" Kora clarifies. "But you said he hated her."

Guy has a mouthful of tea. "He did."

"Did he tell you he was the father?"

He shakes his head. "Mum let it slip one day, or maybe she wanted me to know, I don't know. It was the day the twins were adopted. I was only three, but I can still remember that she told me to say goodbye to my sisters because I'd never see them again. Dad went ballistic and sent me out of the room. When I was older, I asked him what Mum had meant, but he got angry with me and refused to talk about it."

"So, you think they had an affair?" Kora asks.

Guy doesn't answer for a moment. The only sound is the crackling of the fire in the grate. When he eventually speaks, Guy's voice is so quiet I can barely hear him. "As I said, I was only three when Rachel died, but I do remember her a bit. She was very quiet and reserved, and rarely smiled. And I remember her being hostile toward Dad. I think… I think he assaulted her."

"Oh God." The blood drains from Kora's face.

"But I don't know," he adds hastily. "It's just a guess."

We all sit there quietly for a moment, digesting that information. Could it be true? Could Simon Rowe have raped Kora's grandmother? It would explain Simon and Harriet's animosity toward the girls. They'd have been a constant reminder of what had happened.

"Did Rachel call the police?" Kora whispers.

"No," Susie says, "and that makes me wonder whether it wasn't assault, and instead they had a brief affair. Harriet hated Rachel with a passion. She made a snidey comment once, about Rachel being a whore. Simon got angry with her and told her not to speak ill of the dead. It's the only time I ever heard them talk about her. The fact that she said to Guy to say goodbye to his sisters means she knew the twins were Simon's. I think maybe Rachel came onto him, or he was attracted to her but tried to fight it. Perhaps they slept together, and then afterward he told her he wanted nothing to do with her. I think that's what Harriet thought, anyway. We'll never know the truth."

"That's just awful." Kora looks distressed. I can't imagine how it must feel knowing your mother might have been born as the result of an assault. And even if Rachel wasn't assaulted, it still means she obviously went through a difficult time without the father of her children beside her. What a tough life the woman had.

"So you're Guy's niece," Susie says, and smiles.

Kora blinks. "Oh, yes I suppose so."

"I'm so sorry to tell you all this," Guy says. "I wasn't sure whether to, but Susie said you had a right to know. I'm still not sure whether she was right."

"I—I'm glad I know the truth," Kora says. I can see in her face though, that she wishes she didn't. I did tell her the truth can be a double-edged sword. I wish I hadn't been such a smart arse.

"Is there anything else you can tell me?" Kora asks. "I don't suppose you have anything left of Rachel's?"

"No, sorry," Guy replies. "My father cleared out the farm when Rachel died. She hadn't left a will, so the farm went to him automatically, and he just threw everything out. Except for one thing."

"What was that?"

"Her teddy bear. I think it was quite valuable. He gave it to the V&A, I believe."

"The Victoria and Albert Museum?" Kora looks astounded.

"We'll check it out," I tell her softly, and she nods.

"I can't remember anything else at the moment," Guy says. "But if you want to leave me your email address, I'll let you know if anything springs to mind."

Kora passes him one of her business cards, and then declares it's time to go. We say our goodbyes, and Guy and Susie promise to keep in touch. I'm not sure if they will, though. Despite the fact that it appears he's Kora's uncle, I don't think they're keen to remind themselves of the past.

Chapter Twenty

Kora

Half an hour later, we're sitting in the bar of a hotel in Exeter, nursing a cocktail. It's time for dinner, but I'm not hungry, so Callum said he's happy to order room service later.

I barely remember the journey here. Maybe aware of my confused emotions, Callum navigated the motorway lanes and the busy roads of the city, leaving me to my thoughts.

Now, though, he's sitting there looking at me, and I know he's waiting for me to discuss what we've uncovered. But I have no idea where to start.

I look around the bar. The hotel is in the center of Exeter, not far from the cathedral, which loomed briefly through the snow as we drove around the green in front of it. Callum told me the hotel is a Grade II listed Georgian townhouse. Apparently the first owner was an officer of the East India Company, and there are photos of Sultans on the walls, rich textured fabrics, and the rooms are named after trade routes—Cotton, Silk, and Sugar. The cocktail bar is exquisite. I couldn't make my mind up about which cocktail to choose so Callum ordered for us—a caramel and apple hot toddy with cinnamon. It's perfect with the snow falling thickly outside, as the two of us curl up on a sofa in front of the roaring fire.

"Are you okay?" Callum sips his drink. We're sitting slightly turned toward one another, so our feet are interlinked. I like to be touching him. I find it oddly comforting.

I stir my toddy with the stick of cinnamon. "Yes. No. I don't know."

"Well, that clears it up."

I give him a ghost of a smile. "I feel completely blown away. And I don't really know why. Essentially, nothing has changed. And yet it feels as if everything has."

"Of course it has. You can't get news like that and not be affected by it." He tips his head to the side. "Do you wish Guy hadn't told you?"

"A small part of me does, but that's the cowardly, selfish part, because it would mean I wouldn't have to deal with it. I've always been a great believer in the truth. And I don't think I'm the type of person to bury my head in the sand. It will be much better that I know. Once I've processed it and figured out what it all means."

We sip our drinks, letting the peace and quiet of the place settle into us. It's a boutique hotel, and it has only six rooms, so it's hardly heaving. Two other couples are in the bar, and they're far enough away that it's almost as if we're alone.

"Come on," Callum says. "Talk to me. Get it off your chest. What's bothering you the most?"

I try to analyze my thoughts. "I suppose my biggest question is how much did my mum know? She was six when Rachel died. When I think back to my conversation with Grandpa, there was a lot he didn't talk about, but I'm not sure if that's because he didn't know, or if he just didn't want to tell me."

"He can't have known about Simon being the father, surely," Callum says. "I can't imagine either Simon or Harriet would have admitted that when your grandparents went to meet them, and there's no other way they would have found out, is there?"

"Probably not, you're right. I wonder if they suspected, though? He told me that Simon and Harriet were abrupt. He and Grandma must have discussed why that was."

"Maybe, maybe not. Not everyone is as analytical or insightful as you. Most people accept things at face value."

"I guess." I hadn't thought of that. Julian once told me I overthink everything. That's probably true—not that I can do anything about it. It's just the way I am.

"I wonder if your grandparents knew how Rachel died, though," Callum says.

"That crossed my mind, too. And if they knew, did they tell Mum? Would she have known about the aneurysm? I'm not sure if they're hereditary?"

"As far as I know, usually not, but I think there are something called familial aneurysms. Rob once had a girlfriend whose family had them, that's how I know—her father and one of her brothers both died from them. It meant she had a higher risk of developing one, something like twenty percent, if I remember correctly. She had to have an aneurysm screening to study the brain arteries."

"I don't remember Mum ever going to hospital," I say. "She was always fit and healthy, as far as I knew. Surely, if she'd known about it, Dad would have taken her for a screening?"

"Maybe she didn't know. Or she did and she didn't tell your dad."

"I need to talk to him." That's become more important to me as the last few days have gone by. "I've got to find out how much he knows."

"You could ring him tonight?"

I nod slowly. "Would you mind?"

"Of course not! If you like you can go to our room, and I'll stay down here."

"You don't need to do that," I say softly, taking his hand. "I don't mind if you're in the room. In fact, I think I'd like you to be there."

"It's entirely up to you. I'm happy to stay with you." He links his fingers with mine and brushes his thumb across my knuckles. It makes me shiver, and for a moment all the tension of the day fades away as my body comes alive, nerve endings firing, the hairs on my skin rising at the thought of his hands on me.

"I know it's been hard for you," he murmurs. "But I've enjoyed our time together."

"Me too."

"You're strong, Kora. Stronger than you know. You'll get through this, and then you'll be able to move on, and you'll be in a better place for knowing what you know."

"I hope so. At the moment I just feel vulnerable."

"I know. Come here." He holds up his arm.

I scoot a bit closer to him and rest my head on his shoulder as he lowers his arm around me.

We sit there like that for a long while, not saying much. Outside, the snow continues to fall, like a thick curtain being drawn across the window. But in here it's warm and cozy, and I feel safe. Callum's body is solid beside me. I rest a hand on his chest, and I can feel his heart thumping rhythmically beneath my fingertips. When I lift my face to look up at him, he lowers his lips to mine, and we exchange a short kiss that's no less sweet for its brevity.

"Is it too early to call your dad?" he asks.

"No, it's nearly nine a.m. there. Dad will be at work by now."

"You want to go call him? We can always come back down to the bar."

I nod. Callum knows it's on my mind. I'm sure he wants me to get it over with before we continue our evening together.

So we finish off our hot toddies, then rise and go up to our room. We're in the Silk Room, which has intricate Chinese artwork, high ceilings, and huge windows that overlook the Cathedral Green. A Devon hamper that contains locally made fudge and chocolate, as well as a small bottle of Exeter Gin, greets our arrival. The bathroom has a roll top bath and a shower. Our bags are already here, brought up by the porter.

We take off our boots, and then Callum pours us both a glass of the gin and tops it with tonic from the fridge as I set up my laptop on the bed, sitting back on the pillows. He brings me the drink, kisses me on the forehead, then sits over by the window. "Just let me know if you want me to go out," he says.

I nod. I've already texted Dad to see if he's available for a call, and after his affirmative reply, I join him on Zoom.

His picture pops up on the screen, showing him at his desk in the office, dressed in a gray suit, white shirt, and blue tie. His white hair is still thick and neatly combed. He's also growing a beard. I'm not sure about it; he's been clean shaven for as long as I can remember. But he likes it, so I don't say anything. He's in his mid-fifties now, but still very handsome. He and Mum were so much in love. It makes me sad to think he's on his own now.

"Morning, kitten!" he states. "Well, good evening, I mean!"

"Hey, Dad." Despite my nerves, I'm still pleased to hear his voice.

"Are you at the hotel? What's the time there?"

"Eight-ish. It's snowing and freezing cold. I've just had a winter cocktail. The height of luxury."

"And why not? I'm glad you're spoiling yourself. What have you been up to?"

I prop the laptop on a pillow in front of me and snuggle back, warm and comfortable. "I've had a very interesting day. I... met someone I knew a long time ago, so we've been catching up."

"A school friend?"

"No…" Suddenly, I'm reluctant to reveal I'm with Callum, especially with him sitting there. He's studying his phone, but I know he's listening. I don't want the third degree, or to have to explain the situation. "Someone else," I reply vaguely.

"A guy?"

I could refuse to tell him, but that would look even more suspicious. "Yes…"

"Okay," he says. "That's cool. He showing you around?"

He's obviously picked up that I don't want to be grilled, and I relax a little. "Yeah. He's on the board of a charity over here and it was their charity ball at Leeds Castle last night, so he asked me to go with him. Dinner and dancing, you know the kind of thing."

"Oh, that was nice of him. I understand that Leeds Castle is beautiful."

"Yeah, it was a lovely evening."

"On Valentine's Day?" His voice turns teasing. I glance at Callum. He doesn't look up, but he smiles.

"That was a coincidence," I say wryly. "But anyway, yesterday he took me to see where the Battle of Hastings took place, and then to Pevensey Castle."

"Oh, you have been getting around. What's the guy's name?"

"Callum MacDuff. He's Stephanie's ex." Shit, now why did I say that?

Dad's eyebrows rise. "Stephanie Prince?"

"Yeah." Suddenly I'm acutely conscious of Callum being there. Why didn't I ask him to wait in the cocktail bar? "I bumped into him at the toy store. I first met him when he was on holiday in New Zealand twelve years ago."

"So you've been catching up. Well… how does Stephanie feel about that? Or doesn't she know?"

"I have no idea. I don't really want to talk about it, it's not a big thing and… Callum's here." I glance over at him.

"Oh, okay," Dad says.

"Dad…"

"It's not a big thing. I get it. Only you're all kinda… glowy."

"I am not glowy!" I blush furiously. Callum glances up and grins.

"It's all right," Dad says, also smiling. "You don't have to tell me everything."

"No," I snap, embarrassed. "Because we don't do that in this family, do we?"

Dad blinks, his smile fading. "What?"

My chest heaves as I fight for control. "Well, you didn't share with your children that their mum was adopted, did you?"

There's a long silence. I know Callum's watching me, but I don't look at him.

Dad glances away, and I imagine him staring out through the window at the view of Wellington Harbour, the sea a little choppy, the sky a bright blue on the gorgeous summer day. Suddenly, I feel so homesick it makes my stomach clench.

"You knew," I whisper.

His gaze comes back to me. "How did you find out?" Even though he doesn't confirm it, his lack of surprise tells me I'm right.

"I went to see Violet Johnson in the retirement home."

"Carol's sister? Wow."

"Her daughter, Fiona, was there too. She remembers Mum, and her sister, Maggie. They were twins, Dad. Didn't you think that was important for me to know? Especially with me and Theo being twins."

"She didn't want you to know," he says quietly. Then he glances to one side and murmurs to me, "Hold on." He smiles at someone off camera, and Elena, his PA, appears briefly in shot as she places a coffee in front of him. "I'm talking to Kora," he tells her, gesturing at the screen.

"Hey, Kora!" Elena bends and waves at me. I like her a lot. She's in her late forties, with blonde hair in a bob and modern rectangular glasses. She looks elegant today in a navy suit and white blouse.

"Hey, Elena."

"Having a good time over there?"

"Yes, thank you. Lots of fun."

"We miss you here."

I blink as tears sting my eyes. "Thank you."

She looks at Dad, then rises and walks out of shot. "Thanks," he calls to her as she leaves the room. His gaze lingers on her for a moment longer before returning to me.

I've wondered before if there's anything going on between them, but I've never had any proof of that. They never touch, never do anything inappropriate in the workplace. I think Elena has feelings for him, but then I suppose it would be weird if she didn't, considering she's worked there for ten years. She was also Mum's best friend, so I'm sure that plays on both of their minds.

"Does Elena know?" I ask.

"I don't know. We've never discussed it. I doubt it, though. I think I was the only person Mum told over here."

"Why didn't she want us to know?" My voice has turned husky with emotion. I've always found it impossible to hide my feelings. Callum told me, *You really do wear your heart on your sleeve, don't you?* And I know he's right.

Dad inhales, then exhales slowly. He leans back in his chair, picks up his coffee cup, and takes a sip. "She saw her move to New Zealand as a brand-new start. She was unhappy in England, and she wanted to put that life behind her. Sometimes it broke through her new happiness, like a wave coming over her, and she just had to wait for it to pass. But in many ways she was a very private person. She didn't even like discussing things with me, and I learned to respect her wishes."

"Dad… I've also been to see Guy Rowe and his wife."

He frowns. "Who?"

"He's Simon Rowe's son. I think… I think Simon Rowe was mum's father."

Understanding dawns, and his frown lifts. "How on earth did you track him down?"

"Just on the Internet, looking at birth and death certificates. I knew there was more to the puzzle, and I had to find out. How much did Mum know? What did she tell you about her parents?"

He sits back in his chair, playing with a pen, sliding it through his fingers. "Not much. What do you know?"

He's being cagey. "Everything," I say. "I know that Rachel Hoffman was Jewish, and she came over on the Kindertransport. Simon's parents adopted her, and Simon and his brothers didn't like her, maybe because she was his parents' favorite, even though she wasn't their natural daughter. They left the farm to her, which made him angry. Guy and his wife told us that his parents dropped hints that suggested Simon was the father of Rachel's twins. They don't know what happened—they could have had an affair, although Guy thinks his father raped Rachel."

I'm cruel on purpose to see his reaction. He winces, but he doesn't look shocked. Jesus, he knew all this. He and Mum both knew everything, but they didn't tell us.

"And Rachel died from a brain aneurysm," I say, tears forming in my eyes. "I'm guessing Mum knew that too."

"Yes," he says quietly.

"And you didn't tell us? You must have known it could be hereditary."

"Yes, we knew."

"Did she have regular scans to see if she was developing one?"

"No."

"Why not? She might have been able to avoid what happened, Dad!" I'm furious and upset at the same time.

"She didn't want to." For the first time, he looks angry. "Do you think we didn't argue about it? It was the only thing we did argue about. I begged her to go to the doctor many times, but she didn't want to know. And in the end, I had to learn to respect her decision. I couldn't force her to go. And it wasn't my place to tell you everything. It was her past, her choice. Would I have told you if I could? Of course. But that's just the way she was. What happened in England with her sister crushed her. She wasn't mentally strong, Kora, she just wasn't. She couldn't deal with those memories. I wanted her to see a therapist, but she didn't want to talk about it or relive it. She coped by shutting everything away. I didn't agree with it, but that's how it was, so I honored her decision, because that's what you do when you love someone. You learn to be there for them, and let them make their own decisions about their own lives."

His outburst shocks me so much that I can't contain the tears. I put my face in my hands, unable to hold them back, and just give into the sobs.

Chapter Twenty-One

Callum

I promised myself I wouldn't interfere with Kora's call, but as I watch her dissolve into tears, I find I can't sit by and do nothing. I rise and go over to the bed, climb on, and take her in my arms, then settle back on the pillows and look at the screen.

"Hi," I say to her father, who looks distraught. "I'm Callum. Sorry about this, but I couldn't just sit there and watch."

"Hello, Callum, it's great to meet you." He runs a hand through his hair and sighs. "Kora, love, I'm so sorry."

She shakes her head, still sobbing. I reach across to the tissue box on the bedside table and bring it back, take out a few, and push them into her hands.

"It's just a bit of a shock," I say to him. "She'll be okay. It's been a tough couple of days for her."

"It must have been very hard," he says. "I'd have told you everything if I'd known you were going to look into it. Kora, please don't think harshly of your mother. Blame me if you like—I should probably have told you everything once she died. But don't blame her. She didn't want you to know about what happened to Rachel. She suspected Rachel had been assaulted because Grandma and Grandpa were sure Simon was the father, and his reaction hinted that their relationship had not been good. She hoped it was just an affair that went wrong, but she always worried that he'd assaulted her, and that thought tortured her."

I can see how it would be incredibly upsetting to think your father had raped your mother. Every child should be born out of love. When that doesn't happen, it must make a person wonder if it somehow has an effect on the child.

Kora's sobs are dying down, and she blows her nose and wipes her eyes. She smudges her mascara in the process, but I don't think she cares at this point.

"I don't blame anyone," she whispers. "I know you'd have told me if you could. I just wish I'd known; I think it might have helped me understand her. Sometimes she was so distant, and I didn't feel close to her, and that upsets me now." More tears run down her cheeks, and she tries to wipe them away.

"You were always close to her," her father says. "You were her only daughter, and she loved you with every cell in her body. She was so haunted by her past, and I think she didn't want you to be haunted by it, too. She felt she was saving you by keeping it to herself. She wanted you to have a wonderful life, Kora. She'd have been so proud of you."

Well, if anything was going to be her undoing, that was it. She dissolves completely into tears, pushes away from me, runs into the bathroom, and closes the door. The sound of her sobs filters out, heartfelt and full of sorrow.

"Oh dear," her dad says. "Think that might have been the wrong thing to say."

"It was the perfect thing to say," I tell him softly. "I think she's still grieving over her mum and her grandfather, as well as her previous relationship, and what happened to Theo over Christmas. It's come together, and it's just overwhelmed her."

"I wish she'd told me she was looking into her family tree. I feel terrible that it came out this way. I didn't agree with Olivia keeping everything secret, but what was I supposed to do?" He looks frustrated, and I understand why.

"I think you did everything you could," I try to soothe, even though I don't know the guy. "Kora's strong. Think what she's been through, and yet she came to England, and she's full of life and energy. She'll be fine."

"At least she has you," Nick says. He gives a small smile.

I look away at that, out at the snow. "I'd better go check on her."

"Okay. Well, it was nice to meet you, Callum. Tell Kora I'm sorry, and that she can call me at any time, will you?"

"I will."

"All right. Look after her. 'Bye." He hangs up.

I close the laptop and sit there for a minute. I can't hear her sobs anymore, but I know she's probably still crying.

I get up, go over to the bathroom, and knock on the door. "Kora?"

She clears her throat. "Yeah?"

"Can I come in?"

She sighs. "It's not locked."

I open the door and go in. She's sitting on the tiled floor, her back against the bath, knees drawn up. She wipes beneath her eyes with a handful of tissue, which doesn't help the panda look.

I lower myself down beside her and sit close, so our arms are touching.

"Sorry to leave you with my dad," she mumbles.

"It's all good. We bonded." I smile.

She fiddles with the tissue. "He's such a bastard. I was so angry with him, and then he went and said that about Mum being proud of me, and it was like an arrow to my heart."

"I think he's very proud of you, too. That much is obvious."

She rests her head on my shoulder. "I just keep thinking about what a burden she carried all her life. All that about her mother, and then losing her twin sister… It would have made it so much easier for her if she'd been able to talk to me about it."

"Maybe, maybe not. Like I said, not everyone feels comfortable analyzing their lives. It makes some people feel vulnerable and confused. Perhaps the only way she could deal with it was to shut it in a box and lock it away."

As I say the words, I know I'm the same, or at least I have been until I met Kora. I rarely spoke about my parents to Stephanie, and I don't talk much about them to Josh or Jim. That part of my life belongs to the past, like a holiday I've had and haven't enjoyed. I've locked the photos and mementoes of that time away in a drawer, and I never take them out.

"I feel so mixed up," Kora whispers. "It's like I'm watching myself react to it all, and the real me is thinking what's the matter, why are you so upset? It doesn't change anything. But I can't help it."

"You're in shock," I tell her. "You've discovered some things about your family that have changed your view of your parents and grandparents on a fundamental level, and it's going to take some time to process it all. Add to that all your grief, and it makes for a right bloody muddle."

She chuckles at that and looks up at me. "You sounded very English when you said that."

"Yis, I did." I copy her accent, and she laughs.

Pleased to see her face light up, on impulse I bend my head and press my lips to hers. I only meant it to be a light kiss, but she lifts her hand and slips her fingers into my hair to hold me there, and it turns into a long, lingering smooch.

"Mmm," she murmurs eventually when she releases me. "I needed that."

We study each other for a long moment. She cups my cheek with a hand, her thumb brushing over the bristles on my jaw. Her eyes are a beautiful blue, her hair bright as the sun. She still smells of cherries. A little piece of summer, held in my hands in this frozen world.

"You're so handsome," she whispers, her voice husky. "You really do make my heart beat faster. You're like a drug. I'm addicted to you. You're all I can think about when we're apart. How am I going to leave you behind when I go?"

"I don't know." My gut twists at the thought of saying goodbye to her.

"I want you." She slides her hand back into my hair and tightens her fingers. "Make love to me, Callum." And she pulls my head down and crushes her lips to mine.

I don't need any further encouragement. I know she's desperate for comfort, for a connection to something that doesn't hurt or disappoint her, and maybe I'm convenient, and she's using me, but right now I don't care. I want her too much to mind.

The heat between us flares fast, as if someone's taken a blowtorch to us. I open my mouth and she plunges her tongue inside, and I'm hard immediately, all the blood in my body flowing to my groin in seconds. She lifts up and climbs onto my lap, straddling me, and she groans as she rocks her hips against me and finds me ready for her.

"You're so fucking sexy," she whispers, her fingers fumbling to find the bottom of my sweater. I lean forward a little to help her, and she pulls it up my body and over my head, then throws it over her shoulder onto the floor. My T-shirt follows, but then I lean back and meet the side of the bath, and the icy marble makes me exclaim out loud.

"Sorry." She giggles. "Come on." She climbs off me, stands, and extends a hand, and I take it and let her pull me up with some effort. She walks into the bedroom, pulling me after her, but instead of going over to the bed, she leads me in front of the fire, then sinks onto her knees on the soft rug.

I go to follow, but she stops me, and instead undoes my belt, then unzips my fly. Finally, she pulls down my boxers, releasing my erection, and in seconds she's taken me in her hand and closed her mouth over the tip.

Groaning, I let my head fall back and sink a hand into her hair as she washes her tongue over me, then slides her lips down the shaft as she takes me into her mouth. Fuck, that feels good. She sucks rhythmically, stroking with her hand at the same time, and I give myself over to the amazing sensation. The scene reveals itself through my hazy eyes—the snow still falling outside, the firelight turning her golden hair a fiery red, and suddenly I want to see it playing over her skin.

"Kora." She lifts her head as I speak, and I put a hand under her arm and help her up. Then I strip off her sweater and tee, help her off with her jeans and bra, and now she's just wearing a pair of sexy white cotton panties and fluffy white socks that I find oddly arousing, although I couldn't have told her why.

Nearly naked, she sinks back to her knees and takes me in her mouth again, and this time I get to watch the firelight turning her skin molten, her breasts swaying gently as she moves back and forth. It's an erotic scene, one I could watch all night, but I'm not going to last that long, and I want to make sure she's satisfied, too. She's the one who needs comfort, after all.

So I kick off my jeans and underwear, while she takes off her panties, and then I drop to my knees. My plan is to lie her down and kiss her all over as I slowly arouse her, but it soon becomes clear she has other ideas. She pushes me onto my back until I'm stretched out in front of the fire, then climbs on top, rocking her hips as she arouses herself on the base of my erection.

"Condom?" she whispers.

"Soon," I promise.

"Now," she demands, reaching over to get my jeans and extracting my wallet. She passes it to me, and, giving her a wry look, I take out a condom and roll it on. Immediately, she lifts up and positions herself so the tip of my erection presses against her entrance, and then she sinks down.

I slide inside her so easily that it's clear going down on me aroused her. She lets out a long, sexy sigh and tips her head right back, arching her spine. The fire lights up her breasts, turning her nipples to gold buttons, and as I roll them with my thumbs, she moans and drops her head to look at me. Her fiery hair falls around her face and shoulders, and her teeth tug at her bottom lip as she begins to rock her hips.

"Callum…" She leans over me, and I fill my palms with her breasts as she bends to kiss me.

It's a change for me, someone wanting me this way, with such desire, such urgency. My hips rise to meet hers, but it's Kora who's driving the pace, and I'm happy to lie there and let her ride me while I admire her body and play with her breasts. She kisses me for a long while, plunging her tongue in my mouth, hungry, needy, desperate, and we spiral toward a climax together as she moves faster. Each breath is a long moan that fills the warm room, and when I tug her nipples it turns into a cry that I'm sure those next door will be able to hear, but I don't care, I'm too fired up, too hot, too turned on. Our skin has turned damp from the heat of the fire, and hers glistens, while her hair sticks to her temples, but she doesn't stop, she keeps thrusting, and I know it's not going to be long before she comes.

And suddenly it's not enough, it's not satisfying my urge to drive the action. So I catch her around the waist and flip her onto her back, surprising her. She squeals, then groans, her concentration broken, and the orgasm that was so tantalizingly close slips away from her. But as soon as I begin moving, her eyes flare, and again she bites on her bottom lip, searching for the elusive end.

I prop myself up on my hands and drive into her, filling the air with the seductive sounds of sex that only turn me on more. Our skin is slick and we slide together, our groans mingling as I bend and kiss her deeply. She wraps her legs around my waist, and her nails claw at my back as she reaches for her climax, and I watch as it finally claims her, second by second—her brow creasing, her lips parting, her breath turning ragged as all the tiny muscles in her belly and between her thighs contract. And then she cries out loud, while I plunge deep inside her, taking my own pleasure, heat rushing through me, enjoying that beautiful, blissful moment that's only seconds long, and yet it's better than anything else on earth, more precious than gold.

Chapter Twenty-Two

Kora

I come to my senses slowly. Callum is lying on top of me, crushing me into the carpet. His chest heaves against mine, and his face is buried in my neck. He's so heavy, but I can't bring myself to complain.

God, I needed that.

Ohhh… life is so cruel. Either that or I'm so stupid. Why did I go to bed with him? Why did I open myself up to losing him? I adore this guy, and it's going to be like removing an arm when I eventually have to leave.

But I can't honestly wish it hadn't happened. How could I think that, when I'm lying here having had the best sex of my life? Bar maybe that first night on the beach. This man seems to know just how to press all my buttons in the right order. Julian wasn't even a patch on Callum. I didn't realize until now how lackluster our sex life was back then.

I don't want to spoil the moment by thinking about my ex. There's no room in my brain for him, anyway. Callum's taken up all my thoughts, all my emotions.

All my heart.

He shifts on top of me, and finally pushes up onto his elbows. His brown eyes look into mine, taking my breath away with the desire that still simmers in their depths.

I opt for sassy. "Oh, so you're letting me breathe now?"

His lips curve up. "Sorry."

"You don't look sorry."

"No, I'm not." He chuckles, then kisses me, taking his time, his lips moving slowly. He kisses my nose, my cheeks, my eyebrows and eyelids, then back to my mouth, and he dips his tongue inside gently this time, tender and careful after his earlier enthusiastic lovemaking.

"I didn't hurt you?" he asks, lifting his head to look at me.

I won't be able to walk for a fortnight, but I'm not going to tell him that in case he stops doing it. "No, of course not."

He kisses my nose. "Good. Come on, let's get you into bed."

He withdraws and gets to his feet, helps me up, and then we go over to the bed and climb on. It's cool under the covers, but we snuggle together, and it's not long before the thick duvet heats us up.

After a while, though, my stomach rumbles, and we both laugh. "Peckish?" he asks.

"Mmm."

"Shall we order room service?"

"Oh yes. I'm in the mood for something rich and decadent."

So we order from the menu—a bacon and egg roll each, a basket of fries, and a couple of pieces of chocolate cake to finish. We cuddle up, watching the snow fall and talking about nothing, until the food arrives, then get out of bed and pull on our sweaters, wrap the duvet around our legs, and sit in the chairs by the fire to eat.

"This is the best food I've ever had," I tell him as I lick bacon grease off my fingers.

"We certainly worked up an appetite." His eyes sparkle as he eats a couple of fries.

"It's your fault."

"Mine?" He raises an eyebrow.

"You're too gorgeous. I can't help it if I have no control over my actions when you're around."

He chuckles softly and has a mouthful of the champagne we also had delivered. His hair is all mussed where I've dragged my fingers through it. I want to do him all over again, but I don't have the energy.

On the table, his phone buzzes. He glances at it, but he doesn't pick it up.

"Who's texting you at this late hour?" I tease. "Not your PA?"

"Nah." He smiles, but it doesn't reach his eyes. The fingers of his left hand curl into a fist on his knee.

Something clicks then. "Stephanie?"

He picks another couple of fries out of the basket. "Yeah."

I surprise myself with the pang of jealousy I feel. He once belonged to her. He came home to her every night, shared her bed, her heart. I know he doesn't any longer, but it's tough to think of the two of them together. She's elegant and beautiful, and they would have made an attractive couple.

"What does she want?" I ask, trying to sound casual.

"To be a major pain in my arse. She's well on the way to achieving that goal."

Reassured by his acidic tone, I finish off my roll. "Is she still hoping you'll get back together?"

He sighs. "I don't know how to convince her it's over. I divorced her, for Christ's sake. How much more final can I be?"

"She'll get the hint eventually, I'm sure."

"Maybe. It's not healthy, the way she's clinging onto the past. It's like I'm trying to climb out of a lake, and she's got one hand around my ankle, and she's dragging me back in."

I sip my champagne. "You're feeling pulled back to her?"

"No. I mean she's dragging me back toward those feelings of hopelessness and frustration I had when we were together. All the time she keeps contacting me, it's so hard to move on."

He pushes his plate away. I can see the anger simmering beneath his composure. He's had enough.

"What you're feeling is perfectly normal." I curl up in the chair, tucking the duvet around my legs. "Life is like being on a raft on a turbulent ocean. When you're in a relationship, it's as if you come across someone else on another raft, and one of you throws a rope, and you cling together, finding some stability for a while. Sometimes you're able to tether the rope and drift together until you find land, like Theo and Victoria did. But at other times, you never reach the island. It's not as if someone comes and cuts the rope, though. What happens is you drift farther and farther apart, and the rope gets longer and longer, until one day you just realize you can't hang on anymore. In a way the divorce is just a piece of paper, it doesn't necessarily cut the emotional ties. It has for you, but not for Stephanie yet. But she'll get there. One day she'll realize you're out of sight, and she'll just let go."

He props his head on a hand and gives me a tired smile. "How did you get to be so wise when you're so young?"

"I'm thirty now. I'm practically drawing my pension."

He chuckles. "Then I've got one foot in the grave."

"You're only three years older than me."

"A lot can happen in three years."

"True."

We study each other, the firelight leaping on our faces. Is he wondering where we'll both be in three years' time, too? Will we still be in touch? Maybe traveling across the world to see each other for a few weeks, to share each other's bed? Or will we have let go of the ropes by then and drifted out of sight?

At the moment there's no way of knowing. Everything's up in the air, and our relationship is like the snowflakes outside, beautiful and glittering and full of promise, but there's every chance that in the morning it'll be gone, and all I'll be left with is gray slush and wet feet.

*

In the morning, we drive slowly back through the snow-covered countryside to London. The gritters are out, making sure the main roads are passable, but the snow is falling continuously like a thick curtain, piling up on the verges, on parked cars, on roofs, and in people's gardens. Schools are closed, and when we drive through the smaller towns, we see children making snowmen and having snowball fights in the parks.

Everything seems clean in the snow, and exciting, as if it's Christmas Eve, even though we're deep into February, and the first snowdrops will be appearing soon.

London is the same, with most of the roads clear, but thick snow building up on the pavements and parked cars. Callum takes us past Green Park, where children are out in full force, dressed in hats and scarves, with red noses and cheeks, their breath frosting as they play. I feel a strange pang at the sight of them. I would have said it's reminding me of my own childhood, but it hardly ever snows in Wellington. With some surprise, I realize I'm feeling wistful at the thought of having a child of my own.

Am I feeling broody for the first time in my life? It completely takes me aback. I've always felt puzzled when my friends have talked about feeling broody. I've not had a hankering for a baby at all. I haven't pictured myself with one in my arms, or felt upset that I haven't yet started a family. It's not that I don't want kids. It's just not been a factor in my life.

At that moment, though, watching a mother walking through the park with one toddler in a pushchair while a young child skips along in the snow, I can suddenly picture myself in the same position.

The feeling is new, different. A kind of deep hunger, a yearning. I've never yearned before about anything, and I never thought it would happen to me. But here I am. Yearning. How odd.

"You okay?" Callum turns the car away from the park and heads up Bolton Street toward Claridge's.

I look at him, and I feel my face flush as he glances at me. "What?" he asks, amused.

"Nothing." I look away at the busy shops. This is nothing to do with him. Everyone tells you a woman is more conscious of her body clock when she turns thirty. It must have just hit me.

We don't speak again until he pulls up outside Claridge's. The porter comes down to open the door, but Callum holds up a hand, and the man nods and moves away politely.

Callum turns to me and smiles. "Well, here we are."

"Mm."

He studies me, tipping his head to the side. "You sure you're okay?"

"Yeah. I've had a lovely time. Thank you so much for coming with me."

"You're very welcome. I enjoyed myself."

"You'd better get back now," I say softly. "I'm sure they're missing you at work."

He looks out of the window. "I thought I might call home, actually. I bet Jim and Josh are in Hyde Park having a snowball fight."

I chuckle. "Are you going to join in?"

"Maybe. I can't remember the last time I did that."

"I don't think I've ever done it!"

"Really?" He purses his lips and thinks for a moment. Then he says, "Want to come with me?"

Pure delight fills me at the thought of spending more time with him. "Seriously?"

"Seriously."

"You really should get back to work."

"I really should." He turns back to the steering wheel. "Buckle yourself in."

Happily, I do as he says, and then he drives off down the road, going around Grosvenor Square so he can head back toward Hyde Park.

"I'd better call Julia," he says. "My PA." He brings up her number and rings her on the speakerphone.

"Good morning, Tower Group," she answers.

"It's me," he says.

"Hey! Are you back in the city?"

"I am."

"Heading in now, I'm guessing?"

"Ah… well… I'm going to be a little longer, sorry." He pulls an eek face at me, and I stifle a laugh.

"Callum… seriously?" She sounds frustrated.

"Why does everyone keep asking me if I'm being serious today?" His tone is almost playful. He's enjoying playing hooky.

"You have a meeting about the South Bank property at two that I've already moved twice."

"Ask Rob to do it."

She hesitates. "Are you sure? I thought you wanted to spearhead this one yourself."

"I did. But something important has come up. Rob wanted to head it anyway. Give it to him."

"He'll bite your hand off, but that's not the point. You have a heap of things to sign and a list of phone calls as long as your arm. I need you here." She sounds slightly harassed.

He pulls up on the roadside, with Hyde Park on our left, puts the handbrake on, and sits back. "I need a bit longer, Julia. I'll be back to work soon. I've never asked you to do this for me before. Tell everyone I've got the flu if that helps."

"Are you okay?"

"I'm fine."

"But—"

"I'll call later." He hangs up, then switches off the engine, then gives me a sheepish glance. "She's been with me a long time. She thinks she's my mother."

"It's good that she's looking out for you." I smile. Suddenly he seems a lot younger than his thirty-three years. His mother has been gone a long time, and he must have had to grow up fast. It's nice to see a playful side to him.

"Come on." He gets out of the car, checking his phone. "Jim just texted me back to say they're still in the apartment. Let's head up there."

I'm going to see his apartment? And meet his family? Suddenly I feel nervous. I'd have given more thought to my appearance if I'd known this was going to happen. I'm wearing dark jeans and a white sweater under my thick black coat. I look smart enough, I guess. My hair has gone fluffy today though, and I'm not wearing much makeup. They're used to Stephanie; I'm going to look like a country bumpkin in comparison.

But I am what I am, and there's no point in worrying about it too much. It's not as if we're getting married and I'm going to meet his parents.

The block is huge, spotless, and expensive looking. Callum walks me through to the elevators, and we ride one up to his apartment.

We don't speak as the carriage rises, and it strikes me that maybe he's nervous, too. He fiddles with the buttons of his coat, looking like a young boy again. That's what his son would look like if he was anxious on the first day of school.

No, no. I mustn't go down that road.

The elevator gets to the top—the penthouse apartment, of course. The doors open, and we walk out into a quiet corridor, and then he unlocks the door to his home.

He stands back to let me pass, and I go inside. I walk into a bright, open room. The windows are floor-to-ceiling and overlook the park. It's all dark wood and cream walls, with white tiles in the kitchen and dining area. It's classy and beautifully decorated. Something tells me he had a firm in to do it. Not that he doesn't have good taste, but it doesn't look… homely.

"Callum?" A male voice calls from the kitchen, and Callum takes my hand and leads me through to it. An elderly man is standing at the table chopping vegetables while a young man who must be Callum's brother is adding tinned tomatoes to a giant crockpot. He looks over his shoulder as we walk in, and his eyebrows rise as he sees not just his beloved brother, but me with him.

"Oh, hello!" Jim looks up in surprise.

"This is Kora," Callum says, keeping a tight hold on my hand, as if he's expecting me to run off in the opposite direction. "Kora, this is my grandfather, Jim, and this is Josh."

"I'm so pleased to meet you." I walk around the table to shake hands with Jim, then immediately turn to Josh and hold out my hand. "I've heard so much about you both."

Josh stares at my hand, then slowly reaches out and shakes it. "Pleased to meet you," he says politely.

I place my free hand on top of his. He's a good-looking lad, smaller than his brother, and with something of Callum's easy grace about him, but he looks tongue-tied, and I can see he's shy. "Callum doesn't stop talking about you," I tell him. "When we went to Hastings, I helped him pick out the knight for you. Did you like it?"

"It was brilliant." He studies my hands as if puzzled that I'm touching him. "It's on my shelf next to the Viking warrior he bought me."

"I've got another one for you," Callum tells him, and produces a parcel from behind his back that he bought in Stonehenge. I release Josh's hands and he takes it from his brother and undoes it eagerly. It's a figure of a man dressed in a tunic holding a bow.

"It's called the Amesbury Archer," I tell him. "He lived in the Bronze Age, and his grave was found at Amesbury—"

"—near Stonehenge," Josh finishes. "I love it." He picks up my hand again. "Come on, we'll put it on the shelf."

"Josh," Jim scolds, "you mustn't grab other people like that."

But I just laugh and say, "It's okay, I'd love to see this famous shelf," and I let Josh lead me through the apartment. His room looks like a young man's, with a Chelsea Football Club scarf hanging from a shelf, music posters on the walls, an untidy desk topped with a computer and a large screen, a hoodie bearing a famous gaming logo on the back of the chair, and clothes strewn about on the floor.

One wall has a long shelf that houses all of his famous models. I can see he's placed them in historical order. There's a Roman foot soldier, a Viking warrior, a Japanese samurai, a few medieval knights including the one we got him at Battle, an English Civil War pikeman, an early nineteenth century figure, an American Civil War soldier, and even a few twentieth-century soldiers.

Josh carefully moves the Roman soldier so he can put the Amesbury Archer in its rightful place at the beginning of the row. "It's fantastic," he says. "His bow even has a string."

"It's a great collection," I tell him. "I love that one, is it Napoleonic?"

"Yes! It's a figure of Richard Sharpe."

"Oh, from the Bernard Cornwell series?"

He looks delighted. "You've seen it?"

"Oh yes, all of them. Sean Bean is one of my favorite actors."

"Me too! I've read all the books," he says proudly, and he shows me them on his bookcase. "Callum bought the box set of DVDs for me too. I've watched them all seven times."

"Wow. I've seen them twice, I think. My brother, Ben, loves historical series and movies, and he adores Sharpe."

"Which episode is your favorite?" he asks.

I suspect I'm being tested. "It's got to be Sharpe's Honour."

"What happens in that one?" His eyes gleam. He knows. He's seeing whether I'm patronizing him by just coming up with a name.

I thank anyone above that Ben is so enthusiastic about the series and likes to share his passion. "Sharpe's framed for a murder and sentenced to hang, and Wellington has to go along with it to placate the Spanish. Sharpe's enemy, Ducos, is behind it all, of course."

Josh grins. "Would you like to hold the soldier?"

"Ooh, yes, please." I'm genuinely eager—I love all toys, and I'm a big fan of figurines of any kind.

As he reaches for the figure, I turn and see Callum leaning against the door jamb, hands in his pockets, watching us. He smiles, and the warmth in his eyes heats me right through. It appears I've passed more than one test today.

Chapter Twenty-Three

Callum

We all go into the park and turn into eight-year-olds for an hour, making a snowman and having a snowball fight that ends up with us all frozen to the bone and with ruddy cheeks and huge smiles. Afterward, we go back up to the apartment and thaw out in front of the fire, warming our hands around mugs of hot chocolate.

Kora is a huge hit. I can already see that Josh thinks she's an absolute goddess. And I can't blame him. Stephanie was a little afraid of him, I think, mistaking his enthusiasm for aggression, and not knowing how to handle his childlike manner. I'm not sure she was ever a child. That's not her fault—she's the eldest of four, and her mum was one of those mothers who teaches their daughters how to apply makeup and comport themselves from the age of about five. But Kora somehow manages to talk to Josh on a level he's comfortable with, without speaking to him as if he's a kid, which he hates.

I can also tell by the way Jim talks to her that he thinks she's wonderful, too. He was never rude to Stephanie, and he's never, ever, criticized her to me. But she saw him as a burden, and that obviously came across somehow, because he tended to excuse himself when she was around. But Kora talks to him about Helen and their life in Hastings, and he responds warmly, enjoying discussing his wife and their life together. And when Kora's hand creeps into mine where we're sitting together on the settee, Jim just smiles, but I know he's seen it, and he loves the small gesture.

It's with some reluctance that Kora eventually states she should be getting back. I know I have to go to work for a while, as it's not fair to leave everything to Julia. So I watch Kora say goodbye to Jim, who kisses her on the cheek, and Josh, who throws his arms around her and gives her a bearhug. She just laughs and hugs him back before collecting her coat and following me out.

I lead her to the elevator and then we stop and exchange a long, luxurious kiss.

"When do you fly out?" I murmur, holding her face in my hands.

"Thursday." So she only has one day left. She sighs. "I'd change my flight but it's my grandma's birthday at the weekend—my dad's mum—and I promised I'd be there as it's her first without Grandpa, so I have to go."

"Of course."

She rests her forehead on my chin, and I give her a hug.

"Would you like to go to the V&A tomorrow?" I ask her. "See Rachel's bear?"

She moves back and looks up at me. "You'll go with me?"

"Of course. How about in the afternoon? I'll get some stuff done in the morning and pick you up at, say, three o'clock?"

"That would be great."

"Okay." Relieved that I'm going to see her again, I press my lips gently to hers.

"Thank you for an amazing time," she whispers when I eventually move back. "I'm so pleased you came with me."

"Me too. Glad I could be there for you."

"I'll see you tomorrow, then?"

"Yeah. Take care."

She goes into the elevator, and we smile at each other until the doors close.

*

I go to the office and lose myself for a couple of hours in work. My heart is only half in it, though. I do what's required of me—sign documents, return phone calls and emails, sit in on a couple of meetings, and nod and pretend I'm taking notes. But more than once my gaze drifts out of the window, as I think about Kora's rosy-cheeked face in the park, and her infectious laughter as she threw a snowball and took Josh by surprise.

Because I asked Rob to take my morning meeting for me, he ends up spending the day in the office, and asks to join my second afternoon meeting too, as it's with Tower's heads of department. I agree because

I can't be bothered to argue, and in the end I let him chair and drive the discussion.

When the HODs finally file out of the room, Rob stays behind. I close my laptop and gather up my papers, and go to head out.

"Callum," he calls, and I stop and turn to face him. "Dude," he says, leaning back in his chair. "What's going on?"

"What do you mean?"

"Taking time off? And even when you are here, you're not here mentally."

"I've got things on my mind."

He nods, playing with his pen. "Care to share any of them?"

"No."

"People are beginning to talk," he says.

"Oh, I imagine they've been talking for some while, Rob." I know the office was rife with gossip when I walked out of my marriage. The atmosphere between Rob and I was so frosty that it was clear what had happened, even though neither of us spoke to anyone about it.

"We can't carry on like this," he says softly. "I know I'm to blame. I fucked everything up. We've had it good for a long time, but it's turned to shit, and it's all my fault. I thought we'd be able to keep it out of the workplace, but it's not fair on Julia and the others if it's not working."

I lean against the post, studying the floor. He's right, and it's been coming for a while. It's just that neither of us wanted to face that fact.

I suppose his admission that he's at fault should placate me. It doesn't. All I feel is tired.

I look back up at him. I've known him for fifteen years. There was a point when I was closer to him than my own brother. We've worked amazingly well together, and created an empire we're both proud of. We've exceeded our goals, and before Armageddon happened, we had more goals planned. But it's foolish to think they're going to come to fruition now.

"I've decided," he says. "You can buy me out and keep Tower. I'll start my own company. I've got other ideas, things you're not interested in. I'm tired of stagnating. I want to do new things, take it in different ways. It's pointless to keep dragging things on like this."

And just like that, it's done. He draws a line neatly beneath everything that has happened.

I'm not sure if he's expecting me to argue. If he wants me to beg him to stay. I look at him, really look for the first time in ages. He and Stephanie stopped seeing each other shortly after I found out about their affair, and now he's dating a twenty-one-year-old model. I don't know whether it makes me feel better or worse that he broke up my marriage and then dumped my wife.

I've got flecks of gray in my temples, but Rob's highlights cover any that might be showing in his. His tan is a little too dark to be real, his teeth a tad too white. He works out constantly, and the sleeves of his shirt stretch awkwardly over his bulging biceps. His watch is too large and flashy. He has a red Ferrari. I know the model is only going to be one in a long line of young women who'll pass through his life. He's not going to age well. The money has corrupted him, and he's not the man I knew when I was young.

Or maybe he is, and it's me who's changed.

It's what I wanted. The company I worked so hard to create can finally be mine and mine alone. I should feel victorious. Rob will have to start all over again, find new premises and staff, and build up credibility. It'll be hard work, and I doubt the new company will ever be bigger than Tower. It's the best option for me. All I have to do is keep the company running. Hardly anything will change in my life.

And yet a small part of me is jealous at the light in his eyes, the lift of his shoulders. He's excited about the prospect. He still has the zeal he had at twenty-one, the drive and ambition. But I don't. Mine melted away, like the winter snow will as soon as the sun comes out.

"Fine." I push off the post and walk away.

*

At just after ten p.m., I watch Kora walk across the tiled floor of Claridge's lobby toward me.

She's wearing jeans and a bright blue sweater that makes her look even more like a piece of summer than usual. Her face is flushed, and her eyes are shining.

She stops before me and says, "Hey."

"Hey." I shove my hands deep in the pockets of my coat, suddenly tongue-tied.

I've arrived at the hotel without an invite, on an impulse, and asked the concierge to ring up and tell her I was there rather than call her on the phone. Restless and unhappy at home, I left Josh and Jim a message, got in the car, and drove, finding myself at Claridge's without meaning to. Or maybe I'm kidding myself. I knew where I was coming all along.

We hadn't organized this. Part of me wondered whether she might look frustrated or annoyed at being surprised. Instead, though, she holds out a hand and says, "Wanna come up?"

I nod and slide my hand into hers, and she leads me over to the lifts. Another couple is waiting, and when the doors slide open, we remain silent as the carriage rises, until they get out a few floors up.

As the doors slide closed again, Kora turns to me, and her gaze scans my face. I wait for her to ask me why I'm here, or what's happened, as I'm sure it's clear to her that I'm unhappy.

But she doesn't. Instead, she walks up to me, grabs me by the lapels of my coat, and pulls me to her for a kiss.

I return it hungrily, wrapping my arms around her, and we're still kissing when the doors slide open. She backs out of the lift, still holding my lapels, still kissing me, and we stumble slowly to her room, laughing as she bumps into the door jamb, unwilling to let each other go for even a moment.

I release my frustration, my hurt and anger, and instead just focus on Kora, on the sweetness of her mouth, her cherry scent, and the feel of her skin as I slide my fingers beneath the hem of her sweater. She's warm and silky, and I grow hard at the thought of stripping off her clothes and sliding inside her.

I didn't come here for this; all I knew was that I needed to see her, but now I'm here and she's initiating sex, I'm not going to turn her away. I know she's seen my pain and she's trying to comfort me. It's an unspoken gift, and I'm more than happy to accept it.

We're soon inside the room, and the door closes behind us. The fire's low and it's coolish inside, but Kora leads me over to the bed, and begins to strip off my clothes. She removes my coat, sweater, and trousers as I toe off my shoes, and then I help her take off hers. Finally we remove our underwear, and then we quickly get into bed beneath the thick duvet, and cuddle up.

She stretches out on top of me, her fluffy blonde hair tumbling around my face, and I let the cherry perfume envelope me as I sink my hands into the soft strands, which curl around my fingers like silk ribbons. She kisses me deeply, her tongue delving into my mouth, and I sigh and return it, enjoying the heat rising between us.

We kiss for a long time, exploring each other's bodies with our hands, stroking, teasing, arousing. I'm fascinated by the shape of her, all smooth curves with no hard angles. The swell of her breasts. The dip of her waist. The flare of her hips. The curve of her thighs. Her velvet folds. The moist warmth of her that welcomes my fingers as I stroke inside her. Everything about her is soft. Her hair, her skin, her nipples, her beautiful bottom. I want her. She's mine, and I want to possess her.

I roll on a condom and, facing her on our sides, I pull her thigh across mine and slide inside her. Within a couple of thrusts, I'm balls deep, and she's wrapped around me as if she's never going to let me go.

We move together as if we're dancing, like ice skaters who've practiced an amazing routine a million times. Our kisses become more punishing, our fingers clutching and grasping, teeth biting, nails clawing at skin. Her cries fill the room, and my voice becomes a growl as the animal in me takes over. She's clamped around me, her thighs like iron pulling me even deeper inside her, and I thrust faster, driving us both to the edge. Eventually we tumble over together, and we clutch at each other as we fall into the abyss, the pleasure so exquisite it brings tears to my eyes.

*

"Are you warm enough?" As I say the words, I realize it's the first thing I've said since I returned her 'Hey' in the foyer. I'd feel guilty about it, but she hasn't spoken either, other than to fill the air with her blissful moans.

"Mmm." She snuggles up against me. "It's toasty under here."

I kiss the top of her head. "I'm so sorry."

"For what?"

"For turning up without calling. For not speaking. For just taking what you're prepared to give."

"I'm glad you did. It's mine to give. I wouldn't have asked you up if I hadn't wanted it to end like this."

I lift her hair to my nose and close my eyes as I breathe in her scent. "I missed you."

"I missed you too."

I kiss the top of her head again, thinking about that.

She lifts up, resting a hand on my chest, and her chin on her hand as she looks at me. "You want to talk about it?"

"About us?"

A gentle smile touches her lips. "About what happened at work today? About why you're here."

I tuck a strand of her hair behind her ear. "I don't honestly know. Nothing happened. Well, I had a meeting, and Rob was there. He stopped behind afterward. He said he wanted me to buy him out. He's going to start a new company."

Her eyebrows rise, and I can see her wondering what effect it's had on me. "It's what you wanted, isn't it?"

"Yeah."

She studies me. "But you don't feel as pleased as you thought you would."

"No."

A frown furrows her brow. "Is that my fault?"

"God, no. It's nothing to do with you. I think it's just that it's made me realize how disillusioned I've become with it all." I look up at the ceiling as bitter disappointment washes through me. "I want to find that excitement, that ambition that's always driven me to do more. I miss it. But it's gone, and I don't know how to get it back."

She kisses my ribs. "It'll come."

"I don't know if it will."

"Callum, you're only human. You've spent the majority of your life working your socks off. You might not think so, but you're a creative person. Anyone with vision like yours has to be. And for all creative people, the well sometimes runs dry. Nobody can work at full capacity continually. Everyone has to take time off to refill the well. Okay, not a well—think of it like a bath. You've had the taps turned on full with the plug in since you were, what, eighteen? Maybe even younger. So you've been overflowing all the time. But for the last year or two, the plug has slowly been coming out, and now it doesn't matter how much comes out of the taps, it's never going to stay in there for long. You need a break, so you can get that plug back in and fill the bath up again."

I let out a long sigh that seems to go on forever. "You're right, I know you're right. But I don't think that's all of it. There's no challenge in it anymore. I've done deals I've never thought I could pull off, and I've made them a huge success. I've worked on enormous projects that have taken years to come to fruition. Everything is achievable if you know how to put your mind to it. And now… It's like I've finally got to the summit of the mountain I've been climbing all my life and I've discovered the view is shrouded in fog. What has been the point? I mean, to earn money, obviously. I wanted to make my family comfortable. I've achieved that and then some. But it can't all have been about money?"

"It's called an existential crisis," she advises me. "We all go through it. What's it all about? Why are we here? We're animals at root, Callum. And animals are born, they mature, they find a mate, they procreate, they provide for their family until their young can fend for themselves, and then eventually they die. That's the meaning of life. Losing Stephanie changed that ultimate goal for you. Whether you discussed having kids or not, it's in your genes to procreate. I'm not at all surprised you feel lost. It's going to make you question everything."

She settles back under my arm, her head on my shoulder. "We've all been there," she says, and yawns. "You're perfectly normal."

For some reason, I find that oddly comforting. I've thought of myself as some kind of superhero because I've found it so much easier to make money than the average guy. But I'm not. I know I'm not. I'm an average Joe at heart, with the same thoughts, feelings, and desires as any other man.

Kora yawns again. "I heard from Theo tonight, by the way."

"How's he doing?"

"Yeah, good, thanks. He said Dad got all my brothers together and told them about Mum."

"Oh? How did they react?"

"Okay, I guess. Surprised, but maybe not as shocked as I was, for whatever reason. Theo knew I'd be upset though."

I kiss her hair. "You have a special relationship with him, don't you?"

"I like to think so." She sounds sleepy. "He said Estella has started to crawl a bit. And apparently she tries to sing along to Wheels on the Bus, although I think Ben's probably exaggerating there. I looked after her when she was younger, you know, before Heloise came to the house. I miss her a lot." She gives a long sigh and falls quiet.

She's right about our basic human needs and drives. It's the reason Jim said about me finding someone and settling down; he wants to leave this world and know I'm safe and content and loved. And I want that, too. Even though I might have pretended to myself that I don't, because I thought it would help lessen the pain of my breakup, the truth is that I do want love, and marriage, and yes, maybe even children.

It's a revelation, as bright as the sun on freshly fallen snow.

And at the same time as it comes, I know it's not going to happen with Kora. I can't ask her to leave her family. And I can't leave mine. Family is everything for both of us.

Kora sleeps soundly in my arms, but I lie awake for a long, long while, looking out into the night.

Chapter Twenty-Four

Kora

The next day, in the afternoon, Callum picks me up and takes me to the Victoria and Albert Museum of Childhood. We go on the Underground, getting off at Bethnal Green and walking the short distance up to the museum.

He left Claridge's around seven a.m. to go home and shower and change, and spent the morning at work. I don't think Rob was in though, so he's in a slightly better mood this afternoon.

He's still a bit quiet, though. I'm not sure whether it's because of his issues at the company, or whether he's acutely aware—like I am—that this is my last day. I'm trying not to think about it. I don't want to ruin our last moments together by being sad.

The museum is newly refurbished, and it reopened only a short time ago. It's both about and for children. There are three new galleries: Imagine, Play, and Design, with multi-sensory interactive galleries to encourage children to explore, and there's also the National Childhood Collection, which is where Callum leads me.

I'm expecting to wander through glass cabinets filled with ancient wooden toys—trains and building blocks and dolls—and I'm surprised when he stops at the desk and informs the assistant who he is, and that Ethan Rouse is expecting him.

I raise my eyebrows at Callum as the assistant goes off, presumably to find this Ethan, but Callum just grins and refuses to tell me what's going on. It only takes a minute or two for her to come back with a man of around Callum's age, slender and dark-haired, with round-rimmed glasses.

"Callum!" Ethan comes up to greet him, and the two men exchange hearty handshakes.

"This is Kora," Callum says, introducing me. "Kora, this is Ethan—we went to university together."

"Pleased to meet you." I shake the man's hand.

"Callum has told me all about you," Ethan says, eyes sparkling. "I hear you're a toy expert from New Zealand. How wonderful to meet another enthusiast."

"Likewise," I say with genuine pleasure. "Are you the curator here?"

"Ethan's the director of the whole museum," Callum replies.

"Oh, goodness."

"Just got the job this year," Ethan says cheerfully. "Worked my way up. Took a few years, but it was worth it. Now, I understand you're interested in something in particular." He gestures for us to follow him and leads us behind the desk and through a doorway.

Callum's fingers interlace mine as we walk down a long corridor flanked by offices. "Yes," I reply, and I explain briefly about Rachel Hoffman, and the fact that she came over to the UK on the Kindertransport. "Apparently when she died, her brother donated her teddy bear to the V&A."

"That's right," he says. "It was a Steiff bear."

My jaw drops. "Oh! I didn't know that." Steiff bears are high quality and made from premium materials. Many are highly collectible and expensive, and they are often produced to mark memorable occasions. One that was made in 1912 to commemorate the sinking of the Titanic went for 128,000 euros in the year 2000.

"Until a few days ago, it was on loan to Prince's Toy Store," Ethan says, not commenting on the fact that my surname is Prince, so I'm not sure whether Callum has told him I'm related to his ex-wife or not.

"Oh… I saw the bear when I visited the store."

"He's here now. We'll be putting him back in his cabinet later, but first I thought you might want to meet him." Ethan smiles and opens the door at the end.

We go down another short corridor, and then through a heavy door into one of the special room where they look after the toys. It's cool in here, and I know the temperature and humidity will be well controlled to keep the toys in top condition.

Rachel's teddy sits on a table in the center of the room, lit by one small lamp, so as not to be damaged by sunlight. We stop by the table, and Ethan hands me a pair of gloves, which I slide on. Then he lifts the bear and places him in my hands.

I'm overcome by emotion at the thought that this once belonged to my birth grandmother, and my chin trembles. I can't cry! Salty tears won't help him at all.

Ethan and Callum withdraw to give me a bit of privacy, talking in low voices in the corner, leaving me alone with the bear.

"Hello," I murmur, lifting him up so I can get a good look at him. He's not in amazing condition, and he's obviously been well loved through the years. I doubt he's worth a fortune—but he'd probably still fetch a few thousand dollars just because of the nature of his journey here. He's a bit limp and looks a little sad, but I'm sure I see him brighten as I beam at him through my tears.

This bear came all the way across Europe, probably from Nazi Germany. He would have been clutched in Rachel's hand, and he survived the raid on the train by Nazi soldiers. He must have slept in Rachel's bed when she was a child, and she obviously kept him until the day she died.

A tear rolls down my cheek, and I wipe it away as best I can on my shoulder.

I feel a hand rest on my waist, and I lean back against Callum's broad chest. "Thank you so much," I whisper.

"You're welcome." He kisses the top of my head. "Ethan was just asking whether you'd like to have Ted on loan at some point, either for your exhibition at the South Pole theme park, or if you do go ahead with your new museum."

I look around at Ethan in delight. "Really?"

He crosses back to me. "Of course. We often send toys on tour to different countries, and I'm sure he'd love to visit Down Under. Send me an email when you get back, and we'll arrange something."

"Thank you so much." I run a finger over Ted's face for the last time, then place him gently back on the table. "I really appreciate this."

"No problem at all."

I take off the gloves, say goodbye to the bear, and Ethan leads us back out to the museum. "How about a tour?" he asks.

I look at Callum in delight. "Do you have time?"

"I'm not going back to the office today."

"Then yes, please!"

So Ethan walks us around the collection, explaining how there are nearly thirty-three thousand objects spanning four hundred years from 1600 to the present day. He shows us one of Britain's oldest rocking horses and lots of other toys that make my eyes boggle, and he also takes us around the archives to show us some of the papers documenting the history of childhood, schooling, and play. This includes the Donne Buck collection I've heard of that contains a fascinating history of adventure playgrounds.

It's with some reluctance that he eventually returns us to the front desk over an hour later. "Sorry, but the museum is closing soon," he says. "Otherwise I could have shown you much more."

"I'm sure Callum is bored enough already," I reply, but Callum shakes his head.

"It's been a fascinating insight into the world of toys," he states, as we both shake Ethan's hand. "Thanks so much, I really appreciate you taking the time."

"Any time, Callum. And I'm glad to make your acquaintance," he says to me. "Maybe if I ever get to New Zealand, you'll show me around your exhibition, too."

"Of course I will, I'd love to."

We wave goodbye, and head out into the snowy afternoon.

It's already dark. We watch the snowflakes fall for a moment, and then I turn to Callum and bury my face in his coat. He puts his arms around me, and we continue to stand like that quietly for a long time.

"That was wonderful," I whisper eventually. "Thank you so much."

"I'm glad you enjoyed it."

"More than you could ever know, and being able to hold the bear was a fantastic finale to my vacation."

"I admit I was thrilled when Ethan suggested it. I thought you'd have to look at it behind glass."

I turn my head and rest my cheek on his coat. "What are we going to do?"

He's silent, and I know he's understood my meaning. Finally, he says, "I don't know."

"I'm sorry," I tell him. "For starting it all. On the beach and here, when we met at the store."

"From what I remember, it was me who asked you to dinner. Begged you, in fact."

My lips curve up. "Yes, it was you. Okay, I take it back."

He chuckles, and I move back and look up at him. "Why don't we find a nice restaurant," he suggests, "and take our time over dinner?"

"I'd like that," I say happily.

So we take the Tube back to Soho, find ourselves an Italian restaurant that Callum knows, and sit there for over two hours, dipping breads in olive oil and salt, eating peppery spaghetti carbonara, and sharing a tiramisu that's out of this world.

We talk about travel and business, books we've read, movies we've seen. We carefully stay away from anything too personal, but of course all the time we're feeling our way around each other, finding out more about our likes and dislikes. And it's impossible not to be intimate, when the waiter lights the candles, and we sip our champagne. The music is gently romantic, and we feed each other small mouthfuls of the chocolate-and-coffee dessert, a taste that will always make me think of him and my time in London from now on.

Afterward, we catch a traditional black cab back to Claridge's, and we sit in the bar and have a couple of drinks, letting our dinner go down, sometimes talking, sometimes listening to the music, and just enjoying being in each other's company.

It's late when we eventually go up to my room. I'm acutely conscious that this is the last time we're going to be together, and I'm sure he is, too. He starts by playing an old love song on his phone, and he pulls me into his arms and we dance to it slowly, turning in the middle of the bedroom floor. He kisses me, softly at first, then more passionately as heat blooms between us. I arch against him, sliding my hands up into his hair, and hold him there while I return the kiss, delving my tongue into his mouth, feeling an urgent need to taste him, to consume him, before he's gone.

Soon our fingers are fumbling at buttons and zippers, stripping off trousers and sweaters and shirts, and it's not long before we're naked and under the covers again, his hot skin sticking to mine. Part of me is desperate to have him inside me, but equally I don't want this to be over, and he seems to understand that. He turns me onto my tummy, then proceeds to kiss me from the nape of my neck all the way down to my toes, his lips gliding over my skin beneath the covers. I close my eyes, half lost in this dreamworld of warm sensuality, murmuring my approval when his tongue traces patterns on the backs of my knees and the tops of my thighs and the dip in the small of my back.

Eventually, he turns me over again, then proceeds to do the same to my front, taking his time to tease my nipples before dipping his tongue in my belly button, then eventually moving down between my legs. Ooh... his mouth makes me feel as delicious as the Tiramisu, sweet and divine. When his fingers join his tongue, it's less than a minute before the orgasm sweeps over me like a wave of rich, dark chocolate, carrying me away as my muscles pulse and I gasp out loud with pleasure.

But he doesn't stop there. He returns to kissing my skin, all the way down to my toes before making his way back up again, keeping me on that plateau of desire, until eventually he reaches my lips and his big brown eyes stare with love into mine. Yes, love—it's silly to deny it. I can't define it any other way.

He dons a condom and then slides inside me, and he continues to keep his gaze fixed on mine as he moves. When my eyelids flutter shut, he kisses me and murmurs for me to open them, as if he wants me to keep him fixed in my mind once we're apart. He doesn't have to worry about that; he's branded on my brain, and these memories are going to take a long, long time to fade.

We make it last for as long as we can, kissing, touching, and keeping our movements slow, but it was never going to last forever. Eventually our breathing grows deep and ragged, and his hips move faster, and we concede defeat and give ourselves over to our climaxes. And it's bittersweet when we come, beautiful and blissful, but also an ending we can't put off any longer, and when we're done, it makes me cry.

*

"I'd better go," Callum says.

It's a lot later, and it's still dark, so it's maybe four or five in the morning. We've dozed a little, but most of the time we've lain there talking and kissing, two people adrift on the ocean, afraid to let go of each other.

"I know," I reply.

He tucks my hair behind my ear. "I had a great time."

"Me too."

"I wish…" His voice trails off.

"Yeah," I say. "I know."

He gets up and dresses, and I rise and pull on the hotel robe, as the fire has died down, and the room is a little cool. I glance out of the window, and the streetlamp shows that sleet is falling, a horrid, cold, frozen rain that's going to turn all the beautiful white snow to slush.

He pulls on his coat, then stops and turns to face me. "What time is your plane?"

He knows because I've already told him, but I say again, "Just after nine a.m. I'll be leaving around seven, probably." I have to pack, but I haven't been able to face it yet.

He nods. "Let me know when you're at the airport."

"Okay."

"And when you get home."

"I will." We have each other's phone numbers and email addresses, and we're friends on Facebook. We have everything we need to stay in touch. But I know that at this moment, I'm wondering if we should, and I'm sure he's thinking the same thing.

He walks to the door, then stops and turns to face me as I walk up behind him. "I don't suppose it'll help if I get on my knees and beg you to stay?"

I swallow hard. "Right this minute, I want to. But I'm homesick, too. I need to see my family. I… I need time to think."

He nods slowly. "Yeah. I know."

"I'm going to miss you," I tell him.

He leans forward and presses his lips to mine. Then he goes out and lets the door close behind him.

I stare at it for a long moment.

Then I go and sit on the bed.

It only takes a few minutes for the tears to come.

Chapter Twenty-Five

Callum

I'm very rarely in a foul mood. I like to think of myself as a sunny-natured soul. But the morning after Kora leaves, it's as if I have a big black cloud over my head that's permanently covering me in cold, heavy rain.

The weather itself seems to react to her going, too, and the rain doesn't let up. The snow disappears within hours, and soon the city is overcast and dull, blanketed with the depressive February atmosphere that makes people's footsteps seem to drag, and strips all the bright colors from the world.

I go to work, because there's nothing else to do, but I stalk my office moodily. It helps a little when Kora texts me to say she's at the airport, but then it's an agonizing twelve-hour wait until I hear from her again when she lands for refueling at Singapore. I'm home by then, and Jim and Josh have gone to bed, tired of my grumpy manner. But my heart lifts when my phone rings, and when I hear her voice, it's as if the sun has come out and turned night to day.

"The flight was fine," she says, "but tiring. I'm so lucky to fly first class; God knows how people cope in economy. I think I've got a cold coming, too, again. Probably something else I caught on the plane."

"Are you going to sleep now?" I ask. I'm standing by the window, looking down at Hyde Park in the rain. London never truly sleeps, but for once I can't see a single soul, and at the moment there aren't even any cars passing by on the road. There's just me, awake and alone, clinging to Kora's voice as if I'm hanging onto the rope of her life raft.

"Once we're back on the plane. I keep thinking about Theo, and how terrifying it must have been for him when his plane crashed into the sea. I didn't think about it on the journey over at all. It's weird. Maybe it's because I have something to lose now."

With some surprise, I realize she's talking about me. "Yeah, don't crash," I tell her. "I'd rather you stay alive, if at all possible."

"I'll do my best." She's smiling. "What's it like there?"

"I've been grumpy all day. Josh actually told me to fuck off tonight. I can't remember the last time he swore at me. And Jim didn't disagree, which says something."

She laughs. "Poor Callum. Well, I'm glad you're missing me."

"I feel as if part of me has been ripped away."

"Me too."

"I've never felt heartsick before, not like this. It's a tad pathetic."

"Are you trying to make me cry?"

I swallow hard and lean on the window, massaging my brow. "I'm sorry. It's just… I miss you."

"I miss you too, more than I could have imagined. I've got to go now, they're calling my flight. I'll ring you when I get home."

"Kora…"

"Yes?"

But I don't know what to say. She knows how I feel. There's no point in begging her to come back, or in trying to define our pain in other, different ways. What else is there to say? "Take care," I whisper.

She sighs. "You too." She waits a moment, then hangs up.

I stay awake for hours, looking out at the rain, but eventually I doze off in the chair, and I'm still there when Jim gets up at six. I wake as he drapes a blanket over me.

"Don't say anything," I mumble.

"Wouldn't dream of it." He goes into the kitchen and starts the coffee machine going.

*

I call my PA and tell her I'm going to be a bit late in, have a coffee with Jim, then take a slow shower. I get a text around nine a.m. from Kora that says she's landed and is currently going through customs in Auckland. It's ten p.m. there, so I know she must be all over the place with the jetlag. But it's wonderful to hear from her.

She rings half an hour later from the domestic lounge, where she's due to catch a flight to Wellington. We talk for forty minutes until they call her flight. I wander through the apartment while we chat, and Jim and Josh call out to her and make her laugh as they bring me over a cup of tea and a chocolate Hobnob, which she grew to love while she was here.

When she eventually has to leave, I go to work more cheerful than I was yesterday, and spend the rest of the morning and the afternoon catching up on all the work I've been neglecting. My heart still isn't in it, but I'm there in body if not in mind, which is an improvement of sorts.

That night, when it's her morning and she's slept for a few hours, we're finally able to meet up on Zoom. I tell her about my day, and she fills me in about her flights and how she's looking forward to seeing her family later. She's going over to her father's, and her brothers are going to meet her there, so she can fill them in with details of her vacation.

We talk for about an hour, and part with promises to call each other the next day.

The next week or so follows a similar pattern. We catch up when I get up in the morning, so she can tell me about her day. Then I call her again in my evening, after she gets up, to tell her what I've been up to.

We don't talk about anything too in depth. We keep it light, but on the first call I end with "Love you," and after that we both say it to each other, and it doesn't seem weird at all.

She texts and emails me too, with photos of her at work to show me her office, shots of Wellington, and also of the South Pole theme park when she calls in there to check on her exhibition, where she points out the place where Rachel's teddy is going to sit when he flies in from London.

I look forward to her next contact eagerly, and the little buzz of my phone in my pocket that announces the arrival of a message becomes the only thing that's really keeping me alive.

*

It's close to the end of February when I come back into the kitchen after talking to her one morning to collect the coffee that Jim has made me.

"Everything okay?" he asks as I sit at the table next to Josh, who's tucking into a bowl of cornflakes.

"Fine." I shake my head when Jim offers the cereal box. "She's about to go out with Mollie. That's her best friend. Mollie told her she's moping too much so she's dragging her to a nightclub. Kora doesn't really want to go, but I told her she should get out a bit more."

I have a sip of the hot coffee, hoping it'll stop my stomach churning. Kora really didn't want to go, and she went quiet when I told her it'll be good for her.

We both know it's possible she might meet a guy while she's out. It's going to happen at some point. At the moment we're hanging onto the memory of our time together and neither of us wants to let go, but we both know it will happen one day. The thought gives me a physical pain in my chest.

Jim exchanges a glance with Josh. Then he pulls out a chair and joins us at the table.

"We want to talk to you about something," he says.

"Oh?" I have another sip of coffee, and it burns the roof of my mouth. Cursing, I put it down.

"You know we're both here for you," Jim says. "Whatever you eventually decide."

My gaze slides to Josh, who spoons cornflakes into his mouth, his brown eyes innocent. "Yeah…" I say.

"But it's clear to both of us that you're crazy about this girl." Jim smiles. "We've never seen you like this before. And we understand why."

"She's great," Josh says.

I give a small smile. "Yeah, she is."

"And we think you should be with her," he adds.

I purse my lips. "I don't think she can move here. She has her family and her job Down Under."

"We know," Jim says. "Which is why you should go and be with her."

I swallow hard. "I can't go."

"Callum—"

"Why are you saying this? Don't you know how hard this is for me?" Anger flares inside me. I'm having enough of an internal battle without the two of them pulling this on me. "Kora and I have both agreed that family is everything. Yes, we had a great time together, but we know it can't work. She can't leave, and neither can I. My life is here. Even if my job isn't what it used to be, you two… you're my family. You're everything to me."

I was half-expecting them to look upset and then to argue with me, but they don't. Jim just waits patiently for me to finish, and Josh rolls his eyes.

"No, idiot," my brother says. "We want to come with you."

I stare at him, then my gaze slides to my grandfather. "What?"

"What Josh said. We've talked about it. And we're all ready for a new adventure." Jim leans forward and places his big bear paw on top of mine. "We know your heart isn't in your work anymore. And we know Rob will happily buy you out. You don't need the money, Callum. You've done an amazing job providing for us, and we're incredibly grateful for everything you've done. But it's time to think ahead. To work out what you really want. You love this girl, don't you?"

My jaw has dropped, and now I close it slowly. "I haven't known her long," I say, as I don't want to admit the truth.

But Jim doesn't listen. "One of you needs to make a sacrifice and, mate, I think it should be you. Sell the company. We'll move to New Zealand. And we can all start over again. You can do whatever you want. Start up a new company. Or not. You have enough money to spend the rest of your life surfing or painting watercolors or doing whatever you feel like. But you have this chance to find love, and the last thing Josh and I want to do is stand in the way of that."

"But your life is here," I say hoarsely.

"I'll survive," he says cheerfully. "I'd like to explore a new country. Make new friends." He smiles.

I look at Josh. "Your whole life is here." He has several friends and a busy-ish social life.

But he shrugs and says, "I want to go to the South Island and see where *The Lord of the Rings* was filmed, and go to Weta Workshop, and Hobbiton. And the South Pole theme park. And the real South Pole—you can fly there, you know. And learn Maori. I can already say hello—it's Kia ora. I want to meet Kora's brothers, especially Ben, because he likes Sharpe. And Theo, because he's Kora's twin."

I feel overcome with confusion. They're only saying this to please me. I couldn't possibly ask them to give up their whole lives and move across the other side of the world.

"Opportunities like this don't come around very often," Jim states. "You have to grab them with both hands when they do." He sips his coffee. "Do you think Rob will want the company?"

"He seemed pretty thrilled to be starting afresh."

"Well he would say that, but hasn't he also been begging you to sell for the past year?"

I don't answer because he's right. And it's not the point.

"How would you feel about leaving it?" Jim asks. "About cutting the ties. Starting again?"

"Give up everything I've worked for?" I'm appalled. "I can't."

"This thing with Kora is powerful," Jim states. "And you're only making it harder on yourselves by keeping in touch like this."

Again, he's right, I know he is. And when it comes to it, I have two options.

Give up everything for her. Or let her go.

Chapter Twenty-Six

Kora

"Well, you're no fun." Mollie blows out a breath and finishes off her drink.

"Sorry," I say guiltily. "You can stay if you want."

But she smiles and shakes her head. "No, of course not. I shouldn't have dragged you out when you didn't want to go."

She leads me out of the noisy nightclub and dials for an Uber, and soon we're on our way home. We're currently sharing an apartment. I was living with Ben after I moved out of the place I shared with Julian, but Ben's house is quite isolated, and I missed being in the city.

It's been fun living with Mollie, but I know I need to get my own place soon. I'm thirty, and I need to start putting down roots. I feel as if I understand the importance of that more now I've discovered where I come from.

I lean my face against the cool window, looking out at the dark streets. February in New Zealand is often hot and sticky, although in Wellington there's always a breeze somewhere to keep the temperature from rising too high. It is nice to be back. But the ache in my heart is so big it's overshadowing everything else.

It'll get better with time, I know it will. Eventually Callum won't be the first thing I think about when I wake up, and the last when I go to sleep. I won't spend every spare moment remembering the touch of his hands on my skin. And I won't compare every man I meet to him, and find them wanting.

If I'm honest, it's part of the reason I didn't enjoy being at the nightclub. Those places are often like zoos and I felt as if I was being watched through the bars. I don't want to think about other men. At the moment, I can't imagine being interested in another man ever again.

"You okay?" Mollie asks as the Uber turns onto our street. "You look quite pale."

"I haven't felt right since I got back." I definitely picked up a bug on the plane. I've been achy and tired all the time. "It's the jetlag, that's all."

"Yeah. Let's get you to bed. Want a hot water bottle?"

"Nah, I'm good, thanks." I'm hot and sticky, if anything, and suddenly the coolness of my bed is highly attractive.

Once we're indoors, I give Mollie a hug and go to my room. She'll be up for a while yet, but I'm too tired to watch TV. I brush my teeth, strip off my clothes, splash my face with water, then get into bed naked. The cool cotton slides over my skin, and I turn onto my side with a satisfied sigh.

I look at my phone and bring up Callum's latest message from a couple of hours ago. It just says, *Miss you. Love you. xx* It came while I was at the nightclub, so I missed it at the time. I've replied, but he hasn't come back yet. I send him one now, *Are you there? Fancy a chat?* I wait for a while, but he doesn't reply, so maybe he's in a meeting.

The phone still in my hand, I close my eyes, and I'm asleep within a minute.

*

I jerk awake sometime later. It's dark and quiet. I'm still holding my phone, and the screen lights up as I move, announcing it's just after two a.m.

I sit up in bed and stare ahead of me into the darkness. Something came to me in my sleep, and the shock of it ripples through me now, making me go cold, even though the air is humid and warm.

I reach over to the bedside table, turn on the light, then pick up my pill packet. I take twenty-one pills and then seven sugar pills to keep me in a routine. Usually I have a light period once I start taking the sugar pills. But I've taken six, and there's only one left in the packet before I start taking the next pack.

No. Surely not.

I can't be pregnant.

I'm on the pill. And Callum used a condom every time. I can't be.

My heart's hammering. I fall back onto the pillows and stare up at the ceiling.

I have to think logically about this. Let's start with the pill. I take it with my breakfast every morning between seven and eight a.m. But of course when I went to the UK, they're currently thirteen hours behind New Zealand, which put all my timings out. Before I left, I told myself I'd take it between eight and nine p.m., but of course I forgot and ended up taking it at the usual time the following morning, around twelve hours late.

That in itself shouldn't have been a problem, but I also had that stomach bug when I first arrived, and I vomited for a couple of days. It was a week before I met Callum, and I forgot all about it, but I guess it could have screwed up my system, and maybe it led to a stray egg making a break for freedom.

But he used condoms! Surely that should have protected us? I'm a realist, though, and I know nothing is a hundred percent effective. One could have broken and, combined with the fuck up with the pills, it might have been just enough to let an errant sperm meet with a rebellious egg.

I rest a hand on my tummy, trying to remember to breathe. It's probably not that. It's almost certainly the jetlag that's upset my system and made me tired and emotional all the time.

But would jetlag affect my period? I touch my breasts gently. They've been tender for a few days, but again I put it down to my whole system being off kilter.

It's silly to get into a panic, because I won't be able to confirm anything until I can get to the chemist and take a pregnancy test. But it's impossible to stop my brain racing.

What if I am pregnant?

First, I know a large percentage of early pregnancies end in miscarriage, so there's no guarantee my period won't start in a day or two.

But what if it doesn't?

I slide my hand down to my belly again. What if, against all the odds, Callum and I made a baby?

To my utter and complete shock, I feel a swell of joy, followed quickly by a rush of tears. It would be a disaster. Either the baby will have to grow up only seeing its father once in a blue moon when one of us is able to travel, or I'll have to move to England.

Would it be the end of the world? Well, yes, literally. But metaphorically? Would it be so terrible if I only saw my family once or twice a year?

I swallow hard, but I'm unable to stop the tears tumbling over my lashes. I liked England, but I don't want to move there. I love New Zealand, I adore Wellington, and I'd miss my family terribly. My dad, my brothers, my baby niece, they all mean the world to me, and although I'd love being with Callum, I'd miss them so much.

It's stupid to cry when I don't even know if I'm right, but I can't stop the tears coming. Why do I screw everything up? Why did I think I'd be all right sleeping with a guy I met twelve years ago? Did I really think I'd be able to walk away without my heart being affected? I'm such a fucking idiot.

I bury my face in the pillow, and let it soak up my tears before I finally fall back into a fitful sleep.

*

When I wake again, it's seven a.m. The first thing I do is check my phone, as there's usually a message waiting for me from Callum, but this morning there's nothing, which I can't help but find ominous. It's a beautiful morning, and sunshine is pouring through my window, but I have a heavy heart, and I drag myself out of bed, doing everything I can not to think about what sprang into my mind last night.

It lasts about thirty minutes, and then I go into the bathroom and vomit into the toilet.

Oh God.

When I'm finally showered and dressed and go out into the living room, Mollie looks up from her cereal bowl with raised eyebrows. "Wow, you look rough. You didn't drink that much, did you?"

"No." I sink onto the sofa and put my face in my hands.

Her spoon falls into the bowl with a clink as she rises and comes to sit beside me. "Oh no, what's happened?"

I wasn't going to tell her, but it only takes her about thirty seconds to wheedle it out of me.

"I can't be," I insist, fighting against tears. "I can't be that unlucky."

"Fate doesn't come into it." She's all brisk and businesslike. "There's no point in discussing what-ifs until we know all the facts. Come on, the pharmacy opens soon. We'll get a test and come straight back and you can take it." Mollie's a freelance illustrator, so her hours are flexible, and because my family owns the toy store, nobody's ever going to demand to know why I'm a couple of hours late.

I let her bully me into having a slice of dry toast, and then we walk the short distance to the shops, and I buy a pregnancy test. We come back home, read the instructions together, and then I go into the bathroom and pee on the stick. I set it on the sink and wash my hands, then open the door. We watch the timer tick down on my phone together.

"I don't want to look," I tell her.

"Do you want it to be positive or negative?"

"I…" I meet her eyes. I want it to be positive. The desire is suddenly so strong that it takes me by surprise.

I can't admit it to her, but I can see by her smile that she's guessed. "Turn it over," she whispers.

I flip the stick over. It says "Pregnant, 2-3 weeks."

"Bloody hell." In my moment of panic, I turn British.

"Oh my God, Kora!" Mollie squeals and throws her arms around me. I laugh and hug her, as tears pour down my face.

"I don't believe it." I pull back and stare at the stick, but I hadn't imagined it—I'm pregnant. "I can't be."

"But you are!"

"Oh Jesus." Now panic washes over me. "He lives on the other side of the world, Moll. What am I going to do?"

She leads me out of the bathroom, and we both sit on the sofa. "Well…" she says slowly, "I suppose the first and biggest question is… do you want to keep it?"

"Yes," I say immediately. There is absolutely no question in my mind. Even if Callum doesn't want to know, or he acknowledges it but we decide to stay apart, I want to keep this child.

"Good," she says, obviously relieved. "Then everything else will follow."

"He's going to want me to move to the UK," I whisper.

"Do you want to?"

"Not really. But I suppose I have to think about what's best for the baby now."

A baby. Oh my God, I'm having a baby.

"Yes and no," she says. "It's also about having support. I mean obviously they have doctors and midwives over there, and you'd soon make new friends. But you wouldn't have your family around you."

I wouldn't have my father, or Ben, or Theo. Lucas and Jacob will both be great uncles, too. Heloise, Ben's partner, would be great helping out because she's a nanny, and she's looked after lots of babies. And I think I could be very good friends with Theo's girlfriend, Victoria. They're getting married soon, and I'm sure they'll be having kids before long, which means their baby and mine would be able to grow up together. But not if I move away.

"You don't have to make your mind up now," Mollie soothes. "Let's take it one step at a time. The first thing we have to think about is your pregnancy. You have to take special vitamins, don't you? Folic acid and stuff. And no more alcohol or… cheesecake, isn't it? I have no idea why. We'll have to do some research."

I nod, try to keep a lid on the panic. She's right. One step at a time.

And the main thing is that I can't tell anyone else until I've told Callum.

*

A couple of hours later, when I've calmed down and Mollie's gone to work, I text Callum and ask him if he's around for a chat. It's ten in the morning there, so he must be up and at work.

I wait for an hour, but he doesn't reply.

I send another text asking if he can just let me know he's okay.

Still nothing.

Now I'm starting to get worried. He doesn't tend to stay up super late, so when it gets to midnight, I know he's not going to contact me until my evening. Disappointed and worried, I consider looking up his home line and calling it, but I don't want to wake Jim and Josh. And besides, Callum has always contacted me immediately when I've texted him. If he doesn't want to message me, he'll have a good reason for it.

I check his last text again. *Miss you. Love you. xx* I have to hang onto that for now and just hope all is well.

*

At midday, Theo turns up at the apartment.

"Hey, you!" I'm still in my nightie, and I know my hair must be all over the place because he gives me an amused look as he comes inside. "What are you doing here?"

"Checking up on you. Elena said you were sick."

"Just a stomach bug. I'll be in tomorrow."

He puts the bag he's carrying on the table. "I brought you a box of chocolates. Probably won't help if it's a stomach bug, but I thought you might fancy one."

"Aw." I slide my arms around his waist and give him a hug. "Thank you."

He squeezes me and kisses my forehead. "Are you okay? You look a bit pale."

"Yeah, I'm fine." I desperately want to tell him, but I know I mustn't until I've spoken to Callum.

"Heard from Callum?" he asks casually.

I move back and sink onto the sofa. "Not since last night." Even as I say it, I know it doesn't sound like very long ago. "It's just that he usually texts me in the morning," I add lamely.

Theo stuffs his hands in his pockets. "I'm sure he's just busy."

"It's the middle of the night there."

"Yeah, true. Perhaps he's working on something important, though. You know what these workaholics are like. They don't keep normal hours."

"I guess." Callum's enthusiasm for his work appeared to have waned, but maybe he's starting to get back into it.

"Well, I won't keep you," Theo says. "I'm meeting Vic in town for lunch."

"All right. Have a lovely time."

"Keep your chin up," he says softly. "Everything's going to be okay."

His words make my throat tighten, but I keep a grip on the emotion and just smile, and he heads out.

Then I let myself have a quiet cry.

*

Later, gathering my courage in both hands, I finally call Callum, but it goes to his answerphone. I leave a bright message saying I miss him and need to talk to him as soon as he's available, then hang up before I start begging to know why he hasn't called.

The day wears on, and I constantly check my phone, but it stays silent apart from the occasional texts from other friends that make my heart race and then plummet each time.

Mollie makes me dinner, and then we watch a movie together. We both know it's only to pass the time. My phone continues to stay silent, and when it gets to eleven p.m., I know there's no point in staying up.

I think he's finally given up on me. Oh God, I hope he's not with Stephanie. Perhaps she got in touch with him and invited him over, and he was lonely, so he went. They could have had dinner together. And maybe they ended up in bed.

Deep down, I'm sure that isn't the case, but I'm not thinking straight, and now I can't get the idea out of my head that because I've gone, he's decided to try to make things work with her.

Mollie gives me a big hug, lost for words because there's nothing she can say to comfort me. I go to bed, and lie there for a long time, looking out at the stars.

*

The next morning, there's still no message. Now I'm getting cross. What the fuck is he up to? I get up in a brisk and practical mood. I refuse to lie around in bed in a funk waiting for him to call. I'm not going to be that girl. Time will pass more swiftly if I go to work. So I get up and shower, vomit into the toilet, have a piece of dry toast, then give Mollie a hug goodbye before heading to the office.

I'm not even going to look at my phone. I have lots to do, and if Callum texts me, he can wait until I have a spare minute to reply.

I get stuck into my emails, sipping from my mug of fruit tea. I miss my morning coffee, but I'm going to have to pass on it for now.

I glance at my phone. Then look back at my laptop.

"Morning." It's Theo again, leaning against the door jamb.

"Hey." I smile.

"You look better today." He gestures at his hair. "More under control."

"Yeah, the fluff got the better of me yesterday."

"Feeling better?"

"A bit. I got bored."

"Fair enough. You got a minute?"

"Sure." I lean back and wait for him to come in. He doesn't, though. Instead, he glances down the corridor, then looks back at me, winks, and backs away.

And then another man comes around the corner and into the office.

He walks a few steps in, then stops. He looks hesitant, wary, unsure of my reaction. He's wearing jeans and a navy sweater, incongruous in the summer weather, so I can tell he hasn't been here long. His hair is ruffled, and I can tell by his eyes that he hasn't slept much.

"Hey," he says. "I… I hope you don't mind. I was passing, and I thought I'd call in." He slides his hands into his pockets, hunches his shoulders, and gives me a small smile.

My jaw drops. My heart shudders to a stop.

And then I leap out of my chair, run around the desk, and throw myself into his arms with a loud squeal.

Behind him, I see Theo's smile as he leans in to close the door behind us. And then I bury my face in Callum's neck and burst into tears.

Chapter Twenty-Seven

Callum

We stand there like that for a long time. My T-shirt is soon soaked with Kora's tears, but I don't care. She's soft in my arms, and I feel a surge of relief and comfort at the familiar smell of her cherry perfume.

Eventually she quietens, but we continue to hug. I think she's as afraid to let go as I am.

Over her shoulder, I can see Wellington Harbour. It's a beautiful summer day, and the sunshine has covered the choppy waves with sparkling diamonds. It's a lovely little city, and it looks as if someone has scrubbed it clean just for me.

"Shall we sit down?" I murmur eventually, gesturing at the sofa and chairs to one side of her large office.

"Okay." She reaches over to her desk and snatches up a couple of tissues before she lets me lead her over to the sofa. I take off my sweater, which is far too warm for the summer weather, and then we sink down together, facing each other, our knees touching. "When did you get here?" she whispers.

"My plane landed in Wellington an hour ago. Theo picked me up."

"Theo knew you were coming?" she asks, astonished.

I nod, a bit guiltily. "I contacted him when I decided to come out here, to ask his advice and make sure he thought it was a good idea. I knew he'd know you better than anyone else."

She looks puzzled. "But Theo doesn't know."

"Doesn't know what?"

"Have you spoken to Mollie?"

"Mollie? She's… your friend, right? No. Why?"

She blinks. "Why are you here?"

"To visit Hobbiton. I understand it's worth the visit." I smile at her confusion. "To see you, Kora Prince. Why else?"

"I don't understand."

I lift her fingers to my lips and kiss the tips. "I have something to tell you. I had a conversation with Jim and Josh yesterday. At least I think it was yesterday. I've lost all track of time. Anyway, they both told me they thought I should move to New Zealand, and that they wanted to come with me."

Kora's jaw drops. "What?"

"I know. I'm as shocked as you are. They both seemed excited by the idea."

"But… your company… your work…"

"I've already spoken to Rob. He's going to buy me out. And I'm going to start again. I don't know what I'm going to do yet, but we're hardly going to be short of money. I've been thinking about some kind of charity work. I'd like to do something for kids who have Fetal Alcohol Syndrome, maybe…"

My voice trails off at the look on her face. All the way here on the plane I've tried to picture how this is going to go. At no point did it enter my head that she might not want me to move here. But there's no joy on her face, no triumph. She just looks… worried.

"Sweetheart," I say, my heart banging away, "what's the matter? I thought you'd be pleased."

"You're not here because…"

"Because of what?"

"I…" She clears her throat. "I've got something to tell you."

Immediately, I go cold. I know she was going to the nightclub with her friend last night. Oh shit, please don't let her have met somebody else…

"I'm pregnant," she says.

I stare at her. That was absolutely the last thing I expected her to say. "What?"

She rubs her nose. "I'm on the pill, and we used condoms, I know. I think I fucked up my schedule with the jetlag, plus I was sick on the first few days in London. And I guess a condom might have split. I don't know how it happened. Well, I do know, obviously, but you know what I mean. Anyway, it's really early, so anything could happen, but I am late, so I took a test, and it was positive." She blinks and bites her lip, obviously aware she's rambling. "It's yours, in case I haven't made that clear. Obviously."

"You're having a baby?"

She sucks her bottom lip, then nods.

For a moment, it's such a shock that I'm completely numb. Kora's big blue eyes widen, filled with hope and a touch of panic.

And then I get a wave of such joy that my throat tightens and I can't speak.

Instead, I pull her toward me and wrap my arms around her. "Oh," I manage to squeak. "Oh…"

"I'm sorry," she whispers, "I didn't mean for it to happen…"

"Oh… Kora…"

"You're not mad at me?"

I move back and look into her beautiful eyes. "No, I'm not mad at you, you silly, silly girl." Then I crush my lips to hers and, for a long moment, I make it very difficult for her to come up for air.

When I eventually let her breathe again, her face is wet, and her eyes are shining.

"I can't believe it," I murmur. I drop my gaze to her belly, and place my hand over it. "A baby. Our baby."

She blows her nose. "I thought you might be upset with me."

"It takes two to make a baby, love. It's my fault as much as yours, not that anyone is at fault. These things happen."

"I honestly don't know how it could have happened when we used condoms too, but I guess we were just unlucky."

"No," I correct. "We were really, really lucky."

She presses her fingers to her lips. "You mean that?"

"I do. Oh Christ, I'm going to have to tell Jim. He's never going to stop smiling. And Josh is going to explode at the thought of being an uncle."

"They really want to live here?" She doesn't look as if she can believe it.

"Yes, they were very enthusiastic about it. They've obviously been talking between the two of them. Jim told me he thinks the change will do Josh good, get him out and about more. As soon as I realized it could work, I rang and booked the next available flight, stuffed a load of clothes into a bag, and jumped on the plane. I'm so sorry if I was out of touch for a while, but I wanted to surprise you."

She gives me a wry look. "Well, you definitely did that! And Theo… he knew?"

"Yeah. I asked him whether he thought you'd mind if I just showed up. He laughed and said as long as I didn't mind your head exploding.

I told him I loved you and I was going to ask you to marry me. He seemed pretty pleased."

"M-marry?"

I take her hands in mine. "Look, I know this is all happening really fast, and I don't want us to rush into anything we're not ready for. But the baby is going to force our hand a bit, don't you think? I came here with the intention of staying for a week or two, spending some time with you so you can show me around your lovely country, and discussing with you the idea of me and Jim and Josh moving here to see if you thought it could work. My plan was that if we decided that's what we wanted, I'd go back and sort out selling the apartment and tying up all the loose ends at the company, and then after a month or two all three of us would move here. That was the original plan, anyway. When I was talking to Theo, the 'm' word just kind of popped out."

"He came to my apartment to check on me," she says softly. "I should have guessed something was up."

I kiss her hands. "I'm sure this goes without saying because we've talked about it, but I want to be clear about everything. With Jim and Josh, well…"

"We can buy a big house and they'll live with us," she says immediately. "Callum, of course they will. I know how important they are to you, just as my family is to me."

I swallow hard. "Thank you. It means a lot to me."

"And it means a lot—so much, you'll never know—that you're considering moving here. I've been thinking about it non-stop, and just going around in circles." She kisses me briefly. "I wanted to be with you so much. I kept telling myself that longing would go away, but I yearned for you." She smiles then. "It's funny, but I thought the same thing when we were watching kids playing in the snow in the park. I've never thought of myself as maternal, but for the first time I felt broody. Now, I think I know why." She rests a hand on her tummy. "I'm so glad you're here. Now I can tell everyone else!"

"You haven't told your family yet?"

"No, of course not. I told Mollie because we live together, and she knew something was wrong. But I wouldn't tell everyone else until I'd spoken to you about it."

As I say the words, there's a gentle knock at the door. Kora glances at it, then gives me a wry look. "It seems it's time to spread the word. Are you okay with that?"

"Couldn't be happier." And I surprise myself by meaning it. I want the whole world to know we're a couple, and that I'm going to make a new life here. "Are you sure you're okay telling everyone, though, when it's still early days?"

"I can't keep a secret," she says. "You never need to worry I'm keeping anything from you! And anyway, if something were to go wrong, I'd want the support of all my family."

It's a nice thought. Still, I feel a little nervous at the idea of her telling everyone. Hopefully they won't think badly of me because I knocked up their little sister. And her father… oh dear.

It's too late to worry about it though, so we stand and go over to the door, and Kora opens it. There's a crowd of people outside, and she laughs as she sees their eager faces, most of them peering inside to see me.

"They wanted to make sure you were okay," Theo says.

"I'm wonderful," Kora states, and everyone laughs. "Come in," she says. "Everyone, this is Callum."

She proceeds to introduce me to them all. Theo I already know, and I recognize her father from the Zoom call. He shakes my hand enthusiastically. "Great to meet you in the flesh, Callum."

"You too."

Kora then introduces me to her other brothers—Ben, the eldest, Lucas, who I suspect is a year or two older than Kora and Theo, and Jacob, who is probably the youngest. They all greet me with big smiles, clearly pleased I've come all this way to be with their sister. There's also Elena, who is Nick's PA, and who gives Kora an extra-long hug.

"There's something else," Kora announces when I've finally met everyone. "It's very early days, so I shouldn't really be saying anything, but you know we all share everything. The thing is… I'm pregnant." She looks at her father. "We didn't mean for it to happen, but it has, and we're both really excited about it. I hope you can all be excited, too."

There's a moment of stunned silence as everyone's jaws drop. I look at her father, who's staring at her with complete bemusement. And then, as one, everyone exclaims and comes forward to congratulate us.

"Kora, that's amazing!" Elena gives her a huge hug. "I'm so pleased for you!"

"Thank you!" Kora's crying again. "I'm so emotional! It's the hormones."

"Like you've ever been any different." Theo hugs her, then shakes my hand. "Congrats, Callum. Welcome to the family."

"Thank you." I'm very touched by his words, and my pleasure only grows as all her brothers come over and tell us how thrilled they are at our news.

Finally, there's only her father left. He takes his daughter by the shoulders, looks into her eyes, and says softly, "You look so like your mother right now, Kora. She'd have been so happy for you."

"Oh, Daddy…"

"Come here." He wraps his arms around her, and she buries her face in his shirt.

Behind her back, he reaches out a hand to me, and I grasp it. "Look after my little girl," he says.

I nod. "I will, I promise."

"She means everything to me." He moves back, cups her face, and kisses her forehead. Then he says, "All right, we'll let the two of you have some peace and quiet. But tonight, everyone's over at my place for a celebration party!"

Cheers ring around the room, and then everyone files out. Soon it's just the two of us, and we stand in the middle of the room, having a hug.

"That went well, I think," I say to her.

"It's all happening so fast." She rests her cheek on my chest.

I kiss the top of her head. "We'll make sure we take it slow now. We have the rest of our lives. There's no hurry."

"The rest of our lives… together."

"Yeah. You can't get rid of me, Kora Prince. I know you thought you could escape by legging it to the other side of the world, but I wasn't going to let you go."

She chuckles. "I'm glad. Do you want a boy or a girl?"

"Oh, love, I don't give two fucks what it is. I'll love it all the same."

"Me too. And I love you, Callum."

"I love you too, sweetheart."

I rest my lips on her hair and breathe in her cherry scent, and watch the seagulls swooping over the harbor, as the warm summer sun beats down on the waves.

Epilogue

Kora

June 21st

It's shortest day in New Zealand, and in Wellington it's cold and blowing a gale. Nothing like February in the UK, though. I doubt we'll see snow here this winter.

Inside, it's warm and toasty—a little too warm, in fact, in the dining room, with all the bodies around the table and the heat from the kitchen. The Yule festival is often more like a Christmas dinner than our summer Christmas one is, so we're celebrating midwinter by having everyone around for a family dinner in our new home. I've been working hard all morning, and, if I'm honest, I've probably overdone it a little.

"Are you okay?" Callum leans close and murmurs in my ear. "You look a bit flushed."

"Just warm—I'm fine." I fan myself with a teeny-tiny fan that came in one of the crackers.

"You should have let me hire a chef." He'd tracked down one of the best in Wellington and was all prepared to get him in for the day to cook our dinner, but, like an idiot, I wanted to do it myself. "Stop fussing," I scold, but I soften it with a smile. I like being fussed over.

Still, he rises and opens the sliding door a few inches to let some of the cool air replace the warm. "Let me know if it gets too breezy," he tells Elena and Mollie, who are sitting at the end of the table with Dad.

Everyone's here—Dad, Ben, Heloise, and Estella, Theo and Victoria, Lucas and Jacob, Jim and Josh, Grandma Belle, Grandma Carol and Grandpa Alan, and, with Elena and Mollie, that makes sixteen of us for dinner without the baby. Our dining table has an extension we can pull out so it seats twelve, and we've added a small square table at the end to fit in the extra four people, covering it all with a red tablecloth so you can't tell.

I asked Mollie to come because her parents are away at the moment, and she's been invaluable since I've been pregnant, coming to antenatal classes with me if Callum is busy, and she's going to come and stay with us for a while when the baby's born to help out. We haven't discussed it as such, but I know she's aware that I don't have my mum around, and she's hoping to fill that space a little.

Also, and again we haven't discussed it, I'm convinced she's got a thing for Lucas. I don't know why because she's very bright and bubbly and he can be quite the grump at times, but I'm certainly going to encourage it if I can, because it's time he settled down.

I asked Elena here because I know she lives alone, and I don't like anyone being alone when everyone else is celebrating. Despite her having worked for the company for over ten years, I actually don't know an awful lot about her, and I'm not sure that even Dad does, although they work in the offices next to each other all day. She's a very private person. I know she was married once but it didn't work out, but I don't know why. She doesn't have any kids. Her parents are still alive but live up in the Northland, and I think she has a sister over in Oz. I know she does yoga and Pilates because she told me once, and she plays the piano. But that's about it.

She wasn't going to come at first. She rarely mixes with us outside work, maybe because she doesn't want to push her way into the family, even though I practically think of her as part of ours. But I managed to talk her into it by explaining there were going to be lots of people there, and eventually she agreed.

I sat her opposite Dad. I don't think either of them have thought anything about that—they probably assumed I did it because they work together. Neither of them have guessed that I have an ulterior motive.

I'm convinced she likes him, and after watching him on Zoom that day and seeing his gaze linger on her, I'm sure he likes her too. But I have a feeling neither of them is going to start anything, so I want to see whether I can help things along a bit.

I look around the table, pleased to see everyone tucking into the dinner. I've never cooked for sixteen people before, and it severely tested my culinary skills, but Callum was a Godsend and let me boss him around the kitchen for most of the morning. Jim and Josh were also great and did jobs like sorting out the table and organizing the seating. I roasted a huge turkey with stuffing, and there's also a ham with an orange glaze, chipolatas wrapped in streaky bacon, hundreds of roast potatoes, several trays of roasted root vegetables, homemade cranberry sauce, and lots of other bits and pieces to make the winter meal complete.

I've been on my feet for hours, and now I feel ready for a nanna nap, but I'm glad I did it. I smile at Jim, who winks at me from his place next to Callum. He and Josh came over in May, a few weeks after Callum and I moved into our new house. I've been worried that they'll find it difficult to settle in here—I can't imagine how hard it is to emigrate and move right across to the other side of the world. But my family has been amazing and made a real effort to include them in everything.

Ben is now sitting next to Josh, and I can hear them talking about the Richard Sharpe series and discussing their favorite episodes. Jacob has also been terrific, and several times he's taken Josh to watch the Wellington Phoenix soccer team at Sky Stadium, and I think the two of them are going to Auckland next week to see the All Blacks play the Wallabies at Eden Park.

Belle has taken Jim under her wing and introduced him to some of her friends, including those at the local bowls club, a country dancing group, and her University of the Third Age classes on gardening and photography. I don't think anything romantic will develop between them, but they both seem pleased to have company at social occasions.

And Callum… he seems to have flourished since he came to live here. Part of it, I know, is making the break with the UK, and with Stephanie. Apparently she cried when he told her he was moving, but since then she's stopped emailing and texting him, so I think she's finally come to terms with the fact that they're not going to get back together.

Despite his assurance that we should take things slow and make sure we didn't rush into anything, during his two-week stay with me at the beginning of March, we began looking at houses, and we found one we liked a couple of days before he was due to return to the UK to settle his affairs. So I started proceedings on the purchase, and by the time he returned at the end of April, the house was ours. We had a couple of fun weeks buying furniture and making the place look nice before Jim and Josh turned up in May. Then, on the first of June, we got married in a quiet ceremony with family and a few friends, and since then things have only gone from great to wonderful.

He's taken a few months off work, and he seems much better for it. That haunted look has disappeared from his eyes, and he seems rested and full of energy. So much so that only last week he flew up to Auckland with my father and met with Brock King and Nikau Rogers, who now runs the We Three Kings Foundation. Together, the guys are going to fund a new charity for kids who suffer from Fetal Alcohol Syndrome, and Callum is going to run it from Wellington. He'll have to put a board together, organize the financial side of it and events to raise new money, and set up communication between the hospital and the new clinic he wants to open. He's full of enthusiasm for it, and the fact that it's a project which will also help children and teenagers in desperate need of help has given him a job satisfaction he never experienced in the UK.

Everyone seems happy, and tears prick my eyes. I wish Mum could have been here to see it. She would have adored having grandchildren. I feel so sad to think that Dad won't be able to share that with her. He's great with Estella, but I can see the loneliness in his eyes when he holds her. He misses Mum so much. Now I have Callum, I can understand his loss so much better.

I look at Elena, who's eating quietly, and Dad, who's talking to Jim, and suddenly I doubt the two of them will ever get together. I don't know that Dad will ever get over losing Mum. Poor Elena. Is she doomed to live forever in Mum's shadow?

"You're not eating," Callum scolds beside me.

"I am," I protest. "I've had two roast potatoes and three sausages."

"You're eating for three," he reminds me.

At my scan, I discovered I'm having twins. No surprises there, I guess, although it was still a shock for us both.

"That's a fallacy, and I don't want to get fat." I sniff and poke at a carrot.

"What's up?" he murmurs, sliding an arm around me and kissing my shoulder.

"I was thinking of Mum, that's all."

"Aw. Yeah. You must miss her most at times like these."

I give him a bright smile. "I'm okay. Everyone seems to be enjoying themselves, and that makes me happy."

After the meal, Victoria and Mollie bully Lucas and Theo into clearing up, and they send the rest of us with me protesting vehemently into the living room. Some of us fall into the sofa and chairs, others collapse on bean bags and cushions. Elena and Heloise take baby Estella for a walk around the garden in her pushchair. Jacob boots up *It Takes Two* on the PlayStation, and soon everyone is in fits of laughter at the sight of him and Josh fighting giant wasps and falling into pits of lava.

I curl up on the sofa with Callum's arm around me, and rest my head on his shoulder. I'm five months pregnant now, and he insists I'm blooming, even though I'm beginning to feel a bit ungainly. He puts a hand on my belly, and one of the babies kicks as if it can feel him, making us both laugh.

We chose not to find out the babies' sex. I like the idea of being surprised on the day, and Callum was happy to go along with whatever I wanted.

Secretly, I'm hoping at least one is a girl. I feel that somehow it will be a replacement for the connection I've lost with my mum. But either way, I just hope they're happy and healthy.

Callum kisses the top of my head, and I close my eyes, content.

Within about ten seconds, I'm asleep.

Newsletter

If you'd like to be informed when my next book is available, you can sign up for my mailing list on my website, http://www.serenitywoodsromance.com

About the Author

USA Today bestselling author Serenity Woods writes sexy contemporary romances, most of which are set in the sub-tropical Northland of New Zealand, where she lives with her wonderful husband.

Website: http://www.serenitywoodsromance.com
Facebook: http://www.facebook.com/serenitywoodsromance